Enthusiastic reviews for Lior Samson's novels –

Distant Sons

" [A] book that will stay with me, probably for the rest of my life, and that I know I'll read again. ... It enlarged my experience of being human."   *—M. Thornberg, author*

The Rosen Singularity

" The plotting is ingenious and the characters come through strongly."   *—Rebecca Goldstein, MacArthur Fellow, author*

The Millicent Factor

" A solid page turner. The author keeps the pace just right with action and chases ... and backroom dealings."   *—RJ Beam, author*

The Intaglio Imprint

" Super-realism and compelling rationale, ... an intricate and incisive creation."   *—George Church, geneticist*

The Drucker Proxy

" An edge-of-the-seat, emotionally gripping, intimate, arousing, techno-legal tour-de-force."   *—Phillip M. Samson, attorney*

Bashert (The Homeland Connection)

" Samson writes with a crisp elegance, like John Le Carré, and weaves his plot magically."   *—James A. Anderson, author*

The Dome (The Homeland Connection)

" An excellent read, and very highly recommended."   *—Midwest Book Review*

Web Games (The Homeland Connection)

" This extraordinary author has the ability to anticipate events. ... You will not put it down."   *—Alan Caruba, critic, BookViews*

Chipset (The Homeland Connection)

"[A] multi-dimensional thriller ... populated by flesh-and-blood characters."
                                    - Avraham Azrieli, author

Gasline (The Homeland Connection)

"[A] great novel . . . high concept, flesh-and-blood protagonist, and realistic action. ... [It] will raise your blood pressure and make you think."   *—Columbia Review of Books and Film*

Flight Track (The Homeland Connection)

"Stunning, compelling, thought-provoking. To the book's broad scope and expert pacing, add three-dimensional, engaging characters."   *—M. Thornburg, author*

Exit Plans (The Homeland Connection)

"Page-turner, nail-biter, thought-provoker [by] one of the two great American writers of near-future-maybe-as-soon-as-tomorrow fiction most worth reading ."   *—M. Thornburg, author*

The Four-Color Puzzle

"[A]n authentic thinking person's ideal mystery; an eloquent feast of words and an excellent story."   *—Jeanie B. Clemmons, author*

BASHERT

TENTH ANNIVERSARY EDITION

BASHERT

by Lior Samson

GESHER PRESS

Gesher Press
Rowley, Massachusetts

5 4 3 2 1

ISBN 978-1-7326091-4-3

Cover and book design: Larry Constantine
Cover photo: Tal Paz-Fridman, talpazfridman.com
Copyright © Tal Paz-Fridman, used with permission
Set in Optima

For Lucy, my *bashert*, whose believing buoys me through my days, and for Frank Samson, z"l, my father, whose lessons in responsibility still reverberate.

~ ~ ~

In memoriam
David Arthur Hahn, 1944-1976

You can't connect the dots looking forward; you can only connect them looking backwards. So you have to trust that the dots will somehow connect in your future. You have to trust in something—your gut, destiny, life, karma, whatever.
– Steve Jobs

Table of Contents

Preface:

Tenth Anniversary Edition

MILESTONES ABOUND. Many of them are arbitrary, based on nothing more than numbers and their origins in counting on our fingers, then further enshrined by our elliptical travels around the sun. A decade. A century. These are only significant if we make them so.

Writers write to be read, to leave some manner of legacy, fingerprints in the minds of readers and footprints in the sands of an unseen future. Most writers likely never know what imprint, if any, they might leave, or whether their writings will even survive them. By a twist of fate, I can say with some confidence that my first novel will still be read in 2067, because a copy was chosen to be included in a time capsule buried at the Massachusetts Institute of Technology in 2017 to commemorate the fiftieth anniversary reunion of its one hundredth graduating class—my class, the class of 1967, and, by no coincidence, also the graduating class of Karl Lustig, a protagonist of the novel.

But those are all just numbers: 10, 50, 100. The real reason for releasing a new edition of *Bashert* is to put in place, while I still can, a definitive record, a "director's cut" of that first novel. The opportunity to fill out the record is irresistable, so fill I will. The book has been re-edited, reset, and reproofed in hopes of finally excorcising the last of the typographical demons and to make this edition easier and more gratifying to read, not only with some more transparent organization, but with the addition of supplemental material that further grounds the story. It is still the same story, but, I hope, told and presented better.

I started the story in 2006, on a day spent bedridden by a bug that had been a nuisance to my children but had laid their father flat. I spent much of the day musing about an all-but-forgotten episode from my college days and wondering about what might have been the outcome had a brash bunch of student friends actually carried through on their fantasied exploits. At the end of the day, my wife teased me by asking what I had accomplished, lying in bed all day, and I told her that I had outlined a novel.

"Oh, really? Tell me about it," she said.

So, I did. And then she told me what was wrong with the storyline, thus establishing the precedent for a highly successful mode of collaboration that has since seen me through thirteen novels and two collections of short stories. I write something, and then she tells me what I need to do to make it work.

It took me a year of research and writing to complete the first full manuscript, a year during which I had been traveling extensively on business, punctuated by teaching a course at the University of Madeira, in Portugal. I had promised that I would finish the manuscript before returning at the end of the semester. On 17 May 2007, I finished the final paragraph of the last chapter and saved off the Word file just as a Lufthansa flight attendant reminded me for the third time that I must shut down and stow my laptop because we were about to land in Boston. One minute later, we were on the ground.

The rest of that year was spent in editing and rewriting, getting further feedback from my wife and other readers, and putting together a private, limited-edition printing distributed to family and close friends for Hanukkah and Christmas presents. Then began the long slog of finding an agent and a publisher.

I was, at the time, already an established, award-winning author. I had sold my first magazine article when I was twenty-one, had a sizable advance on my first book before I turned thirty, and had subsequently placed nearly a dozen books with major publishing houses, but, three years after finishing my first novel, I was still agentless and without a publisher. Keenly aware of the ticking clock and the flipping calendar, I reluctantly decided to take things into my own hands. My background in publishing went all the way back to the computer consulting start-up I launched before I finished college, in which my diverse duties included editing and doing cover art and book design for its publishing arm.

When the first, privately published edition of *Bashert* appeared, my then school-age son read it and enthusiastically encouraged me to write more about the characters I had created. So I did. And again.

In the three years plus that I spent looking for an agent and publisher for *Bashert*, I continued to write, finishing two more novels, *The Dome* and *Web Games*, which meant that the newborn Gesher Press published three titles in its first year. All three are being re-released in new Tenth Anniversary Editions. Technically, I was not (ugh) self-publishing; Gesher Press actually began as an imprint of the publishing division of a full-blown corporation—the consulting company owned by my wife

As Steve Jobs once said, we do not connect the dots ahead of time; the dots connect in retrospect. After a gap of four decades, I was returning to my early roots in publishing, trying my hand at modern book design, and relearning the manifold pitfalls of the manuscript-to-print process. When I first started, the state-of-the-art for small publishers was IBM's novel Magnetic Tape Selectric Composer and photo-offset printing. By the time of my return, print-on-demand had arrived, complexified by the requirements of electronic publishing for Kindle and other eBooks.

In writing and polishing *Bashert*, I had already mapped out, not always with fully conscious intent, an itinerary for a journey that would finally extend through six more novels and come to be known collectively as The Homeland Connection. In returning to the 2010 editions of the first stories in that long story arc, I have been confronted with how much of what followed grew from well-prepared ground. The dots connect.

Here, in this story, is where the dotted line began. Whether you are entering for the first time this particular world of adventure and discovery, of ordinary people caught up in extraordinary circumstances and facing exceptional challenges, or whether, like me, you are retracing a road once traveled, I hope your journey proves rewarding.

Also coming in 2020, with new material -

The Dome: Tenth Anniversary Edition

Web Games: Tenth Anniversary Edition

BASHERT

Prologue

1963 — THE DOOR WAS UNMARKED. Every other door along the gray-green basement corridor had a number, as did, to the best of Mitchell Rossing's knowledge, every door to every office, lecture hall, bathroom, or storage closet anywhere on campus. He ran his hand through his sandy, crew-cut hair and stared. He had passed the door on his rounds for weeks without paying any notice, but now, intrigued, he reached for the master key on the ring hanging from his belt.

Mitchell was not supposed to have the master key, but then Mitchell was not even supposed to be at MIT, much less working the night shift as a janitor. In the student records, he was a nineteen-year-old sophomore physics major, class of '66, living, until recently, in Burton House, one of the on-campus dorms; in the personnel records of Buildings and Power, MIT's maintenance and custodial services department, he was twenty-two, a resident of Somerville. To a few close friends—a very few—he was a brilliant, bored kid from Milwaukee who had faked his high school records to get into MIT at the age of sixteen. His friends fully expected him to graduate in a few years at the top of his class. Or end up in jail.

The master key had been easy. By comparing every office key he could get his hands on, he had deduced what he needed to file away to turn one of his restricted keys into a master that would open any door he wanted.

He glanced up and down the hallway, listening for a moment to the muffled chuffing of a vacuum pump in one of the labs. When he was sure no one was coming around the corner, he inserted and twisted the key. It didn't budge. He jiggled it in and out a few times before the pins dropped into place and the cylinder finally turned.

The door was unexpectedly heavy, and Mitchell had to heave his chunky body against it to get it ajar. He slipped in and partly closed it behind him before turning on his flashlight. The room was narrow and deep and appeared to be nearly full of metallic cylinders in waist-high wooden shipping frames.

"Holy shit!" he whispered as he backed quickly out of the room and closed the heavy door after him. The resonant bang, like the closing of a vault door, echoed down the empty corridor.

Fate … is a name for facts not yet passed under the fire of thought—for causes which are unpenetrated. – Ralph Waldo Emerson

Part One: Karl

1

2003 — THE DISTANT THRUMMING grew louder as the gurney bounced and rattled down the endless gray hallway. Karl's head hurt and his back ached. What was he doing here? How had he gotten here? He struggled to sort out his surroundings. A nurse leaned over the gurney, a look of concern and annoyance on his face. Suddenly, an astringent mix of aftershave and disinfectant assaulted Karl's nostrils, jerking him fully awake. The gurney dissolved beneath him, and the hospital corridor morphed into the gray and gold interior of an Airbus 340. With courteous impatience, a Lufthansa flight attendant stood beside him, holding out a hot towel saturated with the airline's strangely medicinal signature scent.

"*Nein, danke,* no thanks," Karl said, waving the towel away while still struggling with his sense of disorientation. For reasons he had never fully deciphered, hospitals had become a recurrent element in his dreams whenever he traveled. They had fascinated and repelled him ever since his emergency surgery as a young man in college.

He twisted around to check the lines at the lavatories four rows back. He was hoping there would be time to wash up and shave. He fiddled unsuccessfully with the elaborate array of buttons on the seat control but managed only to get his seat part way toward vertical before he gave up and muscled himself erect. A consummate techie, Karl prided himself in his ability to decipher any new technology, but he had a special place on his personal blacklist for Airbus engineers, who, in his opinion, never seemed to get the human factors right, an opinion he was more than ready to express to any traveling companion fortune might put in the adjacent seat.

The line at the toilets was still three deep when the seat-belt light flashed on and the captain came on the PA to request that everyone return to their seats. Karl, one of those rare Americans who truly believed that rules and regulations were for the greater good of all, was the only one who headed back to his seat. As he squeezed past the flight attendant he nodded toward the queue at the back, smiled, and shrugged, as if to say, "What can you do?" It seemed to Karl that modern society, particularly in his own country, was drowning in entitlement, in people who thought themselves somehow exempt from the rules.

Karl pressed button after button on the control unit in the arm of his seat until it was finally restored to its fully upright position. He sat down and settled in. He was already thinking about his Plan B, a stop at the Lufthansa lounge before leaving Frankfurt airport. The whole trip had been improvised: an unplanned response to a last-minute call from one of his oldest clients who wanted him to sit in on a product review at the request of a subcontractor in Israel. It did not impress him as cost effective and was not likely to be all that interesting, but he hated to turn down good money.

Boston-Frankfurt was yet another routine that Karl Lustig had mastered in his enduring struggle to order the chaos of his peripatetic life. The moment he boarded the flight he would reset his watch to European time, stare at it for a few moments, then shake his head saying aloud, "Whoa, way past my bedtime." Resetting the mental clock, he called it. Rejecting the trendy tee-totaling approach to air travel of the water-bottle toting set, he always accepted the proffered champagne before takeoff, followed it once airborne with two glasses of whatever passably good German white was being served, and then collapsed into dream-tormented sleep for the remaining five hours over the Atlantic.

As other passengers downed the last bits of what passed for breakfast in an era of airline cutbacks and minimalist amenities, Karl flipped absent-mindedly through the duty-free catalog, then drifted in and out of sleep until the plane hit the tarmac.

The flight, which had been delayed out of Boston for never-specified mechanical reasons, was more than an hour late, so by the time Karl reached the maze of Terminal 1, Frankfurt Airport was becoming an absolute zoo awash in every variant of the human animal. Even the Lufthansa business-class lounge was wall-to-wall with travelers between flights. Karl pushed through a knot of Russian businessmen to reach the bathrooms. On returning, he looked around for a vacant seat. Seeing none, he headed toward the racks of newspapers and searched for the comforting peach color of the *Financial Times.* Slipping one under his arm, he strode back past the courtesy desk and headed down the stairs again. With his laptop over his shoulder and his mono-grammed Tumi trailing behind him, Karl zigzagged through the crowds, stopping briefly at the Hertz Gold counter to pick up his keys before heading for the car park.

A light dusting of dry snow, as fine as confectioner's sugar, eddied and swirled on the road as he pulled onto the A3 heading toward Nürnberg. The sun, now risen just above the tree line, sparkled through the airy waves of crystal washing over the Autobahn, creating tiny evanescent rainbows. Accelerating hard, Karl deftly shifted into the high-speed lane with one hand while tuning in *"Antenne Bayern"* with the other. The mostly American rock interspersed with light chatter in German provided just enough stimulation to help keep him alert without distracting him from the demands of driving.

Traffic was heavy but steady at a hundred-and-forty for several minutes before some perturbation sent a double dotted red line of flashing brake lights zipping toward him. Karl smiled. He slowed and expertly shifted lanes in the quick ogive favored by European drivers. To him, this was sport, like a sort of 3D video game requiring three-sixty-degree situational awareness and hair-trigger reflexes. Nearly two hundred kilometers-an-hour one minute and down to eighty the next, with only a car length or two between you and the Mercedes in front. For Karl, the only child of two engineers, it was not a matter of thrills but the challenge of meshing with precision as one more cog among thousands in the fast and fluctuating German highway machine.

Totally absorbed in his driving, Karl almost missed the exit sign for the *Rasthof Weiskirchen*, the rest area that had become his customary stop for coffee and pastry en route. He checked his mirror, then slowed quickly, calibrating his braking by the blue-and-white striped marker posts streaming past, counting down each 100 meters, all the while conscious of the Fiat on his tail that followed him onto the exit ramp. Once in the rest area, he drove past the pumps and the café to park his blue Audi well down the lot and away from other cars. He tucked his newspaper under his arm, and headed back to the café, striding briskly in the crisp air.

Inside, the café was bright and noisy. A line had already formed in the self-service area, but there were still plenty of empty tables, particularly in the central non-smoking section. As Karl grabbed a tray, a middle-aged woman in business attire pushed ahead, limping slightly, to slip into line behind him, just edging out a group of loud-talking young Germans. As he slid his tray along past the glass cases filled with sandwiches, pastries, and salads, he fished out a ten-Euro note from his passport wallet and placed it beside his plate. Hearing the woman behind him mutter something in English, he turned just in time to see her fish a credit card from her purse and lay it on her tray. She smiled at him and said, almost apologetically, "I meant to stop at the *Geld-automat* to get some cash. I really hate to charge just a cup of coffee."

Karl nodded and smiled back. Then he noticed her credit card and laughed.

"What?" she said.

"Just this." He fished his wallet out of his jacket again and placed it on his own tray, opened to show an identical credit card: MIT Alumni Association. "Good school," he said with a nod.

"You went to MIT? What course? When?"

"Course 6, class of '67. You?"

"No way! I was class of '67, too. Course 2. I can't believe this. What a coincidence. Imagine the odds. Here we are in the middle of Germany, and ... and a classmate just happens to want coffee at the same time at the same rest stop." She said the last with just the faintest hint of sarcasm, almost as if she didn't believe in mere coincidence. "Fate maybe?" she added with a grin and a tilt of her head.

As she talked, Karl studied her, tracing the lines of her boyish, pleasantly plain face. The auburn highlights in her thick, short hair and her makeup—more than Karl usually liked—showed attention to detail, as did the Hermes scarf pinned artfully around her shoulders. She managed an elegance that made her seem taller than she was. He might have pegged her as being in her mid-forties had he not already known when she graduated from college.

"It really has been a long time," he said. "It was all numbers to us back then, but now I don't even remember what course 2 means. Not that that sort of thing makes a lot of difference in the long haul. As for me, I may have been an EE major, but I never actually did any electrical engineering. I got completely corrupted by a course whose number is still etched in my mind: course 6.41, Introduction to Automatic Computation. It was a life changer. Once I'd written my first Fortran program, I was hooked. Then my fate was sealed by way too many weekends wasted programming on a PDP-1 computer in the basement of building 26. I've been a computer geek ever since in one manner or another.

"Oh, sorry for being rude and not introducing myself properly. I'm Karl Lustig." He put out his hand.

She took it gracefully but firmly. "Maryam Cashman. Good to meet you. What brings you to Germany in the dead of winter?"

"A couple days of meetings in Nürnberg." He shook his head. "Really crucial." He made quotes in the air with his fingers. "You?"

"A trade fair, *Spielwarenmesse Nürnberg*. I'm a buyer for a chain of children's stores."

"Ah, yes, the famed International Toy Fair. So, it's your fault I couldn't book a room within 20 miles of my meetings," he said with a wink.

"I suppose then the least I can do is buy you breakfast. No, I insist. *Bitte, alles zusammen*," she said to the clerk, gesturing at both their trays. "I hope you don't mind. Would you like to join me over coffee?" She nodded toward a table in the center section with a *"Nichtraucher"* sign on it.

He let her lead the way. She emptied her tray on the table, then slipped it down beside her chair. "Mechanical," she said as she sat down.

"Wie bitte? Er, I mean, say what? You have to forgive me, I'm in my 'It's-Tuesday-so-this-must-be-Germany' mode."

"Mechanical engineering, course 2, my major at MIT. That ultimately led me into industrial design. In fact, I studied at the *Hochschule für Gestaltung* in Ulm, here in Germany, then got into toys and games. But that's another story. *Sie sprechen gut Deutsch,"* she said, praising his German.

"Nur ein bißchen. Only a little. *Falo um pouco de Português. Jeg taler en lidt Dansk.* I speak a little of a dozen languages and not much of any. I suppose it's iconic. My life has always been a lot like that: a little of this, a little of that, a little here, a little there. Never a lot, but always enough to manage."

She held her mug in both hands and sipped slowly at her coffee. "So, let me guess. You are a consultant."

"Yeah, sometimes. Is it the sign on my forehead? Also sort of a journalist. I write a column for a rag called *iTech Weekly* and have a blog that draws pretty well. The column, advertising on the blog, and a gig now and then for Microsoft or GE or whatever keep me in beer money. Things are not as hot as they were a few years back with the millennium bug scare, but I'm doing all right. Not exactly what I would really want to be doing, but I do get to travel—although more than I would like some of the time. Still, with nothing really to tie me down it's not a bad life."

"You're not married, then," she said, a statement more than a question.

"No. I was … briefly … when I was young. Too young, really. And you?" He snuck a quick glance at her left hand. No ring. She shook her head and took another sip of coffee. "Are you a road warrior, too?"

"In spurts," she answered. "Mostly to major fairs or to check in on a supplier that is not performing up to par. Haifa is home for me now. A long way from Cambridge, but life can take unexpected twists and turns. The voyage begins with such brilliance and direction, doesn't it? In college you think you are going somewhere, somewhere in particular. Usually it's somewhere big. Then you end up in Haifa, buying and selling toys and game." They both laughed, a quiet puff of a laugh.

"Haifa, huh? It's a real mess in the Middle East these days, isn't it?"

"You can leave off 'these days.' We have had a lot of practice in living with conflict. Maybe too much. Crisis can become habit, just another part of everyday life. Of course it has gotten even messier since your president decided to take on Iraq."

"He's not my president. We didn't even elect him, he just took office. I don't know about you, but my life has certainly gotten a lot more difficult with all the extra security stuff now. Business travel is certainly more work and less fun, not that there ever was a heap of fun in sleeping sitting up."

"So, what exactly would you like to be doing, then? If you could pick anything in the world, what?" She tilted her head and looked at him expectantly.

"Am I being interviewed for your blog? You do have a way of getting to the point," he said with another quick laugh. "Okay, that's all right, I like that. I think. Well, I suppose I would be writing. Novels. Giving Dan Brown a run for his money. I have a dozen files on my laptop with the first pages of what I am certain could be best sellers, really, but somehow I never get around to writing the rest of the pages. I keep promising myself that I'll spend time writing on the plane or in my hotel room but then I break my promise and…" He trailed off. "You know how it is."

"Maybe you ought to aim higher," she said.

"What? Higher than Dan Brown? Higher than the best-selling author since God?"

She looked at him earnestly. "Well, David Mamet for literate dialog. John Irving for subtle character. Or Francine Mathews for fast-paced complexity."

"I know Mamet and Irving, but not Mathews."

"You should check her out. But Brown is a good plotter." She looked briefly out the window behind him then smiled broadly at him. "That's plotter, not plodder."

"Uh huh. What about you? What would you be doing?"

"I don't know, but it's time I was getting out of supply-chain management," she said, absent-mindedly swirling her coffee. "Yes, it is time. I think I've had more than enough of the toys. And the games. Everything has gotten so complicated lately. It all seemed so much simpler in the beginning.

"Speaking of beginnings, MIT really was such an amazing place when we were there, wasn't it? MIT. The 'Tool and die works,' as we called it then. We thought we were 'tooling' away at our studies so hard we would die. I suppose it still is amazing, but you always remember your own years in college as the glory days. Anything was possible." She paused, taking another sip of coffee while staring intently past him out the window. As soon as Karl noticed, she shifted her gaze back to him.

"Do you remember the hacks?" she asked. "Inspired insanity, so many brilliant stunts! I think my favorite of all time was The Great Pumpkin hack. You remember that one? The undergrads who pulled it off had to work feverishly in teams to dangle black painted sheets from the Great Dome and rig the floodlights with orange gels in the few minutes of dusk before the outside lights were turned on. When the floods on the Dome did come on, Boston was treated to the sight of the Great Pumpkin rising across the Charles River."

"I didn't see it myself, but I heard about it. I do remember this one guy," said Karl, "a real character, the consummate hacker. He was absolutely brilliant. And absolutely crazy, I suppose. Also rather charismatic in a geekish sort of way. He drew people to himself, drew them into the circle of his plots and machinations. Do you remember how everything was a 'comm,' like the Judicial Committee was JudComm? Well he had formed this unofficial cadre of pranksters that called itself HackComm. They fancied themselves real masters at orchestrating over-the-top stunts.

"One morning the first subway train into the Kendall Square Station fails to stop. The engineer puts the brakes on full, but the train just sails right on through the station and finally stops halfway across the Longfellow Bridge to Boston. They found lithium grease spread along the tracks. The spokesperson for the T went on and on about how dangerous the stunt was but failed to mention that they had found a handwritten sign at the exact spot where the train had finally skidded to a stop. The guys who pulled it off had done their physics homework and knew it was safe."

Maryam smiled broadly. "No shortage of chutzpah, that's for sure. Although actually it wasn't a sign, just a chalk mark running across the tracks at the point where the front of the first car would stop." She paused, then added, "If I remember correctly." She paused again. "Yes, MIT was sure a hotbed of hackers, a lot of smart kids with no sense of limits. You don't happen to remember the name of that guy, do you."

"Mmmm, Michael something. No. Can't think of it now. Funny. I can picture him. He had this easy-going good nature and a knowing smile that never left his face. I was just a freshman, but we became friends for a short while, even planned some hacks together." He stopped for a moment, deep in thought. "I lost interest in it all before he did. Maybe I was starting to grow up. Or maybe I just was carrying a heavier course load. I was on a scholarship and didn't want to lose it."

She nodded with an understanding smile. "Do you ever wonder what happened to the hackers? Like this guy. Did he ever grow up? Did he succeed? Or end up in jail? What would you imagine, Mister Next Dan Brown?"

"Never thought much about it. I have no idea where he went or what he did. I have never been very good at keeping track of people. Always moving on, I suppose. Next job, new clients, new apartment, that sort of thing. I think I have always been too busy thinking about what lay around the next curve."

"You know, you could just make it up. The life of an errant genius could make a good novel, don't you think? You could call it," she paused, feigning deep thought, "maybe something like 'Catch Me if You Can.'" She arched her eyebrows as she gave him a silly grin, then glanced out the window over his shoulder again. As if suddenly remembering a forgotten appointment, she quickly pushed herself back from the table. "Well, I better be hitting the road if I'm going to have time to check email before my first vendor meeting. Oh, good luck at Siemens."

Karl started to ask how she figured he was headed for Siemens, but she was already out of her seat and collecting her things off the table. He rose, too, smiling. "Maybe we'll bump into each other in Nürnberg," he said hopefully.

"Doubtful," she said as she brushed past him. "I've a really full calendar this week. But good luck with your novel. I'll look for word of its publication in the alumni news." She winked, then headed for the parking lot.

Karl nodded to her back as he watched her leave, first noticing how she favored her left leg slightly, then shrugging his shoulders for no particular reason. He sat back down to finish his coffee and scan the *Financial Times* before picking up his wallet and bussing the tray back to the drop-off point.

As he returned to his car, Karl didn't notice his new acquaintance watching from a Fiat squeezed in among the lines of parked soft-sided trailer trucks with Eastern European license plates. He was long gone on the Autobahn when the driver rolled down the window and squinted up at a man's face, too silhouetted against the brightening sky to make out, and said, quietly, with a mix of resignation and uncertainty, "Lev?"

2

THREE DAYS OF CONSULTING all day and mandatory business dinners every night had taken their toll on Karl, who was, despite his gregarious professional persona, an introvert at the core. He also hated the end-of-day return flights from Europe, preferring the brutally short night of the outbound flight to the one ungodly long day on the way back. To make matters worse, for some reason his anticipated upgrade to business class had not cleared, so he had been stuck in cattle class with the tourists and those whom he thought of as the business and professional also-rans.

At Logan Airport, he dragged himself through the serpentine lines of immigration and wearily handed his passport and customs declaration to the agent, who glanced at the passport and said, mechanically, "Welcome back, Mr. Lustig. What took you to Germany?"

"Same old same old, meeting with clients."

The agent scanned the passport nonchalantly, turned the declaration over and marked a red swirl on it.

Karl had expected more scrutiny on his return, given the heightened security, but was actually most anxious about the "food police" from Agriculture. The dogs who sniffed his bag, however, were obviously more interested in drugs or explosives than the cheese he was bringing back from Germany. He zipped through the green line without a hitch, then stopped off in a men's room to freshen up. Alone in the room, he studied himself briefly in the mirror, giving his tousled salt-and-pepper hair a quick brush and straightening his tie before deciding to take it off altogether. He thought about getting the brush-off from the woman he had met at the rest stop and wondered, as he studied his face, whether he was just getting too old and unappealing. A loner, that's what I am, that's my karma, he thought, as he left and headed for the vast concrete gloom of Logan Airport's Central Parking.

~ ~ ~

In the tunnel heading for Boston, traffic was already past peak, but Karl had to twice flash his brake lights at some guy tailgating him. One way or another, there were headlights in his rearview mirror all the way to his Beacon Hill apartment. He was just making the final turn into his street when the lights in his mirror started flashing blue.

Shit, what now? Karl thought. He pulled over as best he could on the narrow street lined with parked cars. He watched as the officer walked up beside his car and shined his flashlight in.

"May I see your driver's license and registration, please?"

Karl stretched to get his registration from the glove compartment, then pulled his wallet from his jacket. His driver's license was not in its usual slot. He checked through the wallet, then started fishing around in his pockets. "I, uh, can't seem to find my license at the moment. I just flew in from Germany and I seem to have mislaid it." He handed his registration to the officer, who studied it under the flashlight.

"Are you the owner of this vehicle?"

"Yes, I'm Karl Lustig. Here, I can show you my passport."

"That won't be necessary. But you had better find your license or get a replacement right away. Do you know why I stopped you? Your left taillight is out and the brake lights are not working. I'm not going to cite you for driving without a license, but you had better get those lights fixed right away. Okay?" He handed the registration back.

"Yes, thank you, officer. I will. I'll take care of it right away. My license is probably in my luggage. I'll find it."

Karl obsessed over the license and the broken light as he drove the last block and a half. In the small parking lot behind his building, he left the car running as he unloaded his luggage from the back. To his surprise, both taillights were working. He groaned as he thought of the hassles ahead. He knew that a loose connection somewhere in the wiring harness could be the devil to track down.

Even though he was bone tired, once in his apartment, Karl started following his coming-home ritual to the letter, carefully hanging his coat on its hallway peg and his suit jacket in the bedroom closet, moving books from one row to another on the bookshelves lining the hallway to make the proper space for the new novel he had been reading on the plane, sorting the mail, and finally checking his messages. There was a reminder on the answering machine from his editor to check in about the book he was writing plus a couple of messages with only background traffic noise quickly followed by a disconnecting click.

The driver's license bothered him most. He was not one to misplace things, and he had never before in his life lost his license. After zipping through his email, he spread his folding suit bag open on the bed and started checking every pocket and compartment. He put the heavily wrapped *Butterkäse* secreted with his shirts into the cheese drawer of his refrigerator, then slid the two bottles of German reds, a Dornfelder and a Lemberger, into the bottom of the little climate-controlled wine keeper in his living room.

As he unpacked his sports jacket, he checked the pockets for the missing license. In the left side pocket his fingers closed on something cold and metallic. He pulled out a small, filigreed cylinder on a silver chain; it danced and glinted in the overhead light. At first he was unsure of what he was looking at, then recognized it as a mezuzah. What in hell is this doing in my jacket? he thought. How did it get there? And whose is it?

Karl walked slowly into the living room, set the mezuzah down on his coffee table, then went to the kitchen to pour himself a glass of viognier from a bottle in the fridge. He returned and slumped down on the couch to stare off into space and slowly drift into an exhausted and anxious sleep. He dreamed he was stuck in economy class with a planeload of kibbutz-bound college students on an El Al flight to Tel Aviv.

3

KARL WAS AWAKENED by the tweeting of his cell phone. The caller ID showed "out of area." He looked at the time and guessed that it might actually be from overseas. Probably Dieter Braun calling from Siemens to follow up on their meeting. He flipped the phone open and put it slowly to his ear. "Yes?" he said.

Traffic noise. Click.

He closed the phone and put it back on his belt clip. Time to get organized, he thought. What day is it? What do I have to do? Take a shower and change, for one thing. Oh, yes, the teleconference with David.

David Edelmann was his editor at Harrison-Interbooks. Karl, who was nearly a year behind on delivering a book manuscript, dreaded even talking with David. Like his unwritten novels, Karl's latest technical book—on the arcana of client-side scripting for Web applications—was only a few thousand words of notes and reams of good intentions. Another apologetic, excuse-filled chat with David was the last thing Karl wanted. He cradled his head in his hands for several seconds. He had long believed that he was immune to jet lag, but in recent years was finding his belief eroding. Mornings like this one sorely tested his faith.

After a quick shower and change of clothes, he marched into the kitchen to pour himself the last cup of coffee from the pot he had, as usual, stashed in the fridge before leaving for Germany, then shoved the mug into the microwave. As he waited for the coffee to heat, he absent-mindedly fiddled with the mezuzah. He had, of course, seen them before, but he had never actually held one. He was surprised when the end came off in his hand to reveal the scroll inside. He pulled it out and unrolled it. The tiny piece of parchment paper was covered with minute Hebrew letters that meant nothing to him but carried the mystique of an undeciphered message in an alien script. He twisted it tightly and stuffed it back into its case.

"Now there's an idea," he said out loud. He looked across the room at the digital clock on the microwave. "Just enough time to make it to David's office." Years of living alone had left Karl with the habit of talking to himself, which he struggled, not always successfully, to keep in check when he was around others.

He stuffed the mezuzah in his pocket, then quickly transferred his coffee into a travel mug. In the living room, he grabbed his car keys off the end table, reached for his laptop beside the sofa, and headed out the door.

Leaving Boston, Karl had to resist staring upward at the dizzyingly elegant patterns formed by the cable stays of the Zakim Bridge. Both his parents had worked on bridges, and this one had become one of his favorite local sights. To him it was the near-perfect expression of an engineering aesthetic that his parents had always preached, one that crafted beauty from purpose.

Heading toward David's office in Woburn, Karl found the northbound traffic on I93 to be particularly heavy for after nine in the morning, and it was several minutes before he became fully aware of the identical black Lincolns crowding him in front and behind. He switched lanes and slowed.

They jockeyed for position and soon were boxing him in again. Damned Massachusetts drivers, Karl thought, even limo drivers are obnoxious these days. He was so preoccupied with the two cars that kept crowding him, that he almost missed his exit.

He checked his mirror, flipped on his signal, and made a quick "S" onto the off ramp, all in a single move. To his surprise, the car on his tail followed expertly. Karl shook his head. It was beginning to seem like he was being followed. A phrase from his in-flight reading flashed into his mind: surveillance awareness. He'd been surprised to find the Francine Mathews spy thriller in an airport bookstore. Remembering that the author had been mentioned by the woman at the *Rasthof,* he had bought it on impulse. No, this is ridiculous, he thought, a paranoid hypothesis if ever there was one. Still, he supposed, there should be a way to test the hypothesis.

He eyed the car on his tail while waiting to make his left turn into the traffic on the one-way street. He tromped the accelerator to pull precisely into a break just big enough for one car, then signaled and zigzagged expertly across three lanes of traffic and into the far lane. As soon as he cleared the underpass, he pulled into the breakdown lane, then guiltily and cautiously backed up to the onramp to head north again on the Interstate. When he reached route 128, he took the southbound exit of the cloverleaf, then looped again to reverse direction back toward his exit from I93. Just like the Autobahn, he thought, only here all the rest of the people on the road are Boston drivers—idiots.

There was no sign of his escort when he turned into the industrial park, but he deliberately passed the entrance for Harrison-Interbooks and pulled into the second driveway.

He parked behind the first building, locked his car, and crossed through the trees that separated the two sections of the park. Ducking behind a van, he waited and watched. Nothing. He felt silly.

At David's office on the second floor of the Harrison Building he knocked, then opened the door to peek around it with a grin on his face.

"Wow. To what do I owe this?" David said, rising from behind his glass and chrome desk and extending his hand to Karl. The desk was an island of modern-design order amidst a reef of chaos, with stacks of books and papers all but surrounding it. David's pastiche of plaid jacket, turtleneck, and blue jeans—sartorial testimony to his artsy past—were a better match for the messy perimeter than the corporate center of his little atoll. Like Karl, he harbored fantasies of writing a great novel. Like Karl, he invariably deferred to the demands of "real" work. "You haven't been to my office in years. I thought we were having a teleconference this morning. I was just about to ping you at your apartment."

Karl grabbed a chair and pulled it close to the desk. "This may seem a bit odd, but, well, we've been friends and have worked together for a lot of years."

David ran a hand through his curly hair. "That sounds like a lead-in for a favor if ever I heard one," he cracked.

"No. No favors. Just thought you'd be able to tell me something about this?" He reached out and opened his hand above David's, dropping the mezuzah into it.

"So, did you finally realize what Ellen has always said? You have a *yidishe neshama*, a Jewish soul. You're really one of us," he said teasingly.

"Not me. I'm a card-carrying secular humanist, Dave, you know that. Humanists don't have souls. Anyway, I don't think I qualify by either ancestry or temperament."

"Look, half my friends at Temple Beth Shalom are humanists. There's room for all kinds in the goodly tents of Jacob. And who knows what surprises might lurk back there in your northern European family tree. I always wondered about that Mediterranean nose of yours.

"But, here, let's take a look at this. Nice mezuzah, looks handcrafted, very intricate design." He turned it over. "Yes, here's the artist's mark, Shira Zemer, an Israeli woman, I believe. I think it's a pseudonym, by the way."

"Why do you say that?"

"Because it's sort of a play on words. 'Sing song.' I don't think anyone with the surname Zemer would name a daughter Shira. But then, I never could imagine a parent naming a daughter Moon Unit, either."

Karl took it back, opened it, and removed the scroll. "Okay, so what's this? Is it a message? What does it say?"

"That's the *Shema*, a Jewish prayer. Well, not *a* Jewish prayer, really *the* Jewish prayer. Here," he reached for the tiny piece of paper and squinted at it. "Yes, see it says '*Shema Yisrael Adonai elohenu, Adonai echad.*' Hear, oh Israel, the Lord is God, the Lord is One." He paused. "But…"

"What?"

David frowned. "This isn't right. The beginning, the first six words, are the *Shema*, but then it has two extra words: '*Zachor, Bashert.*' Remember. Fated. Then it continues as it should, except the calligraphy is uneven, too heavy in places. This is impossible."

"Why? I don't understand."

"These things are written by *sofrim*, scribes who are real *frumis*, you know, very pious. They work under strict rules and the work is always thoroughly checked. One mistake,

even the tiniest, and the scroll is invalid and has to be ritu-
ally buried. I can't imagine how work this bad could slip by.
Unless it was deliberate. Where did you get this? And what
are you doing with a mezuzah, anyway? You're a self-con-
fessed card-carrying humanist. And while we're doing the
interrogation thing, where is the manuscript you owe me?"

Karl laughed. "Always the editor, eh David? As for the
mezuzah, I really don't know. I found it in my jacket pocket
when I unpacked last night. Don't know how it got there, but
I must have acquired it somehow in Europe. I am beginning
to have an uneasy feeling about it. This probably sounds paranoid, but twice since I got back from Germany, I thought
somebody was following me. And my driver's license is missing. You know me." He slowed to punctuate his words. "I
do not lose things."

He stood and leaned over the desk. "Look, could I borrow an office and an Internet connection for a couple hours.
Is that okay?"

"Sure, as long as you're working on the book you owe
me," David said, then held up his hands in mock defense.
"Just kidding. Here, you can use my office. I've got meetings
all morning, anyway. Some former spook from Israeli intelligence wants us to publish his memoirs. So, make yourself
at home. Use my computer, too. With our security systems it
would be way too hard to get your laptop to work on our
network." He grabbed a sheaf of papers off the top of a stack
beside his desk and headed out the door.

Karl sat down at the desk, launched a browser, and started to work. First he went to the mass.gov site to order a replacement drivers license, then switched to the spartan fa-
miliarity of the Google homepage, where he typed in "Shira
Zemer."

It was several hours before David Edelmann poked his head back into the office. "Any luck?" he asked. Karl nodded. "Good. Look, I need my office back, but Ellen says you are invited to dinner at our place tonight, eight o'clock. I think she figures if we feed you, you'll feel obligated to finish the book for me. You can fill us in tonight about whatever you found out."

4

KARL HAD KNOWN ELLEN much longer than David—he had, in fact, introduced them to each other—but he was surprised by the slender, middle-aged woman who opened the door. "You ... you look great!" he stammered.

"Thanks," she said with obvious pleasure. "I've lost weight, been working out."

"Here," he said, giving her a slow up and down as he handed her a gift bag decorated with multicolored grapevines.

"What's this? Hmmm, let me guess." She shook the bag gently and pretended to listen for a rattle before pulling out the bottle and feigning surprise. "Wine. How nice," she said, turning the bottle to read the label. "This looks interesting. A Lemberger? Never heard of it."

"The German reds are virtually unknown here and unfairly unappreciated, not least of all by the Germans themselves. This one is a Württemberger I just brought back from Germany. It's really good, surprisingly dense and subtle. If it doesn't go with what we're having tonight you can always save it for another occasion."

"Well, we are having comfort food tonight, pot roast, my grandmother's recipe. What do you think, will it work?" Karl nodded. "Okay, let's do it. Come on in."

She took his coat and hung it in the oversized hall closet, "Dave and the boys are waiting," she said, pointing toward the living room.

Dinner was deferred for a compulsory parading of the Edelmann's twins before they were sent off to bed. Karl tried to show interest and make small talk about soccer and model airplanes, but he was not, in his own words, a "kid person." Both boys gave their father one of those eye-rolling heavenward looks as they left the room.

"Don't mind them," David said. "They don't particularly like talking with me either. It's a ten-year-old boy thing."

Once dinner started, he and Karl talked shop until Ellen interrupted. "Enough about publishing and consulting. I want to hear about something interesting. David says you're researching Judaica now," she said teasingly. "Did you uncover any treasures today? Or was it Talmudic truths you were seeking on the Web?"

Karl took a quick sip of wine before answering. "I don't know what David told you, but it has been one weird thing after another ever since I got back from Germany this week. I lost my driver's license, would you believe, apparently while I was overseas. And I spent most of the morning trying to find some clue about this mezuzah I discovered in my jacket pocket." He laid it on the table. "All I was able to learn was that the silversmith who made it is an artist who lives in Haifa. She goes by the name of Shira Zemer, which David says is a kind of multilingual joke. According to her website, she grew up in England but studied in America before moving to Israel. I sent an email to her with a photo of the mezuzah asking if she might know anything about it. No reply yet, but that's no surprise, time difference and all.

"On the other hand, I drew a complete blank on this woman I met in Germany, Maryam Cashman. I was curious. She claims she graduated from MIT the same year I did, so I thought I'd check the alumnae register. Nothing. She said she lives in Haifa, so I search the online telephone books for Haifa. Zilch. Now I am really intrigued, so I phone MIT pretending to be an HR guy and claiming she's applied for a job, and, naturally, I wanted to verify her application. There were not that many coeds—no wait, Ellen, remember, that's what they were called back then—so we checked through them all. No Cashmans and no Maryam anybody enrolled at MIT at the time."

"Well, maybe she changed her name at some point," Ellen said. "Cashman could be her married name or Maryam might be a variant of her original name or something else."

David put up his hand to stop her. "Remember, Karl is a consultant. I am sure he tried all those things. He researches stuff on the Web all the time as part of his job. If he can't find anything, there probably isn't anything to be found."

"Sure," she said, "he may have tried the World-Wide Web, but did he try the Jewish Web? No, I'm serious. Jews know Jews. You should talk with Jews you know. I mean six-degrees, that's all that separates any of us, right? For Jews, it's only four." David had lowered his head almost to the table and was shaking it slowly. "No, no, I'm serious," she continued. "Use the network. Thelma down the block has a cousin in Haifa. I should ask her. You should ask your other Jewish friends, Karl."

Karl laughed. "I have no other Jewish friends, so I'm asking you."

"What do you mean? You have no other *friends*," David said with a grin. "I'm only half joking. You certainly have a lot of colleagues, but not many friends. Not that I know of, in any case."

Ellen interrupted him and said, "Speaking of which,

when are you ever going to get married again and settle down? No. I'm serious, too. It's never too late. And you're a good catch. For an over-the-hill hermit, anyway."

David put his hand on Ellen's arm. "Now, don't abuse the man. Let him eat. But Karl, surely you know lots of Jews. You must have had many Jewish friends over the years besides Ellen ... and me, of course. You went to MIT, after all. Whether you were aware of it or not, the place was probably crawling with Jews."

Karl paused with his fork halfway to his mouth. "You know, that is funny, because this woman from Haifa that I met in Germany was talking about hacks—you know, stunts, practical jokes—and I do remember this one woman who was part of this group of hackers, except she wasn't at MIT. She went to Boston University and was a member of BU Hillel. I remember that because I had to ask what Hillel was, which is how I found out that she was Jewish. I was pretty clueless about those sort of things then.

"Deborah Geffner. Wow, I can't believe I remembered her name. Well, I did have a thing for her. She was a sharp little firebrand of a girl." He looked over at Ellen who gave him a scowl. "Okay, woman. Well, no, girl, really. Cute as all get out. Voice like Joan Baez. Had fantasies about going to Israel to join a kibbutz."

"Make *aliyah*. That's what it's called, *aliyah*, go up. Did she?"

"I don't know. I lost track of her. Who knows."

"Well, how about dessert before you go? And how's that for a segue? You know, somebody has to feed the poor bachelors of the world. It's a *mitzvah*," Ellen said with a smile. "Blueberry pie. You can have it ala mode if you like. And, yes, we had meat for dinner, but we're not very big on keeping kosher. Funny how often I feel the need to explain those things. I think it's the plight of the modern Jew. We may be liberated from our legacy intellectually, but for many of us, we are still self-conscious about it."

"Well, I don't keep kosher either," he said, laughing. "But no thanks. I am really too full. Still, thank you for a lovely dinner. I think I'll just call it a night."

"You don't fool me, Karl Lustig. Remember, I know you. You want to get back to your apartment so you can spend half the night on the computer trying to track down this Geffner person."

"You always did have my number, Ellen. Which is probably the real reason you left me and married David. Aside from the fact I'm a goy and therefore surgically imperfect. But, you also know firsthand that I'm hopeless, impossible to live with."

"And who's saying David is such a prize?" she said. David grimaced and feigned being stabbed in the chest.

As David was retrieving Karl's coat from the closet, Ellen disappeared into the kitchen. She returned with a slice of pie on a plastic plate covered with cling wrap. "To give you energy for your late-night surfing," she said.

On the drive back into Boston Karl started thinking again about the flawed scroll in the mezuzah. *Zachor, Bashert*, it had said. Remember. Fate. Maybe it was meant for him. Remember. But remember what? He smiled, thinking about Debbie Geffner and how he had met her. It had been in Mitchell's apartment. Right. Mitchell, that was his name, not Michael but Mitchell, Mitchell Rossing. He was the hacker who had pulled off the subway train stunt. I am on a roll, Karl thought, congratulating himself. Nothing wrong with my memory.

The car struck him from behind without warning. Karl heard the grinding crunch of metal on metal, the sound of shattering glass as he was pushed into a line of parked cars, and the sharp bang as the airbag went off. Dazed, Karl tried to figure out what had just happened. Suddenly, a tall man in a ski jacket jerked open the driver-side door.

"Are you all right?" he asked, leaning into the car. His face, mere inches from Karl's, was blotchy, with a texture like gravel on a beach. He grabbed at Karl as though trying to lift him out of the car, then pulled back quickly.

"Yes … I'm okay …. What the hell? Why the hell did you rear end me? Wait a minute!" Karl wrinkled his nose. "Shit, the car's on fire." He pawed at his seatbelt, struggling to undo it quickly. He scrambled out of the car and stood back from it, watching, but there was no sign of flames and only the faintest haze of smoke.

"Don't worry," the man beside him said. "It's just the charge in the airbag, the explosive. You'll be all right."

Karl turned around, but the man was already getting back into his car. He revved the engine and pulled out quickly, missing Karl by inches. Karl recognized it as a Lincoln, but had no time to get the license number.

Too shook up by the hit-and-run to do much of anything, he sat down on the curb and stared at the crumpled rear of his car. Well, at least now they won't have a problem figuring out why the taillight doesn't work, he thought. I guess I better call the police. He pulled out his cell phone to dial 911. As he waited for them to answer, he idly reached into his pocket to finger the mezuzah. It was gone.

5

1963 — DEBBIE GEFFNER HAD WALTZED briefly into his life back in 1963 when she bounded up the two flights to Mitchell's Back Bay apartment and nearly collided with Karl.

She was a living whirlwind with long black hair, which she straightened by ironing it, and even longer speeches, which were twisted and curled and liberally peppered with Zionism. She had a 150 IQ, which she frequently touted, and a 34-22-34 body on a 5-foot-one-inch frame, statistics which she was also known to announce on occasion. She had held Karl enthralled from the moment he saw her. Debbie, however, regarded both Karl and Mitchell as just fellow nerds, pals and conversationalists who might sometimes be nice for a platonic cuddle on a cold New England night, but nothing more. Born and raised in Austin, Texas, she hated the northern winters. Karl had always suspected that, for her, a big part of the appeal of emigration to Israel was the climate.

Karl was standing on the landing, about to knock, when Debbie pushed past him and threw open the unlocked door. "Everybody decent?" she called out. "Girls on deck."

Mitchell, wearing an apron with Maxwell's equations embroidered on the front, pushed through the bead curtain across the door from the kitchen. The embroidery was his own work, for which he had been roundly teased back in the dorm. "Oh, it's you," he said.

"Is that any way to greet Boston's only folksinger mathe-matician?"

"What about Tom Lehrer?"

"Doesn't count. He's from Cambridge. What's cooking?"

Karl poked his head hesitantly into the apartment, which was packed like a warehouse with second-hand furniture, odd bits of machinery, and cardboard boxes overflowing with electronic parts. Mitchell had been kicked out of MIT's Burton House for tripping the circuit breakers one too many times. When the janitors discovered the extra Romex he had run from the floor below to power the war surplus radar set-up in his dorm room, it had been the last straw. The radar and sundry other equipment now filled the apartment.

Karl was more than a little awed by Mitchell and his ex-otic schemes, his off-campus lifestyle, and the circle of Bo-hemian friends into which Karl was slowly gaining entry. "Hey. It's me," he said. "Is this a bad time? I brought back your physics text and notes. Thanks." He looked around for someplace to set them down and settled for a wooden fruit crate upended beside the door. "And I have a question for your roommate."

Mitchell, who was chewing on something, waved him in, then pantomimed shutting the door. Karl complied with the non-verbal command.

"My asshole roommate," Mitchell said, swallowing. "Wasserman the Weird is away for the weekend, back in New Joisy." Wasserman, the butt of frequent jokes among Mitchell's friends, was a mathematical wizard with the social skills of a grade-schooler. But his family had money, and he paid more than his share of the rent just to be near Mitchell, on whom he was imprinted, like one of Lorenz's goslings.

"Damn. I am completely snowed by this problem set on

gradients. I'm so lost I'm not even sure what questions to ask," said Karl. "I'm beginning to wish I hadn't done AP calculus in high school."

"Calculus? Gradients? I thought you were here to help plan the Kresge Auditorium hack. We need a way to light the flag atop the dome once it's planted. And you didn't have to return the physics crap. I'm long done with that. You know, conscientious Karl, you are just too damned responsible."

"Maybe, I suppose, but I didn't even know there *was* a Kresge hack," he said, sniffing at the air. "What's cooking? Smells like shit."

"You wouldn't know good shit if you stepped in it," Mitchell said. "It's bratwurst and sauerkraut, and its gourmet Midwest fare, numbnut. But you wouldn't know anything about that, having had your taste buds burned out by too much of that synthetic dorm food carefully 'Krafted by Stouffer's'."

Karl groaned at the pun. Stouffer's, which had the contract for food services in the MIT dorms, was a perennial target of student jibes. As Karl stepped over and around boxes to cross the room, he tried not to stare too intently at Debbie.

"Hi, I'm Karl, one of Mitch's MIT friends," he said, flopping down on the far end of the ratty, flower-patterned sofa, carefully avoiding a greasy stain of uncertain origin.

"I'm Debbie, one of Mitch's BU friends. Where you from? You don't sound like the other natives."

"I'm from Michigan. Upper Peninsula. A tiny little town above the Bridge. My parents are both engineers. They worked with Steinman on the Bridge and never left. You know about the Mackinac Bridge?"

"No, can't say as I do. I'm from Texas. Where is this bridge?"

"Upper Peninsula Michigan. It's the longest suspension bridge in the world. Well, if you count between anchors. It is a pretty amazing piece of engineering. Steinman was a genius. You know about the Tacoma Narrows bridge, of course, the one that tore apart in the wind back in the 1940s?" She shook her head bemusedly. "They've got a great film of the Tacoma Narrows bridge collapse over at MIT. You should see it sometime. Really wild the way resonance with the wind started it buckling and twisting until it broke apart. Well, Steinman was the one who figured out how to avoid that." She did not look impressed.

"You staying for dinner?" he asked, changing the subject.

"Naw, I've got a BU Hillel meeting in an hour," she said, kicking off her penny loafers and turning sideways to lay her feet across Karl's lap.

Karl tried not to act surprised. Then, with uncharacteristic boldness, he started rubbing her feet. "What's Hillel?" he asked.

"What, you don't know Hillel? If not now, when? Hah, hah. Torah while standing on one foot?" She kept looking for a sign of recognition. "Hillel, Hillel the Elder, to be exact, *was* a Jewish sage. Hillel *is* a club for young Jews. But, you keep doing my feet like that and the next thing you know I could convert, become a Bokononist. Only I'm not sure whether a Jew can engage in Bokononism. Idolatry is definitely not kosher, but is it forbidden by *halacha* to follow the fictive practices of an imaginary sect? Even though, of course, said sect is ultimately grounded in a Jewish sensibility, an almost happy fatalism. Then again, look at the author and it's hardly a surprise."

"What, pray tell, are you talking about, young woman?"

"The gentle and erotic art of boko-maru, sole-to-sole union. That's s-o-l-e, my salacious compadre, footsy to the rag-gedy-assed masses. I'm not kidding, you should try it. Mmmm." She closed her eyes and licked her lips. "We are clearly part of the same karass, like a 'Chinese dentist and a British queen, all fit together in the same machine,' to quote The Fifty-Third Calypso, which is, of course, to quote Kurt. We are," she waved her finger melodramatically, "impelled by God to a common end, laboring away, jointly or sever-ally, on our one small piece of that grand and glorious plan, unknown to us mere hominids though it may be."

Mitchell emerged again from the kitchen amidst a clatter of beads. "And I may have found our wampeter."

Karl looked from Mitchell to Debbie and back. "I have no fuckin' idea what you two are talking about. Karass? Wam-peter? What language is that? Hebrew again?"

Debbie tipped her head down to peer over her glasses. "You, my benighted Tech tool, are spending too much time on Advanced Calculus for Engineers or whatever you tools do with yourselves when you are not drooling over flat-chested MIT coeds. Are you telling me you have not read Kurt Vonnegut's new novel, *Cat's Cradle?* No? Well, a karass is simply all those people who, whether they know each other or not, are working on the same piece of God's work. When they meet, they recognize each other in an instant, are drawn to each other out of some deep inner, even uncon-scious awareness of their essential connectedness. Like you and Mitch, Mitch and me," she stopped for a moment. "And, it seems, you and me, kid. Don't believe me? Well, tell me, do you do this," she nodded toward her feet, "to every BU coed who sits on a couch with you? No. I rest my case. Ours is no granfalloon, no false karass. This is *bashert*, fated. We are on a mission to somewhere. God only knows where, but we are bound for a promised land. So there!" She then launched into a twenty minute discourse on Vonnegut's imagined doomsday weapon, ice-nine, his place in American literature, and the roots of modern geopolitical folly, while Mitchell stood grinning in the doorway and Karl continued to massage her feet.

Finally Karl said, "So, a wampeter is the purpose of a karass?"

"No, no, only the object, real or conceptual, around which the karass revolves." She punctuated her point with gentle jabs to Karl's arm. "The purpose, the piece of God's work, is something else, something beyond that. This apartment could be our wampeter. It brought us together. Our purpose might be anything, like returning Jerusalem to Israel or making the desert bloom or putting a man on the moon. Hang on," she said, suddenly sitting up. "What was that you said about finding our wampeter, Mitch?"

Mitch arched his eyebrows and grinned broadly. "Maybe more than that. Last week I found something that could be worth a lot, something important, maybe material for a truly humongous hack. We just have to figure out exactly what we can do with it."

6

2003 — KARL WAS AWAKENED by his apartment door intercom. It was past ten in the morning. He had, indeed, stayed up most of the night online, trying, unsuccessfully, to track down Deborah Geffner, learning about the 613 *mitzvot*, the laws that governed the lives of observant Jews, and digging around in online archives of *The Tech* and the *Boston Herald* for stories about famous MIT hacks. When finally he had fallen asleep slumped in his chair, it had been to dream of a young girl, with black hair down to her waist, singing a song of longing and loss.

The intercom buzzed again. Karl wiped his face quickly, stretched, and went to the door.

"Yes?"

In the wide-angle view of the intercom camera the image of an outstretched hand holding some kind of official-looking identification loomed so large that it almost obscured the two men in non-descript dark suits standing at the building entrance. "Police. We'd like to talk to Karl Lustig."

Karl buzzed them in, then slipped the security chain back onto the door before opening it. "Could I see your identification?" One of the men held up an identification card toward the crack in the door.

"This says Interpol," Karl said. "I thought that was like some kind of interagency thing. Does Interpol have jurisdiction here?"

The shorter man in back leaned forward and flashed a badge holder. "He's with me and I'm FBI. Agent Eric Broome. And we do have jurisdiction. Are you Karl Lustig? Can we come in? We'd like to talk with you."

Karl hesitated for a moment, then let them in. He gestured toward the sofa. "Please, sit down. Can I ask what this is about?"

Agent Broome entered, looked around the room slowly, then held the door for his colleague, who crossed in front of Karl and sat down on the leather couch. Broome closed the door and leaned against it, slouching casually, with his hands in his pockets. His partner sat and stared impassively at Karl without seeming to blink. My god, Karl thought, it's just like the movies. "Could either of you gentleman tell me what this is about?"

"Where is your driver's license, Mr. Lustig?" asked Broome.

"I don't know. I really don't. I think I lost it in Germany. Is this now some kind of international incident? Look, I had it when I arrived in Frankfurt. I know, because I had to show it to the Hertz people. Did they find it? Is that what this is about? Wait a minute, let me guess. I probably forgot it at the Hertz counter and, like, somebody used it for identification or something." God, now I am in trouble, Karl thought. Next thing I know I'm going to be on some watch list. Maybe I already am. Slow down, Karl, slow down. "I'm really sorry. I hope I haven't caused any trouble. I mean, I know I should be more careful. I *am* sorry." Karl had shifted almost unconsciously into one of his well proven coping modes, trying to trump the cards on the table with profuse apologies instead of denials or challenges. It usually helped.

The two men just looked at him.

"Er, look, can you just tell me what this is about? Should I have a lawyer present?"

"You tell us," said Broome. He had the clean-cut, generically handsome look of a cinematic secret service agent, but his voice had an irritating, whiney overtone that didn't jibe with his appearance. "*Do* you need a lawyer, Mr. Lustig?"

The man across from Karl was much older, with wavy hair graying at the temples. His looks were harder to place, with a swarthy complexion that could have been Spanish or Italian or that of any number of ethnic groups scattered around the Mediterranean. He held up a hand to his partner, then slid a small plastic object across the table toward Karl.

"Do you recognize this, Mr. Lustig?" He spoke without a prominent accent but with somewhat exaggerated slowness, as if English were not his native language.

"Yes, it's my driver's license. How?" Karl reached for it but the man drew it back.

"We'll keep this for now. You won't need it anyway, because the replacement you applied for on the Web is already on the way, right?" Karl tried not to express surprise that they knew he had requested a new license. "But perhaps you can tell us, Mr. Lustig, how it is that this one, this driver's license that you said was yours, was found on the body of someone killed this week in Germany. Do you know this man, Mr. Lustig? Did you have some involvement with him?"

He slid a wallet-sized photo across the table, a picture of an older man with thick white hair and a round, unwrinkled face. He looked vaguely familiar to Karl, but not in any specific way, more as a particular type, as though Karl might have seen the man's sister or cousin at some point or as if such people came from a particular part of the world. "Is this the man who was killed? No, I don't think I know him."

"You don't know him or you don't think you know him?" asked Broome, still leaning against the door.

Again, the Interpol man raised his hand to stop his partner. "I think that will be enough for today." He leaned forward, in a mock conspiratorial manner. "Please forgive my sometimes abrasive partner. He's American.

"And you, we must ask not to leave the country for now. We will be in touch with you if we have any more questions. If you think of anything about your license or about this man," he tapped the photo, "please call us. Agent Broome will give you his card."

Karl thought about the mezuzah, then decided to say nothing. It was, after all, already gone. He waited a moment before speaking. "I didn't get your name."

"Lev," he said, then paused as if thinking about what he had said. "Lev Novikov. Eric will give you his card. You would probably not be able to reach me, anyway." He stood up. "You needn't show us out. We'll find our way."

Karl's heart was pounding as he watched the two men leave. He picked up the small photo from the coffee table and stared at it, trying to figure out how it was that the man looked vaguely familiar although he didn't know him. He turned it over. On the back, in small, neat script, it read "Michael Rosen." Karl took the photo with him as he headed for his study.

It took Karl nearly an hour to dig past the hits for Michael Rosen the poet, Michael Rosen the jazz musician, Michael Rosen the dentist—the name was just too common. Finally, though, Karl found a German-language piece on a Michael Rosen, reputed spy and alleged arms dealer, who had been found shot, execution style, in a rest area not far outside Frankfurt, Germany. Karl was able to translate well enough to put together the gist of the story. There was a photo of a blood-spattered Fiat with the article. In the background, the sign on the building was partly obscured, but Karl recognized the bright green trim around the entrance and knew what it said: *"Rasthaus Weiskirchen."* It was the café at the rest stop.

7

KARL WAS STILL GOOGLING around when the gentle ding from his computer announced incoming email. Aside from a couple of offers for dubious impotence cures that had slipped through his spam filter, the only message had one of those generic free email addresses favored by spammers, scam artists, and impecunious young people. Karl was about to reflexively delete it unopened when he recognized the subject line as a reply to one of his own emails.

From: silver09@freebiemail.com
To: Karl Lustig [klustig@itechweek.com]
Subject: RE: artwork

Mr. Lustig,
I am sorry for taking so long to reply, but I was very much puzzled by your email and did not know whether or how to respond. I do recognize the mezuzah in the photo you sent. It is definitely my work, but I must ask you how you happen to have such a picture, because it is a piece I made for my husband, Migdal.

At the moment Migdal is away on business in Europe and has not replied to my email. Are you a friend or business associate?

Regards,
Shira Markham Rozeyn (Shira Zemer)

Karl reread the message several times until something clicked. Migdal Rozeyn. Michael Rosen. Mitchell Rossing. It was a guess, but Shira's husband was most likely dead. Killed. And somehow Karl had ended up with his mezuzah, which was now missing. Stolen. There must be some connection with the woman he had met in Germany. Now he wished he had at least gotten the license plate off the car that had struck him. It was a puzzle in which too many of the pieces had fallen out of the box. Somehow he had stumbled into something complicated and maybe dangerous. Perhaps he should go to the authorities, he thought. He still had the number of the guy from the FBI. But too many things did not quite fit, and not knowing who might be after him or why, he did not know whom to trust. Karl was used to doing things for himself, so, true to form, he decided to puzzle things out on his own as much as he could before taking a chance with anyone else.

Karl fetched the photo from his coffee table, then scanned it in and attached it to his reply. What could he say? "Is this your husband?" He figured he already knew the answer. "Your husband and I went to school together. I think you and I need to meet." He changed the reply address to a Web-mail address he rarely used. His index finger hovered above the F9 key. What was he doing? What was going on? He stabbed at the key, then watched as the progress bar crawled across the screen in front of him. It stalled at the halfway point. The send operation timed out with an error. He tried again. No luck. He launched a browser and waited for his Yahoo home page to open but got only an "unable to open page" message. He ducked his head under the desk to check the cable modem. The connection light was flashing, indicating Internet activity. That's odd, he thought. He closed down all the open applications, but still the blinking continued. He double-clicked to check the log on his firewall software only to find that it had been disabled. He tried to enable it again but nothing happened.

This is getting a bit spooky, he thought. Or maybe I am really becoming paranoid. What do you mean "becoming," he chided himself. He had always had a deep streak of paranoia, although he was able to keep it in check most of the time or to channel it in another direction, such as his need to order and control everything around him. He knew one thing: he could no longer trust his computer or the Internet connection. He needed to start thinking like a pro.

As if an eighteen-wheeler truck were rapidly closing on him from behind, Karl shifted into his Autobahn driving mode and started moving with swift precision. First, he disconnected the Ethernet cable from the back of his computer, then he dragged a bunch of files to a strong encryption folder that he kept in the corner of his Windows desktop to store sensitive client information. Next he plugged the tiny thumb drive on his keychain into a USB slot on the computer, dragged the encrypted folder to the drive icon, waited, yanked out the keychain, and stuck it back in his pocket. He then digitally shredded the files he had just copied to the external drive, making them unreadable and virtually unrecoverable.

What next, he thought? If this is a real threat, I need to cover my tracks. He first opened a directory to scan through a collection of security related software that he had collected for a client project the previous year. When he found what he was looking for, he switched to a command prompt to install special software that would completely wipe out all traces of his temporary files and recent data and allow him to reset the computer to a replica of an earlier state. He drummed his fingers impatiently as the hard disk churned and churned. When the disk activity stopped, and he was finally returned to the desktop, he reopened Outlook to check. Everything was just as he remembered it had been a week earlier.

He went to the living room, pulled the laptop from his briefcase, and set it on the coffee table. He muttered a short curse at Bill Gates and company as he waited for the computer to take its sweet time booting up, then proceeded to do much the same thing as he had done with the other machine. Now what? he thought. Get away from here and find someplace to do research without being trailed. There you go again, thinking like a paranoid schizo. No, I'm not, but I am being careful. See, there you go, talking to yourself. "Yeah," he said out loud, "but people are being killed, and it has something to do with me, and I don't know if I'm next."

He closed the laptop without turning it off, grabbed his ski jacket from the peg in the hall, and headed out of the apartment and down the back stairs. Once out the metal service door, he turned right and trotted down the alleyway. He cut through the narrow gap between two brick buildings, vaulted the low wrought iron fence blocking his way to the street, and started looking for a cab.

8

1963 — THE SMELL OF BRATWURST and sauerkraut still hung in the air in the tiny student apartment. Karl, whose attention was on neither food nor conversation, was studying Debbie, noticing the faintest spray of tiny wrinkles that framed her eyes when she squinted in concentration or when she smiled. He was following the rhythmic in and out of her nipples under the gray BU athletic department tee shirt, unconsciously synchronizing his breathing with hers.

"But how do you know what this stuff really is?" she said to Mitchell. "I mean, what did you see? You saw some round things in wooden frames. Big deal."

"Hey, I'm a physics major. I went back," he said dramatically, "with this." He grabbed the handle of a yellow box the size of a milk carton and held it up so they could see the MIT logo and the meter on top, it's needle quivering as he turned it toward them. "I checked it with the scintillation counter. Then I spent some time at the library and got some details on the construction of the MITR-I research reactor that went critical back in 1958 and on the fuel it uses. There's no doubt, this is the real stuff. In fact, this is likely one of the few spots on the planet where highly-enriched nuclear fuel is stored in an unguarded facility with nothing but a regular lock on the door. Think of the possibilities. And I have a key."

Debbie seemed to be deep in thought, so Karl ventured

in. "What possibilities? It's not like we would irradiate pigeons or build an A-bomb for a hack."

Mitchell rubbed his hands together. "But it's worth money, lots of it."

Karl snorted. "To whom? I know you are always thinking about business deals, but it's not like you could take it down to Haymarket on a Saturday and see what you could get for it." He deepened his voice. "Hey, lady, you wanna buy some nice fresh nuclear fuel? Nice and hot. You look nice and hot yourself. I can give you a good price. Cash and carry."

"There are plenty of people who would pay dearly to get their hands on that stuff," Mitch said. "Plenty."

"We'd have to have a buyer lined up in advance. The right buyer," Debbie put in.

"Look," Karl said, punching at the air with his index finger. "The only people interested in some hot fuel, no pun intended, would not be your neighborhood nice guys. You would not want to sell to the Soviets, would you? Well, would you?"

Mitchell shook his head. "No, even among thieves there is honor, be they Tech hackers or otherwise. We would have to find somebody among the good guys, or at least among the not-so-bad guys, somebody who was trying to develop a nuclear program."

Karl pushed Debbie's feet from his lap and stood up. "Are you serious? You're not thinking of actually stealing nuclear fuel, are you?"

"Easy, friend, it's just an intellectual exercise, the challenge of designing a really cool hack."

Karl held up his hand. "But I thought the rules of Hack-Comm were clear. A legitimate hack means nobody gets hurt but everyone knows about it. Like the train at Kendall Square Station."

"Okay, bright boy, then we bend the rules a bit for the sake of argument. Nobody gets hurt and nobody knows. We just end up rich. So how would we do it?"

Debbie was smiling and biting her lower lip. "Israel," she said. "Israel wants the bomb. They need the bomb. They are no doubt trying to catch up right now. I bet they would be interested in a bunch of extra nuclear material to get them there faster. Hey, and they're the good guys."

"Says you," mocked Mitchell. "Okay, okay, good is relative."

"Listen, my goyishe friend," she said with an edge in her voice. "Israel is an ally, an important and loyal one. And Jews have the absolute historic right to *eretz Yisrael*, the land of Israel, but under the unrealistic borders imposed by the U.N. it's only about 20 kilometers across at Tel Aviv. The whole country could be wiped completely off the map in one concerted Arab strike. Israel needs a deterrent capability."

"All right, so maybe you have your buyer," Karl interjected, as much to keep things on a friendly tone as out of genuine interest. "Potential buyer. But you would still have to get the goods and deliver them somehow without getting caught."

"Easy as pie," Mitchell responded. "The research reactor isn't run continuously, so refueling is infrequent and they don't replace all the rods at once. I don't think they take inventory all that often. I mean, it's obviously a kinda informal operation, to put it diplomatically."

Karl scowled. "Okay, I admit this is an interesting problem. We could take rods from the back of the storeroom and carefully distribute the remaining fuel. If they are as rinky-dink about security and monitoring as they sound, it could be a long time before they discovered the loss. A year maybe. Maybe more. That would be enough time for the trail to go cold.

"But look, I gotta go. I gotta figure out this damned calculus and tool for a chem quiz. You work out the rest of this imaginary skullduggery on your own with your Zionist girlfriend."

Debbie reached out and grabbed Karl's arm "Friend," she corrected emphatically. "Most definitely girl. But not girlfriend." She looked at her watch. "Mickey's hands are almost together. I'll be late for my meeting. But don't make any more decisions until you talk with me. Okay?" She waltzed over and gave Mitchell a peck on the cheek. Over her shoulder she said, "See you, Karl What's-His-Face. Watch out for your friend here. I think he's too smart for his own good, even though my IQ is 16 points higher."

Karl watched her as she left, her waist-length hair swaying behind her.

Mitchell was looking at Karl with his ever present grin. "What?" asked Karl.

"She is something, isn't she?" Mitchell said. "Hey, listen, I'll give you a ride over to MIT." He wiped his hands on his apron, lifted it over his head, and threw it on the couch.

"A ride? You got wheels now? How can you afford it?"

"I bought this panel van at an auction. It's amazing the stuff you can get government surplus. Took me awhile to figure out the system. The trick is to pick a lot you think nobody else is likely to bid on and put in the minimum qualifying bid. It worked; I got two vans for a hundred bucks. The catch is you have to take them with you or forfeit your deposit, so I used the one that *would* start to tow away the one that *wouldn't*, which now lies among the other wrecks at the bottom of an abandoned quarry south of here."

"What about gas? How do you afford to keep it running."

"Five-finger discount, courtesy of B&P. Hey, Buildings and Power has to keep gas on hand for the lawn mowers and plows and stuff. I just help myself to five gallons at a time. Come on, let's split."

The van, a badly battered, dull-brown panel truck, was double parked on one of the side streets, an official looking "Delivery" sign displayed inside the windshield.

"What do you think?" asked Mitchell.

"I'm no expert, as you said, but it looks like shit to me," said Karl. "I think I'd rather walk."

"You'd brave the Harvard Bridge, trudge all 364.4 smoots plus-minus an ear in this wind rather than ride in the luxury of my chariot? Come on, get in." He jerked at the door, which rattled open after the second tug, and climbed in. After a lot of cranking, the engine wheezed and sputtered into life.

Reluctantly, Karl walked around to the other side and got in. "You sure you can handle this thing among Boston drivers?" he chided. "You are not in Kansas anymore, Toto, nor Wisconsin. The rules are different here."

As he pulled ahead, Mitchell looked over at Karl. "I know the rules. It's all the other idiots out there who don't know the rules. Of course, the only real rule for driving in Boston is 'The oldest, biggest car has the right of way.' So, no problem.

"Hey, have you got time to go with me and help pick up some equipment at a warehouse in Somerville?" Mitchell didn't wait for a response, but immediately turned into a side street to make a U-turn.

"Sure, sure. Who needs to study anyway, right?"

The warehouse turned out to be a two-car garage stapled onto a gray-shingled triple-decker, and the equipment turned out to be a rusting monster of a gas-powered electric generator for which Mitchell paid $20.

"What are you going to do with this thing, anyway?" asked Karl wincing as they struggled to lift the generator into the back of the van. "It probably doesn't even run."

"Doesn't. But I can fix it. Then I got all the power I need whenever I want it." He brushed his hands on his pants as he climbed back behind the wheel. Karl walked slowly around to the passenger side and winced again as he climbed in.

They had gone only a few blocks when they approached a light. A white sedan making a left turn from the on-coming traffic had nosed around past the center island just enough to block the van, forcing Mitchell to yield.

"I hate this," Mitchell said, smiling incongruously. "They do this crap all the time. Stick their noses out far enough so you have to give way. And look, not even a signal. Well, I've had it with Boston drivers." He pulled the van straight forward until it was only about an inch from the other car's front bumper, blocking it from turning. "Roll up your window," he said to Karl as he shifted into neutral and pulled on the emergency brake.

"What are you doing? You're nuts." The other driver was screaming and shaking his fist. The light changed and cars from the one-way cross street started honking as they swung around behind the van, which was now stuck in the middle of the intersection. The driver in the sedan was going crazy, laying on his horn as he screamed a steady stream of obscenities. His fist had changed into a finger, which he shook violently up and down. When the light changed again, the driver stormed out of his car, climbed between the two vehicles, and started kicking at the front of the van, all the while screaming at the top of his lungs.

Mitchell just stared straight ahead, the same pleasant smile on his face, for all the world as if he were waiting for a train to pass or for the light to change.

"Mitch, Mitch, please. Let it go. This guy is going to kill us." Mitchell said nothing. The other driver leaned toward them and started pounding his fists on the windshield. Karl could see the stubble of a day's growth on his face, the nicotine stains on his teeth. Mitchell continued to stare straight ahead, smiling the same quiet smile.

The light changed again and the man turned and stomped back to his car. "Now we've had it, Mitch. Let's get out of here." More cars on the cross street swerved around them, horns blaring.

Finally they had the green light again. Karl fully expected the other driver to come at them with a tire iron or something, but instead, the man threw his car into reverse, backed up, and, with tires squealing, made a wide swing around behind the van. Mitchell released the parking brake, put the van into gear, and continued through the intersection. "I hope he learned something," Mitchell said, still smiling.

"I doubt it. But I'll tell you one thing: I sure did. Just remind me never to get involved in any more of your projects." He started to laugh, then suddenly doubled over. "Oh, man! That hurts," he said, grabbing at his mid-section.

9

2003 — DAVID OPENED THE FRONT door in his bathrobe. "What in heaven's name, Karl? It's the middle of the night."

Ellen appeared behind him. "Let the man in, dear. It's freezing out there."

Karl rubbed his hands together to warm them. "Forgot to grab gloves. I've been in the library and riding the T much of the day, so it hasn't been too bad, but the walk from the circle was pretty chilly."

"You walked all that way from the circle? Why didn't you call? We would have picked you up."

"I didn't want to use my cell phone and didn't want there to be anything on your phone records. You know how easy it is for people to get their hands on that sort of data nowadays. I probably shouldn't even be here, but I needed a place for the night, and I figured it was late enough so nobody would notice me on the street. Your neighborhood's pretty well buttoned up."

"Well, you are certainly welcome to stay," she said. "I'll go make sure the guest room is ready. David, you get some tea or something to warm him up. I just hope you don't have frostbite or catch pneumonia, Karl."

David led Karl down the photo lined hall to the kitchen and gestured to one of the ladder-back chairs. "You have got to tell us what is going on, Karl. This is not like you. You're as steady-handed as they come. You don't do wild stuff like wandering the streets after midnight. Are you in some kind of trouble?"

"I don't know. I just don't know." Karl looked at his friend for long seconds. "I suppose I should tell you, but I am not sure it's a good idea." He grabbed a chair, spun it around, and sat on it backwards. "Maybe the less you know the better. Besides, I'm not sure I really know what's going on."

From the doorway, Ellen said, "Karl, now you're scaring me." She crossed the room and put her arm around her husband.

Karl filled them in on his day, starting with the email he'd received and his problems with the Internet. "I spent the afternoon at the library using the public Internet access. I managed to find a JPEG on someone's personal pages taken at a wedding twelve years ago. Here, this confirms it." He pulled a folded sheet of paper from his pocket. "Not very good in black-and-white, had to print it out at the library. That's Shira Zemer, the silversmith who designed the mezuzah I found stuffed in my jacket when I returned from Germany. I recognize her from the head shot on her Web site. Next to her is her husband, Migdal. I knew him as Mitchell Rossing, and the FBI photo I was shown today makes him as Michael Rosen. I didn't recognize him in that picture—it's been almost forty years since I last saw him—but in this earlier shot from the Web it's easier to see the resemblance to the kid I knew in college. The mezuzah, it turns out, was a birthday gift to him from his wife. He's dead now, killed—assassinated—this week in Germany at the rest stop where I met that woman claiming to have gone to school with me. There's a connection, I'm certain, but I have no idea what it might be. I also recognized this man standing behind him.

"Oh, and there was a caption in Hebrew with the photo. Here, any chance you can read it? I think I copied it down correctly." He pulled another piece of paper from his shirt pocket and handed it to David.

"Sure. Let's see. It just says, 'Lev and … and, ah, the crew at Migdal and Shira's place after the, ah, big event.' And you know this guy?" He pointed. "So do I."

Karl held himself rigid, trying not to show any reaction. David continued, "I met him the other day. He's the ex-Mossad agent who was trying to peddle a tell-all to us."

Karl frowned. "Mossad? But he identified himself today as being with Interpol. The guy with him claimed to be FBI. So, I guess I don't really know who the hell they are or who they are with. But they had my driver's license, so that means," he paused. "That means diddly. They could have been the ones who killed Migdal, for all I know. Tell me what you know about this guy."

"Well, he said his name was Levi Novikov. Showed up out of the blue carrying a letter of introduction from our European office—some Acquisition Editor I never heard of—but it was our stationery, all right. One of our senior editors brought him by to introduce him to me just before you arrived the other day, which is how my morning ended up so packed with meetings. He had no outline or sample chapters, but he talked a good line. He even insisted on giving me a quick Internet tour of some of the stuff he said should be classified but is freely available on the Web. He…"

Karl interrupted. "He used your computer?"

"Yes, for a few of minutes. He also showed us some stuff on one of those little flash memory drives. To me it was just a blur of diagrams and text; I can't speed read Hebrew. Even after an hour meeting, it was not clear whether he really knew what it was he wanted to write about. Something to do with how easy it is for the intelligence community or even outsiders to get stuff on the Internet. You know, that song and dance. I don't think any of us were all that impressed. We asked for some sample chapters and sent him downstairs to talk with Legal. Haven't heard back from him yet. 'Course it's Helen Duckworth's bailiwick. I only got drawn into the initial meeting because of the technology angle."

Karl bit his lip. "Look, tell your network security people that your computer has begun to act flakey. Get them to take it off the network and give it a thorough going over for worms, viruses, Trojans, whatever. Insist they give you another system on loan while they work on yours. Do not, repeat, do not transfer your address book or any other files to the loaner. Use your PDA if you can't remember an appointment. I assume you keep it synched. I think this Novikov character may have installed a keystroke logger or some other sort of spyware on your system. That would explain how he knew about my license being ordered. He must be tracking everything. How else would he just happen to show up before I arrived and just happen to use your system. I think we should assume that by now your phones are bugged and your email accounts are being tracked, too."

Ellen looked genuinely scared. "Are we in danger? Are you?"

"Truth? Somebody killed Mitchell Rossing. These people, whoever they are, think I had something to do with it. Or maybe they just want me to think that. Or maybe they whacked Mitchell. I don't know. It all seems related in some way, but something bothers me. Like, why would Novikov tip his hand by letting on he knew about my license? Was he showing off, trying to impress me with how much he knew, or trying to scare me? Or did he just slip up, which seems unlikely. And if Novikov was already at Harrison-Interbooks, who was tailing me on the way there? And then what about the pebble-faced guy who rear-ended me, then lifted the mezuzah?

"Whatever the case, this is a big hairy mess, and I'm just a computer consultant, not some CIA case officer. Maybe I've just been reading too much espionage fiction lately. Who knows? I don't want to get you involved any more than you already are, but I could use a couple of favors."

"Sure. How can we help?" David said, then flinched slightly as Ellen squeezed his arm a little too tightly. "Hey, Karl is our friend," he said to her. "He's in trouble. And he's a guest in our house."

"But the boys," Ellen interrupted in a loud whisper. "We can't …"

Karl put his finger to his lips. "Listen, you don't have to do anything, but it would be a big help, Ellen, if you could go to my place and retrieve a few things for me. And David, if you could, go in person tomorrow to your travel department—don't use the phone or email—and get them to book a couple of flights for me, starting with a round-trip ticket in my name for Detroit Monday, open return, then Tuesday Boston to Tel Aviv via Frankfurt with a return in two weeks. I am not supposed to leave the country now, so have them do the second trip as an e-ticket in the name of Carol Listing. Make sure they get the spelling: C-A-R-O-L L-I-S-T-I-N-G. I'll straighten it out at the airport, but it might delay tipping off our 'friends.'" He did finger quotes in the air.

"Are you sure you want to pick right now to go to Israel?" David asked. "Bush will be marching the troops into Iraq any day now."

"My old project management sense tells me that this is a hands-on problem that can't be sorted out by email or on the phone. I need to talk with this woman in person.

"Ellen, if that guest room is ready, I think I should get some sleep. I'm exhausted and I want to be out of here before sunrise. I'll leave a list of things to get from my apartment. If you are willing, I mean."

Ellen hesitated but nodded yes, then led him back down the hall past all her photos of the twins. "Try to sleep well," she said quietly as she opened the door to the guest room for him. "Do you want an alarm clock?"

"No, I'll be okay. I can wake myself up pretty much whenever I want to." On impulse, he leaned over and kissed her forehead. "It'll be all right. Thanks for being such a good friend."

She smiled back at him, a small, quick, uncertain smile. "You know, it really wasn't because you weren't Jewish. My family went nuts when they found out I was dating a gentile, but by the time we got married, I think they were resigned. And that was never the issue for me. It just didn't work.

"You and I, we're just wired different. You and David do have a lot in common, as well you know. That's probably a big part of why you two manage so well, given our history. But he's not as … as protected as you are. You've always been so self-sufficient, which is a real strength, I suppose. But I'm not, and maybe that's a kind of strength, too. I needed someone who was more like that, more like me. Does that make sense to you?" Karl nodded. She took a deep, slow breath, then left.

Karl slipped off his shoes and flopped down on the bed in his clothes. He fell almost immediately into a deep sleep.

He was awakened with a start by light streaming in the

window. My God, I've overslept, he thought. He checked his watch: 3:30. He looked back toward the window, which was dark again. Must have been a passing car, he thought. Got to get back to sleep. But his heart was pounding and sleep wouldn't come. Finally he gave up, grabbed his shoes, and tiptoed to the back door. After closing it behind him, he checked to make sure it was locked.

It was long before dawn, but the sky glow from Greater Boston made it easy to find his way. As he rounded the corner of the house, he saw fresh footprints in the snow outside the guestroom window. He jammed his hands deeper into his pockets and tried to suppress a shiver as he quickly picked his way past the swing set in the yard and out to the street. The sidewalk, which must not have been properly cleared after the last storm, was crusted with a choppy layer of ice. Karl slowed and walked gingerly, being careful not to slip.

He heard footsteps. Should I turn? Pretend I don't know? What?

From behind he heard a familiar voice. "Karl, wait up." It was David, a parka thrown over his pajamas, Bean boots on his feet. "I thought you might need these. I think they'll fit." He handed Karl a pair of gloves with one hand, then, with the other, slipped some carefully folded bills into Karl's hand the way one might do when tipping a doorman. Karl turned his hand over and started to protest. "No," David said, locking eyes with Karl. "Don't worry about it. You can pay me back when you get back from Israel. Whenever that is." He turned to head back to the house.

"David, thanks," Karl called after him in a hoarse, near whisper. "I'll find some way to contact you. I will. Thanks, really, for everything." He trudged off, thinking about how to kill the two days before his flight without being found out.

10

WHAT AM I DOING, Ellen thought. This is nuts. She looked up and down the street, not knowing what it was that she was looking for. She pulled her coat tighter and waited until a small knot of thirty-something women walked past her. She slipped in close behind them, then veered off when she got to Karl's building. She tried not to fumble the key as she let herself in. Two smartly but plainly dressed men with brief-cases were coming down the stairs just as she was starting up. She turned away from them and opened her purse as if checking for her keys as they passed.

She congratulated herself on her quick thinking, although she was hardly sure it was necessary, then continued up the stairs. At the door to Karl's apartment she hesitated again, listening before opening the door with the second of the two keys given to her.

She suppressed a gasp as she entered. The apartment was a shambles. Shards from a broken vase and hundreds of books from the shelves that lined the entryway were scattered across the floor. She looked around the corner into the small study. A computer, it's metal case bent open, blocked the way. Files and papers were scattered everywhere.

Ellen found the cheap suitcase she was looking for among the overturned drawers piled on Karl's bed. The zipper appeared to be broken, but she was able to work it back and forth until it closed for all but an inch at the end. She opened it again and started filling it with the things from the list Karl had left for her. She found most of the clothes fairly quickly. Even in the mess dumped on the floor, Karl's belongings seemed to retain the outlines of their former order. The bottle of wine Karl had requested was lying broken in a sticky red pool in the living room. She picked another that was still intact.

In the study, as she searched for the two thumb drives Karl had put on the list, something blinking caught her eye. Climbing over the debris on the floor, she reached the fax machine. Out of paper, it flashed. Out of paper. She looked around for paper to feed it, settling for a sheet from the floor that had already been printed on one side but was unwrinkled. She lined it up, sussed out which way it went into the paper feed on the fax, then followed the prompt to hit the start button. A soft buzz filled the silence as the machine slowly printed a page. It was a handwritten note in Hebrew.

Ellen had trouble reading some of it, but at the end was an address for a café in Haifa: *Yafeh Nof*. The note was signed, "Shira." Ellen folded it and put it in her pocket. At the door to the apartment she gave one last compulsive look around, then left. As she turned to go down the back stairs as instructed, she heard footsteps coming up. She backed up and started down the main stairwell as silently as she could. Just before her view was cut off, she looked back over her shoulder and realized, too late, she had not closed the apartment door.

She reached the landing and rounded the corner, then listened to footsteps approaching the door, the rustle of paper and the crunch of glass as someone took a few steps into the apartment, then long seconds of silence. She held her breath until she heard the footsteps continue deeper into the apartment.

Ellen tiptoed down the stairs into the empty lobby. She considered going out the front door until she realized that she could still take the back way out as she had been told to even if she hadn't come down the back stairs. As she passed a bank of brass-fronted mailboxes, she noticed mail in the box for Karl's apartment. There was a third, smaller key on the ring that Karl had given her. She tried it. The box opened. She quickly pocketed the letter and headed out the back. As she exited the service door she almost ran into a sallow-skinned man standing there. He glanced down at her suitcase.

Somehow Ellen felt compelled to explain. "Sorry," she said, "I'm in a hurry, don't want to miss my train." She started down the alleyway trying to look as if she knew where she was going. As she turned into the street, she could see the man still standing there, looking her way, talking into a cell phone.

When she caught up with Karl at Government Center, she told him what had happened and apologized profusely.

"It's all right, Ellen," he said. "Just our spook friends, most likely. I know I can't stay more than half a jump ahead of them anyway. Let's hope it's enough." He took the suitcase from her and set it down on the brick step. He put his arms around her and whispered, "I never stopped loving you. David is very lucky." She said nothing but held onto him until he said, quietly, "Gotta go. Did you get everything?"

She shook her head as she pulled away. "No thumb drives. And I had to substitute the wine."

"I hope it's kosher," he said, smiling. "Anything else?"

"Oh, yes. You got mail. Here, I think it's your driver's license. And you got a fax." She pulled the paper from her pocket and handed it to him.

"Oh, great, it's in Hebrew. Now I'll have to find someone to translate."

"It's from Shira. I'm not as good as David, but I think it says to meet at this café, *Yafeh Nof,* in Haifa. Next Friday, before Shabbat."

"Wait a minute, I thought Friday was Shabbat."

"No, she means before sundown, when Shabbat starts. Anyway, be careful Karl. I wouldn't want to lose such an old and good friend." As he turned to go she said, quietly, "I love you, too." It was lost in the sounds of the crowd and the wind that always swept the plaza.

11

"THEY BEAT US TO IT," Eric said, surveying the mess in the apartment.

Lev frowned. "Someone else, too," he said.

"What makes you say that? This job says Tariq Mustafa all over it."

"Mustafa may be crude, but he is not careless. He would not leave the apartment door open. No, someone else has been here since Mustafa and company went through the place. Pay attention. Maybe we can figure out who got what." He bent over the computer with its twisted cover. "I'd say it was Mustafa who got the hard drive out of this. Let's hope Lustig is as sharp as we think he is and covered his tracks. I'd rather we be the ones to finish this operation.

"Hey, stick a sheet of paper in that fax machine. It's blinking. I think it needs paper."

Eric looked around, found the paper tray from the laser printer in a pile of junk on the floor, and put a handful of sheets from it into the feed of the fax machine. After a brief buzz, the machine spit out one sheet, then went silent. "It's blank. Nothing." Eric tossed it on the floor.

Lev bent to pick it up. It was empty except for the identifying line of text across the top. "That's interesting. Look at the date and time stamp. This fax hasn't been sent yet." He reached over to the fax and started playing with the keypad.

Eric gave him a disapproving look. "What do you mean?

What are you trying to do?" Lev had a way of leaping to conclusions and being irritatingly right about it most of the time.

"This was sent from another time zone some hours ahead of us: Europe, the Middle East maybe. That blank sheet is an overflow page that printed because the original was on A4 paper, which is too long for the standard letter paper used here. The first page is most likely still in memory. Ah, here we go." The machine fed another sheet of paper from the stack and buzzed into life again. When it stopped, Lev took the sheet and handed it to Eric.

"Well, we can make a good guess where our Mister Lustig is headed. I'll take the next leg on this operation. I do speak the language. Meanwhile, see what else you can find here, then report back. You can reach me through the usual channels." He stepped gingerly through the debris and headed out of the apartment.

Eric surveyed the mess in the study, unsure where to begin. He respected the dispassionate certainty with which Lev approached everything. He also resented it. But there was a lot at stake, and Eric knew how important it was that they work together smoothly.

The distant sound of a metal door slamming drew his attention. He stretched across the desk to peek out of the one small window in the room. It looked out on the narrow alleyway that cut behind the building. Toward the end of the alley he caught a glimpse of the back of a well-dressed woman incongruously carrying a battered suitcase. He leaned even farther to peer straight down into the alley. From such an acute angle he couldn't identify the person talking on his cell phone, but he had a good guess about who the man worked for. Eric checked his shoulder holster as he scrambled out of the apartment and headed down the back stairs as quickly but quietly as he could.

12

1963 — THE PIZZA PARLOR was crowded with students and a smattering of older people from the neighborhood. Mitchell smiled. He liked the family that had started the place during the summer, and he wanted them to succeed. But whenever he would try to talk with Gabe about business or financial planning or advertising, he got the same response: "Hey, look, people always gotta eat. They gotta eat somewhere. Here is somewhere." That was the sum total of both his business plan and his personal philosophy. At the moment it looked like the Antonellis might make it, but Mitchell knew the odds were against them. No one would ever rave about the pizza or the spaghetti Bolognese, but, as Gabe would say, here is somewhere. It had become a place where people met and where the neighborhood strata mixed, even if incompletely. And the owners were nice people, particularly their daughter, Francesca, who always made Mitchell feel welcome and who seemed blissfully oblivious to the way the young men from BU tried to hit on her.

Deborah leaned across the table and gave Mitchell a big smile. "Pretend you're flirting with me," she said.

"What?"

"Mitch, just go along. Pretend like you adore me. I have something to tell you."

"I do adore you, but I know it's hopeless. I'm a gentile and you, well you are just this gorgeous Jewess who won't even let me get to first base."

She leaned all the way across the table and kissed him slowly, her tongue playfully darting in and out. "There, you've made it to first base. Cooperate for once and you might, just might, someday get to second. I have something to tell you, but I want you to pretend like we are just this happy young couple adoring each other."

"*I* don't have to pretend. I told you, I do adore you. But what in God's name? Don't tell me you got knocked up. Who's the bastard? I mean, who's the lucky bastard?"

She kicked him under the table. "Listen you schmuck. This is serious, so just act interested and keep your voice down."

"Deb, this is Antonelli's. Who's listening and who cares? Nobody can hear you. Hell, nobody can hear anybody in this din. Just tell me."

"Mitch, they're interested. They want to meet. Tomorrow afternoon. By the swan boats. Mitch, this is real, it's really happening."

"What are you talking about? Who wants to meet?"

"The Israelis, you schmuck. Who else would I be talking about?"

"What Israelis?"

"The ones who …" She stopped and held up her hands. "Okay, I'll start over. I just thought you were tracking me. I mean, we are part of the same karass. We talked about this. We agreed. So I went to the Israeli Consulate downtown."

"You what? Wait a minute, we didn't agree about anything. If you're talking about the stuff at MIT, I mean, I was just musing about a possible hack."

"Mitch, keep your voice down, people will think we're having a spat." She looked around, but all she saw were people with pizza and Pepsi laughing and talking with each other. "I went down to the Consulate to talk about making *aliyah*. That's what I said, but then I asked this nice guy if he knew who I should talk with if I had something that could help Israel's nuclear program, and he said there was no nuclear program, but he got up and left the room abruptly. I waited maybe ten minutes and was just getting up to leave when this really cute Israeli comes in. I mean this guy, Paul something, is gorgeous, maybe in his late twenties. And he starts talking with a slight British accent and, well, anyway, he started asking a lot of questions, but I mean not real direct, and I am really liking this guy. So I just up and tell him that I know some people who can get their hands on a substantial amount of reactor fuel. He stops me and says, 'There's somebody who should hear this.' And he leaves and comes back with this really old guy, I mean gray hair, maybe fifty. Old. This guy wants specifics, like how much, what percent uranium this and uranium that, how is it packaged, how did we get it, where is it, how much do we want—all that stuff."

"Shit, I hope you didn't tell him anything," Mitch said, a note of anxiety entering his voice.

"Do I look like a dumb bunny to you? No, I told him I didn't know details, and we wouldn't say where or when until we had a deal. But I did tell them how much I thought we could deliver. They want to deal, Mitch. They asked me how much we were looking to make from the deal and I said two million. They never batted an eyelash."

Mitchell whistled. "How did you come up with that figure?"

"It sounded good. Enough to let them know we were serious and smart enough to know this was worth something more than pocket change. Besides, it tests whether they are serious, too."

"Look, we don't even know who 'they' is."

"*They* is the Israelis. Haven't you been listening?"

"Yeah, but what Israelis. Look, I saw 'Exodus.' Some of these guys play rough. And we are talking about a program that is top secret—or whatever the Israeli equivalent is—and that isn't even supposed to exist. I mean, it's one thing to put lithium grease on the tracks at Kendall Square Station, but this, this is beginning to sound like it could be dangerous."

"Look, what's to worry? I'm Jewish. I want to make *aliyah* after college. They're not going to do anything to me."

"That is naïve. And I'm not. Not naïve, not Jewish, and not going to go to Israel after college."

"No problem." She held up one finger. "I'll meet with them. Anyway, I thought you didn't get scared, that life was about taking risks. Don't sweat anything, you say. Just go for it. Play it by ear. So, sweetheart, can't you hear me banging out Chopsticks? This is an amazingly improbable chance to do something right and get rich in the process. Bang. Just like that. I say let's do it. We are two of the smartest people on the planet. We are smarter than they are. We will figure all the angles and cover our asses. I am not talking about being stupid or going off halfcocked, I am just talking about meeting with them by the swan-boat dock tomorrow afternoon. It's the Public Gardens, it's Sunday, there will be lots of people. What could happen?"

"You're going to do this, aren't you. You're serious." He started to grin. "Two million dollars. You don't fuck around, do you. Two million."

"In small, unmarked bills," she said. "I know how these things are done. That's what I told them. Half in advance, half on delivery."

Francesca arrived then, carrying a pepperoni pizza above her head. They both leaned back to make room for her to set it down between them. Deborah leaned forward again after Francesca left and gave Mitchell a playful whack on the side of his head.

"Adore me, huh? I saw you looking at her." They both laughed. "By the way, what about your friend, the Tech tool. He's part of this. We need to bring him up to speed. Where is he anyway? Wasn't he supposed to meet us for pizza?"

"Didn't you hear? He's in the hospital. Had to go in for emergency surgery. He ruptured himself lifting a generator into my van. Can you imagine? I thought that was for old farts. I mean a hernia. He's just … just our age. Stuff like that doesn't happen to people our age."

13

2003 — KARL FELT THE TUG from his old hernia repair as he ran awkwardly along the subway platform with the suitcase. He slipped onto the Blue Line train for Revere just as the doors were closing. I'm getting too old for this, he thought. The first repair, an emergency, had eventually needed to be redone. By his second operation decades later, the technology was better, but he figured he had more than his share of scar tissue and plastic mesh in his lower abdomen.

He cursed silently as he looked for a seat. Under normal circumstances, he would never take the train to the airport. He hated the chipped paint and graffiti, the rock-hard plastic benches, and the mind-wrenching squeal of steel on steel every time the train rounded a curve. But most of all he hated the interfaces: waiting for the right train, then waiting again to change to the right bus at the airport. It galled him that transportation planning in Boston was so poor that they kept building ever more massive parking facilities rather than making it easier to commute to and from the airport.

But, he would be the first to acknowledge, these were not ordinary circumstances. He wanted the anonymity of the crowded subway. He did not want some cabby to be able to say later, "Yup, I remember him, took him to the airport, terminal E, looked anxious."

Karl noticed the two men in black wool coats glancing his way. He got up and moved to put more people between himself and them. They kept looking. He stared straight ahead, right into his reflection in the window opposite. There was a smear of red-brown lipstick on his cheek where Ellen had kissed him while they embraced. He wiped at it with a tissue and smiled as he looked back toward the two men, who gave him a nod and smiled back.

At the airport, his heart started pounding the moment he got off the shuttle bus and entered the international terminal. As he expected, the Lufthansa lines were long, but he went past them to stand next in line at the First Class counter. He tried to calm himself, reminding himself that the more nervous he appeared, the more suspicious his story would sound. Without speaking, he handed over his passport with his top-tier frequent flier card on top to show he belonged in the line.

The woman at the counter either recognized him or was very good at reading names upside down. "Where to today, Mr. Lustig?" she said with just a trace of a German accent. "Let me guess, the 4:40 flight to Frankfurt."

"Yes, well, I'm going on to Tel Aviv this time."

The agent typed away at the computer, then frowned. "I don't seem to have a reservation for you, Mr. Lustig. Do you know the record locator?"

"Yes, of course." He pulled out a slip of paper and she typed as he rattled it off to her.

She laughed. "I see the problem. It seems somebody badly misspelled your name. I am sorry," she said, reaching for a phone, "but being an international flight and going to Israel and with all the heightened security, I'm afraid I am going to have to check with a supervisor. I hope you don't mind. This is only a formality and shouldn't take more than a moment." She turned deliberately away from him as she spoke into the mouthpiece in German that was much too quick for Karl to follow.

Karl tried to maintain his studied nonchalance. Finally the agent turned to smile and nod to him as she said over the phone, "*Alles klar. Ja, ja. Vielen dank. Tschüss.*" She started typing away into her terminal. "There, all fixed. How many bags will you be checking? None? Just carry-on? Okay. Please put it on the scale." She fiddled with the printer behind the counter, then handed him back his passport and card. "Your Mileage Plus number has been entered. Here are your boarding passes and your itinerary, that's your gate. Boarding is at ten past four. You are welcome to use our First Class lounge in the meantime, of course. Have a nice flight."

Karl looked down at the itinerary and hesitated. "Is everything all right?" the agent asked.

"Yes, everything is right." David probably had thought he was doing a favor by putting Karl in first class. Things are beginning to get real expensive, Karl thought.

Instead of going to the lounge right away after clearing security, Karl looked around for a public Internet terminal. He logged on, then hesitated when asked for his credit card. He had plenty of cash with him and knew better than to leave a trail with his credit card. Suddenly inspired, he headed for a cart vendor offering prepaid international cell phones.

He picked out the most expensive phone and an equally expensive plan that would not only work in most any other country, but in the United States as well. There was also a substantial deposit to cover if the phone was not returned within the one month rental period. When he started counting out bills, the clerk looked at him and shrugged, but rang up the sale without checking Karl's identification to see if it matched the application form.

In the Lufthansa lounge, Karl dialed into a telephone email service that charged back to the cell phone, then used it to log into one of his newly created anonymous email accounts. He laboriously entered a long text message to a friend in Germany, then checked for email messages with the service's text-to-speech feature.

A developing storm with mixed snow and sleet had slowed departures, and, for a while, Karl worried that his flight might be canceled. After two hours of anxious waiting in the lounge, boarding was finally called. Once on board, he settled into his regular Boston-to-Frankfurt routine, but having gone two days without much to eat, hunger changed his mind as soon as he saw the dinner menu: cabernet-braised duck breast served over garlic-butter sautéed kale with rösti potatoes on the side. Dinner was a mistake, however, nowhere as good as the menu blurb made it sound, and afterwards he slept only fitfully. When he finally dropped into deep sleep, a little over an hour or so before landing, he was plagued by nightmares of being chased along subway tracks and through hospital corridors by men in black wool coats.

14

IN FRANKFURT, INSTEAD of going to the gate for his connection to Tel Aviv, Karl exited through Passport Control and headed for the Hertz counter, where he rented an Audi for cash. On the Autobahn, he passed by the *Rasthof Weiskirchen* without stopping for coffee and a pastry. Then, instead of continuing as usual toward Nürnberg, after Würzburg he turned south onto the A7 toward Ulm.

Intermittent snow began, turning the Autobahn into a white sheet and slowing traffic to a crawl at times. When Karl finally pulled into the driveway of the small house on a rise overlooking Ulm, it was already afternoon. As he approached the bright red front door, it opened. A burly bear of a man in a grey and blue ski sweater emerged and held out his arms. He started to sing in a dramatic baritone: *"Warum ist es am Rhein so schön? Warum ist es am Rhein so schön? Warum ist es am Rhein so schön,"* he held the note for several seconds before finishing, *"am Rhein so schön?"*

Karl laughed, then sang in reply as he approached: *"Weil die Mädchen gern küssen und die Burschen das wissen. Darum ist es am Rhein so schön, am Rhein so schön."* He finished with a dramatic flourish.

"You remember, Karl. You remember why it is so beautiful on the Rhine. You remember about the girls who are so eager to kiss the boys. And how long has it been? How many years? And suddenly you ask me for a car. What made you think I would do it?" His English was clear but heavily accented.

Karl embraced his friend. "Ulrich, I didn't think you would do it. But if you remember, I always have a plan B."

"Come in, come in. It's too cold to talk out here. You must tell me what you are doing and what all this mysterious stuff is about. And all your plans: A, B, C, the lot of them."

Although they had not seen each other in decades, Karl found himself almost immediately at ease. It was the spell of Bavarian *gemütlichkeit* that Ulrich Bremer had always been able to cast over people, and the two of them spent the entire afternoon talking over a succession of glasses of *dunkelbier* from a local brewery. Karl regretted that he had not made the effort to drive over this way before on one of his many trips to Germany, but then, it was precisely the lack of contact that had made Karl feel it was safe to meet with Ulrich now.

Ulrich was no longer the wiry athlete Karl had known in graduate school, but his voice still rang with the haunting resonance of a bass clarinet. It sang even when he spoke, which was all the time that he wasn't singing. Singing had brought them together in college, and they had become good friends and frequent drinking buddies with the kind of baseless bond that grows between young men, not from intimacy but from long hours of simple presence. If they were going to drink together, Ulrich had insisted back then, Karl would have to properly learn the traditional German drinking songs. He had started with *"Warum ist es am Rhein so Schön."*

"Do you sing still?" Ulrich asked, about the time the sun was setting. "I mean seriously, in a group. I have a rehearsal tonight, but we can have a late dinner together after. I sing in the choir at the University and with a community concert opera group. We do Mozart and Handel and that. I had a solo last year in 'Judas Maccabeus.' You?"

"No, I haven't had much time for music in recent years. Not much time for hobbies of any kind. You were always the hobbyist. Do you also still collect weapons? I seem to re-member some trouble you once got into over a saber you tried to carry on a flight to Washington National."

Ulrich smiled broadly, making the scar on his left cheek—the souvenir of an illicit fencing match when he was a young man in Heidelberg—suddenly stand out. "Yes, yes, of course. Come, I'll show you." He led Karl down a curved flight of stairs to what might have once been a brick-lined wine cellar, but the walls were now covered with swords and knives of every description.

Karl listened with deliberate interest as his friend told all about the collection and how each piece had been acquired. When Ulrich finally paused for breath, Karl asked, "What about more modern things, you know, the state-of-the-art? Or does something have to be at least a century old to in-terest you?"

"Well, yes. But the new stuff is not so pretty on the walls. Here." He opened a drawer in a row of cabinets. "These are ceramic and titanium alloy, what people are now calling tac-tical knives." Karl reached for one to pick it up. "Careful, those are razor sharp."

"What about that one?" Karl said, pointing to a dun-colored knife in a snug case.

"Oh, that's a limited edition Dieter Pohl design, a cera-mic knife with a tight fitted case of the same material, so it is all but impossible to detect with x-ray scanners. And, of course, no metal, so no problem with metal detectors. Not exactly illegal but not widely available, either."

"I like it. Clever. And guns? I don't suppose you collect guns."

Ulrich gave him a look with his head half turned. "This is not the U.S., you know, where everyone owns guns. You aren't with some authority are you? No, of course not. Well, yes, it is the case that I started a few years back to get interested in some modern handguns. I even wrote a piece for an academic journal on user experience issues in designing handguns. You know, the 'look and feel' of weapons."

"Yes, I know."

"You do? Oh, yes, of course. The Web. You can find or find out almost anything on the Web. But that means you have been doing research, and this visit is not only no mere impulse but is maybe, I think, about my hobby in some way. Yes, I am right, *nicht wahr?*" Karl nodded. "Then I think there is much more that you need to tell me about your life. Sit down. Please. Tell me. Please. Before I have to leave for rehearsal."

Karl gave him an edited recounting of recent events. "I don't know if you remember me telling you about Mitchell Rossing, the brilliant young kid who faked his way into MIT back when I was there, but he was killed in Germany recently, and now someone is after me, I think. It doesn't make sense, but I am trying to figure out what is going on before I end up shot in the head in some rest stop. The thought of dying without ever knowing why is what scares me worse than just dying. Well, maybe not. Maybe it's nothing but unadulterated terror."

"Wait a minute, *ein Raststätte*, you said. I remember reading something about that." Ulrich opened a cabinet on the wall to reveal a discreetly concealed computer. "Part of my home network," he declared. "What did you say his name was?"

"Rosen, actually, Michael Rosen. At least that is one of the names he used. He was killed at the *Rasthof Weiskirchen* off the A3 the same day that I happened to make a stop there, which is also when I met this woman, Maryam Cashman, an MIT grad. At least she said she had gone to MIT, although I was never able to find any trace of her in their records or anywhere else. If I remember right, she said she also studied design here in Ulm, at the design school. Perhaps you know something of her or could find out."

Ulrich typed as he talked. "I don't recognize either name, but I'll check about the woman. But the man, yes, yes. There was quite a bit about it in the papers here, because it was, what do you say, gangland style. And it is said that he had some connections here in Germany. I mean by that connections with parts of the government. Ah, here." He twisted the screen so Karl could see it better. "Apparently he had been with Israeli intelligence and may have been involved in some operations with the federal police. German Muslims, terrorists, or 'alleged terrorist,' I should say, as the newspapers always do. Not all the details are known or explained, of course. But here, this one blog entry claims he had left intelligence work to become an arms dealer or might have been dealing secrets with the wrong side. All speculation and innuendo, of course, but it might explain his death. Right?"

"Right. Wait. You said Israeli intelligence? You mean Mossad? Whoa, this is really getting complicated. Hard to tell the players without a scorecard. Hey, any chance I could see these handguns that you collect out of so-called academic interest?"

Ulrich nodded and led Karl through a low passageway to another part of the cellar where he switched on a bare bulb in the ceiling. A workbench, with tools arrayed in neat rows, stood along one wall. Ulrich stooped down to open a safe under the bench, then slid out a tray. "These are all rather special in some way, each a different way. This is a vintage American .38 police special. The original owner had it bright nickel plated and personalized the trigger." He opened it and spun the cylinder to verify that it was empty, closed it, cocked it, and handed it to Karl. "You remember, I am sure, from when you were target shooting in college. Just take aim down the corridor, and when you are ready, pretend to fire."

Karl held his arm out, expertly braced it with his other hand, and aimed at the lamp in the other room. The click of the hammer seemed to come at the very instant he decided to fire; the trigger had not seemed to move at all.

"I see you remember this also. You were good on the pistol team. I also recall that it was not by natural talent that you became so good, but by obsession. Am I right? I would not want to guess how many thousands of rounds you fired on the practice range. You were like a machine. You would load the round into the chamber, raise the pistol, and fire. Others would steady themselves for long seconds, hold the breath, freeze the sights on the target, but you would just load, raise, and fire, again and again, for hours, until you could get a one-inch grouping at twenty-five yards."

"Fifty. But that was then. And this," he shifted the pistol in his hand, "is amazing. But I would think that a hair trigger would be dangerous, particularly in police work where you don't want to fire unless you mean it?"

"No, this will not fire unless you want it to. The trigger pull requires the normal force but only a millimeter of travel.

It is almost as if you only have to think 'Now!' and it knows. Agreed, that is not state-of-the-art, but I like it—a certain purity of experience design and function. This is maybe what you had in mind." He picked up a smooth, dull gray semiautomatic, from which he removed the magazine and verified that it was unloaded. He handed it to Karl, who took it, turned it over in his hand, then sighted along it.

"Nice, a little small, light, but still a nice feel. What is special about this one?"

"Well, you see, it is a Glock, but not a Glock you can buy at any gun shop." He reached for it. "This one breaks down—instantly." He made a couple of quick twists like a magician demonstrating a trick and opened his big hands to show three nearly nondescript pieces plus the magazine. "And it reassembles in an eye blink." Almost as quickly, the gun was intact again. "Perhaps you know some of the 'urban legends' about Glocks, mythology perpetuated by Hollywood, that Glock pistols are made entirely of plastic and do not show up in x-rays or trigger metal detectors. The truth is not so colorful. There are many metal parts, and even the polymer frames and other plastic parts on conventional models are a radio-opaque composition that is easily seen on security x-rays.

"Except for this one" He handed it back to Karl. "Myth and legend almost always begin with some basis in fact. What you hold is the fact, the stuff of legend, an exercise in extreme design by an errant Austrian genius, a former student of mine, who set out to see how far he could go with ceramic composites and special laminations that foil most metal detectors, with ambiguous shapes that are hard to decipher in x-ray images. It also comes with this." He fished out of the tray what looked like a penlight flashlight.

"It's a laser pointer, you know, like the ones used by us lecturers to point at slides and such." He pressed on the pocket clip and a bright red spot appeared on the wall opposite. "Except this one slips onto the special Glock like this, click, click. And now all you do is point and pull the trigger when the spot is on whatever you want to hit. It comes off again like this and goes into your shirt pocket, and now nobody knows you are not just another lecturer from the university."

Karl looked his friend in the eye. "How much? I mean, how much is something like that, all that, worth?"

"Who can say? It is one of a kind." He took out a cloth from the drawer and began methodically wiping the gun all over. He held it in the cloth and handed it to Karl. "It's yours—for now. I have this thought that you might have some need of it. Just return it when you don't need it anymore. Now, I must go to rehearsals. I'll be back in three hours, and you can explain what is this thing about my car."

15

1963 — THE TREES MADE LONG SHADOWS across the path as Deborah entered the Public Gardens from off Boylston Street. She found herself nervously looking around to note where people were standing and talking or watching their kids play. The swan boat dock near the end of the stone bridge was closed, and the swan boats for which the pond was famous were long gone, retired to their scattered storage back in September. Deborah shivered despite the warmth of the hottest October on record. She had arrived early and now hung back in hopes of seeing her contacts before they saw her.

Behind her, a quiet voice said, "Hi, you're early." She whirled around and almost collided with the young man from the Consulate. "This is Tsvi Landau, from, ah, from the Institute," he said. "Tsvi, Deborah Geffner, the student I told you about."

Tsvi placed his hand on Deborah's elbow and said, "Let's take a little walk. We can talk as we head over towards the Commons. Paul here tells me you may have something to sell. First tell me one thing, please. How does a college girl end up with material like that?"

"I know someone who has access," she answered.

"Ah, yes, 'access.' And where is this material to which he has access? You're a Boston University student. Is he one of your professors? Is the stuff under your bed at the dorm?"

Deborah bristled. "Look, if you are not taking this seriously, then we have nothing more to talk about. I told Paul here and the other guy at the Consulate that we would not talk about the location or other details until we were sure we had a deal. I thought that was why we were here today: to make a deal."

"But, young lady, you are asking us to take much on faith, and you are also talking about a great deal of money. You will have to say something or do something more to convince us that you have what you say you do and can deliver. So, exactly what is it that you have."

"Okay, okay, we have reactor fuel assemblies, nominally 75 millimeters by 75 centimeters long, made up of plates of highly enriched uranium in an aluminum cermet matrix."

"Not as convenient to us in that form. Too bad you can't just supply highly enriched uranium. How much do you have?"

"You can take delivery of nine once we have a deal."

"Is that all you can come up with? That's not a lot for a million dollars. Fuel assemblies like that would not run more than, maybe, ten thousand each."

Surprised by the numbers, Deborah decided bravado and bluff were her best response. "We said two million. It's the law of supply and demand. You may have the demand, but the supply of highly enriched fuel and people willing to sell it to you on the open market is extremely limited. Besides, it's enough to help jump start your program."

"I think we would have to have a sample before we can even think about negotiating the price. Again, without intended offence, we still find it hard to believe a mere college girl would have reactor fuel to sell. Bring us a sample that we can evaluate. If it really is what you say, and it is something our scientific people say would be of use, then perhaps we can start negotiations. But first you have to prove that you really have it. Or can get it. Go back to this man who you say has access and tell him to get us some. Or better yet, just tell us where it is, and we can pick it up ourselves, save you the trouble."

"Do I look stupid or something? I will have to talk to my partners and see about a sample. How do I get in touch with you?"

"Through the Consulate. Just talk to Paul. Come on, Paul, we need to leave Miss Geffner to think about what she is doing." He turned and started off at a brisk pace toward the entrance to Park Street Under.

Deborah stood there for a minute as she watched them go. It was beginning to seem that they probably didn't really believe she could get them the fuel, but in any case they were going to make it more difficult.

She decided not to go straight back to Mitchell's apartment. She realized it was time to start acting like the game was for keeps, so she headed first to State Street Station, took a Blue Line train for one stop, milled around in the station before switching to a Green Line car for Lechmere, where she immediately turned around and headed in again to Back Bay.

At the apartment, she knocked but got no response, so she let herself in with the key Mitchell had given her, then went into the kitchen to fix herself a cup of tea.

"Hey, what're you doing here?" It was Wasserman, his pudgy face screwed up in an open-mouthed scowl and his left hand absent-mindedly resting atop his nappy hair.

"You scared me," she said. "I knocked but no one answered."

"I was asleep. What are you doing? Does Mitchell know you have a key? Did he say it was all right to use his tea?" He rocked back and forth whenever he talked. To Deborah it made him look like he was davening, as if he were some Chassid rocking in prayer. She suppressed a smirk.

"Wasserman, do you ever run out of questions?"

"How could I run out of questions? The number of syntactically and semantically valid interrogative constructions is infinite. Conversation is finite."

"Right. Okay, Wasserman, okay. Look, could you take a walk or something? I need to talk with Mitchell about something important."

"He's not here."

"Yes, I know he's not here, but he will be, and I need to talk with him. Alone. Okay?"

"Whacha gonna talk about? I'm his roommate, you know. Maybe I should stay."

"No, Wasserman, you shouldn't stay. Here, go for a walk. See if you can work out a proof for the Four-Color Theorem."

"That's a tough one. And it's really a conjecture, not a theorem. I don't think I could do that on just one walk, you know."

"Well, then take two walks. Go see how much progress you can make on it before supper. But don't come back before six unless you solve it."

"You mean if I prove it, I can come back early? What if I find a counter-example, if I disprove it? Should I come back early then?"

The poor slob was absolutely sincere, Deborah realized. "Look, Wasserman, if you find a counter-example, a map that takes more than four colors, you call the New York

Times. No, you call the Fields Medal committee and tell them that a nineteen-year-old nerd from MIT just scooped the best mathematical brains of the world."

"But I don't know their number. Do you know their telephone number?"

She shook her head. "Look, you prove—or disprove—the Four-Color Theorem … Conjecture, and just come back here. I'll call them for you. Trust me. Just don't come back before six."

"Unless I solve it, right? Then I can come back before six, right?"

"Right, just go." She ushered him out the door.

Mitchell was coming up the stairs as Wasserman was going down.

"What's this about the Fields Medal?" Mitchell said as he flopped down on the sofa. "Wasserman was muttering something about the Four-Color Conjecture and the New York Times and the Fields Medal."

"Oh, I was just pulling his leg to get rid of him so we could talk."

"Be nice to the guy, he's a friggin' genius, you know. Someday he may win the Fields Medal, then you'll say you knew him when."

"He's a basket case."

"No, just socially awkward, sort of an idiot savant, like. People don't make sense to him. Equations and proofs do. Anyway, what's up? What happened?"

She told him the news, and his incessant smile blinked off ever so briefly. "Okay, so how do we do this?" he mused. "It's not like we could go in there and saw off a chunk to give them. You know that uranium is pyrophoric; fine chips can burst into flame. Plus I don't relish carrying a chunk of

Lior Samson

reactor fuel around in my pocket irradiating the family jewels. Besides, we don't want to risk going in more than once.
And we certainly can't just give them one of the rods. Do
you realize uranium is some 65% heavier than lead. And
those babies are this high." He held out his hand. He mumbled to himself as he tried to do some quick math. "With the
shielding and the shipping frames they must weigh, I don't
know, maybe close to 200 pounds each. Wasserman could
probably tell you in an instant to the milligram. No, there
has to be another way to convince these Israelis that we
have the stuff."

"You know, Mitch, sometimes you sound a lot like Wasserman, which may have something to do with how you can
put up with him as a roommate." Deborah squinted, which
she did whenever she was deep in thought. "How about a
dosimeter? We could leave it overnight in the storage room,
then show it to them so they could tell from the exposure
level how radioactive it was."

"No, I don't think that would work. For one, the rods are
well shielded, so I am not sure the level would be all that
high. I don't remember what the scintillation counter registered, but it wasn't so high as to make me run screaming
from the room. For another, how would they know we didn't
doctor the dosimeters. It wouldn't be hard." The phone rang,
and Mitchell reached for the receiver on the wall.

"Hello?" he said into the handset. He held up a finger to
silence Deborah. "What makes you think she would be
here?" He put his hand over the mouthpiece and turned to
her. "It's your guy, Tsvi. He wants to talk with you. He
knows you're here. How the hell, I don't know. What should
we do?"

"Look, I'll just talk to him. It seems obvious he had me

followed, so he undoubtedly knows about you, too." She reached for the phone, and Mitchell stretched the long coiled cord over to her. Into the phone she said, "Yeah, okay, I'm listening," then went silent, nodding reflexively every now and then. Finally she said, "Yes, I understand. No, we will have to talk it over. Okay. Bye."

She walked solemnly over to the wall set and hung up the phone.

"What?" Mitchell said. "Tell me, tell me."

She pursed her lips and squinted again. "We don't have to give them a sample. They are quick, they already figured it out. They know all about the MIT reactor program. They know that's where we are getting the fuel from. They figured that out once they knew about you, since you work there. But they have no intention of trying to bypass us because they are perfectly happy letting us take the risks by stealing the stuff. We get caught and its us who go down in flames. But there's a hitch or two—three, no four really. They want an even dozen rods, they will pay only a million, they will pay only on delivery, and they will take delivery only in Israel. We have to get it there ourselves. They will give us exact instructions, which we are to follow to the letter or the deal is off. Oh yeah, and we have a deadline."

Mitchell took several breaths, each one deeper than the last. "Hey, it's just problem solving. We have a ton of reactor fuel that we have to get from Cambridge to Israel. We can't mail it. We can't put it in a truck and drive it there. I have some idea how international shipping works, because of my Polaroid deal, so I know it would not be easy to get an export permit for radioactive cargo. Course, as I also know, we don't have to say what we're shipping, but we do have to have a plausible story. We might need to take on a business partner that's legit, and that starts getting messier than cow-pies in a summer rain."

She interrupted. "You said shipping. That gives me an idea. I think I know where we can get some expert advice. I know a kid from Northeastern whose family is in the shipping business in some way or another. Jef is a tool like your MIT friend, another EE major. He's cool. He may have some suggestions. I think he would find the problem interesting. I'll find an excuse to drop in to see him after work and start a conversation. He's on co-op this term."

~ ~ ~

It took Deborah a couple days to track down Jef Vries. He was working as a technician at a local acoustic engineering firm, bread-boarding circuits and servicing equipment for experimental setups. When Deborah caught up with him later in the week, she found him standing at a workbench covered with tools and electronic parts, running his hand through his crew cut as he stared at the irregular dance of light of an oscilloscope trace.

"Hey, hey. This is a surprise," he said. "They let you come back here?" He reached over and switched the 'scope off.

"I told them I was another co-op student interested in a placement next semester. Wanted to check it out with you. It's remarkably easy to fool people when you just act like you know what you are doing and have every right to be where you are. Here," she said, handing him a slightly greasy paper sandwich bag. "Cookies from home. My mom always sends more than I can eat, and I know how much you like chocolate."

"Wow! Thanks. Mmmm, these smell good. *My* mother never makes me cookies."

"But I thought you said your mother was a cook, like on a cruise ship or something."

"No, no, that was only when she was young. She rotated on a lot of jobs on board before she met my dad. But then she quit working, got fat, and had me." He grinned.

"So, do you know anything about shipping and stuff like that?"

"A little bit. That's the business my father's whole family is in. They own Nederlands Atlantic. It's one of Europe's smaller freight lines, but it's obscenely successful. Why do you ask?"

"Well, I am working on a puzzle. Say you had a ton or two of something you wanted to get from here to the Middle East without anyone knowing about it or being able to track it. How would you do that?"

"I don't know about anyone else, but I would just take my uncle's yacht, the Delft."

"Your uncle's yacht can go from here to," she thought quickly. "Say to Lebanon?"

"Sure, no problem. You got to understand, this is no ordinary yacht. My uncle is stinking rich. He inherited this monster from my grandfather, who started Nederlands Atlantic and wanted something grand to tootle around the world in. So, he bought a surplus navy ship, an APD it's called, a kind of fast troop carrier, then paid millions to have it converted into a humungous private yacht that could take him almost anywhere."

"You gotta be kidding me. You ever been on this thing?" Jef nodded. "But if your family is that rich, why are you working a co-op job?"

"Well, for one thing, the Vries clan believes in learning by doing, in making our own way," he laughed. "But more importantly, my father was cut out of the will when he married my mother—not a proper match, they would say. So my grandfather left it all to the other sibs, and my father was too proud—and too hurt—to protest. So now he works in a shitty make-work job that pays more than he could make anywhere else but leaves him the poorest of the whole clan. Not for me. I want to be an engineer. Screw ships and shipping. Except for the yacht, which my uncle has promised to me when he dies. Only I may not be able to afford to keep it. Very expensive to berth. Fuel? Forget it. But it would easily go from here to Lebanon. The engines have been souped-up and all the controls modernized and automated so that even a landlubber could pilot it. She can make a sustained 30 knots with a range of 6,000 nautical miles. I'd have to check some charts, but I think that would make it to Lebanon. What's in Lebanon? What would you be taking there?"

"That's another story. Just out of curiosity, where is this super yacht."

"It's right here in Boston Harbor until it heads down to Florida for the winter. When it's up here, my uncle lets us party on it a couple times a year. Want to see it sometime?"

16

2003 — KARL AWOKE WITH A START to find Ulrich standing over him. "I am sorry to be back so late, but I was doing some checking after rehearsal. I think it best that we do not go out to eat. I will fix us something here."

Over bread and cheese and a bottle of Riesling, Karl filled in his friend about his plans, and Ulrich told about what he had learned. "Also, I am not a spy," Ulrich said, "but I am an academic, so I do know how to research things, and I do know some people in political science who know some people who know where to look and who to ask. I found the name of Migdal Rozeyn on a membership list of Trade Now, an organization promoting trade and economic cooperation between Israelis and Palestinians. It was formed five or six years ago with a rationalist agenda of peace through prosperity, the argument being that improving the plight of the Palestinians not only makes them less likely to become terrorists but creates markets for Israeli goods. They work at the grass roots level, helping Palestinians set up factories and other businesses and brokering trade arrangements between buyers and sellers on both sides.

"My Muslim colleague at the university—who also sings, by the way—believes that it was the Israelis themselves who killed Rozeyn to prevent such an agenda from succeeding. As for me, I do not know. It seems the argument could be made either way. Israelis. Palestinians. On both sides are those who want peace and those who do not.

"And also, your lady friend, Maryam Cashman, she did not study here at the *Hochschule*, that I am sure. I checked. But, come, we must sleep. Tomorrow I teach. In the morning we talk; in the afternoon I teach my students about industrial design. In the evening we will talk yet again before you leave for Israel. You will find a bag I give to you in the hallway—better than that ragged thing you brought with you. I have moved your things; I hope that is okay. I do not think you should stay too long in Germany. Although I did not learn details, I did get the impression that the investigation of the killing is very active because, my Muslim colleague notwithstanding, the authorities are worried that it was Islamist terrorists here that were responsible."

Karl, however, did not wait as requested, but arose once again before dawn, then quietly pushed his friend's car down the drive before starting it in the street. He drove out to the Autobahn and headed for München. Ulrich was supposed to drive Karl's rental car to Frankfurt to return it, then take the train back down to München to pick up his own car where Karl was to leave it. Karl had previously confirmed with the airline that he would be able to swap his Frankfurt to Tel Aviv ticket.

The whole elaborate ruse would not foil anybody for long, but it raised an extra hoop to jump through for anyone trying to track him. All he wanted to do was buy some time. If his followers were any good at all, they would by now or soon would know he was still in Germany. He regretted not being able to take the Glock, but there just was not time to figure out how to pack it, and leaving it behind cut the risk of being caught. Besides, he thought, it's been a lot of years since I was on the pistol team, and I've never even fired a

Glock.

There were few trucks and only a handful of cars on the road so early. Karl breezed along at a steady hundred-and-fifty. As he neared the München airport in Freising, he could see flashing blue lights. On one of the overpasses, a whole string of police cars were lined up, and overhead a police helicopter circled.

Uncertain what to do, he drove on into the terminal grounds, past the Hotel Kempinski, and into the car park. He parked in a vacant spot in the general vicinity of where Ulrich had told him to leave the car. He knelt down to slip the car keys and parking ticket atop the left rear tire as arranged, then pulled up the handle on the rolling duffle bag Ulrich had left for him. As he was leaving the garage, he noticed a man approaching wearing an airline uniform and towing a flight case.

"Entschuldigung. Können sie mir sagen was ist los? Warum die viele Polizei?" Karl asked in his clumsy German, trying to seem only casually interested in why there were so many police.

The man gave him a blank stare. "Are you talking to me? Sorry, I don't speak German."

"I'm sorry, I was just asking about all the police, the choppers and all. Do you have any idea what is going on?"

"Oh, yeah. Don't know all the details, but they caught a sniper camped out on top of the Kempinski. Seems he was spotted by one of the planes on approach early this morning. Needless to say, security is pretty tight. But they got the guy, so I don't think there is anything to worry about."

Karl nodded. "Thanks. I'm sure you're right." He started to walk on, then stopped and turned. "They don't know anything on what it's about yet, do they? I mean, like who was involved or that?"

"One first officer in the ready room said the guy was Middle Eastern, but I don't really know. CNN probably already has more detail. You know how it goes."

Karl thanked him again, then headed for the check-in hall. It was less crowded than usual, but crawling with security people and federal police with automatic weapons. Karl was starting to have second thoughts about his plans. Perhaps it would be better to wait a day or two, he thought. But, of course, that would just increase the chances that whoever was after him would track him down.

The ticket change seemed to take forever, and, at one point, Karl was beginning to think it had all been ill advised. He was about to offer to buy a new ticket when the counter agent finally finished with what seemed to be endless typing and retyping.

"There," she said. "Everything is set. Here is your itinerary and your boarding passes to Zurich and then on to Tel Aviv."

Karl thanked her and apologized for all the trouble. As he approached the security checkpoint, he started to get nervous again. He had to concentrate to keep his hand from shaking as he handed over his boarding pass and passport. But then his bag went through the x-ray, and he got through security without a hitch. He was glad he had come to his senses and not tried to pack the Glock.

The short hop to Zurich was routine, and security at the Zurich airport was considerably more relaxed than in München. With only an hour before his flight to Israel, Karl had no time to stop in the lounge to check on the news, but when he passed a monitor he spotted a reference in the crawl at the bottom of the screen to terrorists at the München airport. He watched for a couple of minutes, hoping to learn more. Instead he read about an FBI agent found shot dead in an alleyway on Beacon Hill. The world is coming apart at the seams, he thought. I may be next.

As his flight took off for Tel Aviv, Karl finally allowed himself to relax for a moment before he reminded himself that he had only just escaped the frying pan and was probably about to land in the fire. Ahead lay what was to him the unknown—Israel.

17

1963 — AFTER MOST OF A WEEK recovering from surgery, Karl found the climb to Mitchell's apartment much steeper than he remembered. He was still feeling a little wobbly, and he got shooting pains if he moved too fast or twisted the wrong way. He had kept up a brave front with his mother, insisting that he was fine, but once she was on the plane back to Michigan, he found he could no longer sustain the pretense. It hurt.

Mitchell was out, but Debbie was there with another friend whom she introduced as Jef Vries.

"I came to tell you and Mitch that I was dropping out of the, you know, the hack thing we, uh, you all have been talking about. You know."

Debbie smiled at him. "No need to be coy about it, Jef knows all about it. Besides, it was just talk, anyway. We're not going to really do it. You didn't think we were serious, did you? It was just an intellectual exercise. Speaking of which, how about a game of Go while we wait for Mitch to get back? You do play, don't you?" Karl nodded, then shrugged. "Good. I'll give you a four-stone handicap." She winked at him as she opened the board and set it on the beat-up coffee table.

Karl declined the handicap, but soon wished he were not playing an even game. He was no match for Debbie, whose moves were made with quick precision and a smart snap as she placed each stone and rapidly gained control over much of the board. Wasserman appeared from the bathroom and began a running commentary on Karl's increasingly untenable position. He and Jef both kibitzed with suggestions for saving face.

The apartment door swung suddenly open and banged against a chair as Mitchell entered, foot still in the air, arms loaded with two swollen grocery bags. "What's up? Oh, hi, Karl, good to see you up and around. How are your war wounds?"

"Still pretty sore," Karl said. As he stood up to give Mitchell a hand, he swayed slightly and his pant leg caught the edge of the Go board, sending black and white stones flying around the room. Karl stood there with a look of horror on his face as Debbie and Jef doubled over in laughter.

"Smooth move, Karl," Mitchell said as he took the groceries to the kitchen. "Let me guess. Deb was winning, right?"

Karl's cheeks started turning red. "I … I didn't do that on purpose. I mean, yes, she was ahead. Some." Jef and Debbie laughed even harder. "Well, a lot." Jef was almost choking. "Well, okay, I bombed. Maybe I had twenty or thirty points, tops."

"Twenty-two," said Wasserman. "You should have conceded. If you want to continue the game, though, I think I can set it up just the way it was."

"No thanks, I'll take a pass on being humiliated." Karl started to bend down to begin retrieving stones but stopped with the first pull of his stitches.

Jef got down on his knees and started gathering the scattered stones. "Hey crip, let the able-bodied clean up your mess," he said. Wasserman just stood by, watching and rocking.

"Hey," Mitchell called from the kitchen, "She beats me all the time, too. It's a tough game. Not like chess. You know what Professor Minsky said in a lecture last term? He said we'd have computers beating human chess champions within a few years, but it'd be decades before anyone could program a computer to be any good at Go."

"You want a hand putting those groceries away?" Karl called out.

"Uh. No, that's all right. Mostly canned goods and stuff. I can take care of it later. You hoping to stay for dinner? Wait, this is Sunday. Don't you have a rehearsal for that group you sing in? The Tooly Tunes or whatever?"

"They're called the InstiTunes," Karl corrected. "And that's on Wednesdays. But I do have a study group at the dorm that I really need to be at. I am way, way behind."

"You want a ride?"

"Not on your life. The last time I rode with you I ended up in the hospital. And almost had to have a tire iron removed from my rectum. Nope. I'll just take it slow. On the level is easy, it's the steps that kill. Good thing Conner has an elevator."

"If you call the rickety Conner Rocket an elevator. Suit yourself. I'll walk you down. I have some more stuff in the van to bring up."

"What are you stocking up for, anyway?"

"Yeah, what's all the stuff for, Mitchell?" added Wasserman, a little anxiously.

Mitchell patted Wasserman on the shoulder. "Don't worry, it's just stuff on sale. You know, three-fors and that. I like to save money by buying whatever is on sale. Last month they had four pounds of hamburg for three dollars at the A&P, so I got sixteen pounds to freeze."

Karl looked dubious. "Where do you put it? Your fridge only has a tiny little freezer."

"Oh, I shove it all in the bottom of a big freezer in the bio-chem lab. Whenever I need more here, I just let myself in when I'm on night shift." He grinned broadly.

Karl shook his head slowly. "I won't ask what else you have stashed around the Institute," he said. Jef and Deborah looked oddly uncomfortable. "Anyway, see you guys around sometime. May not be for a while. I am really going to have to scramble to catch up this semester."

"You want some help with the advanced calculus?" asked Wasserman, trailing after Karl. "You want me to walk with you? You want to see my Fortran program? I'm working on the Four-Color Problem. Do you know what that is?"

"Thanks, Wasserman, but no thanks. Just … I don't know … just get lost. Find some place to go."

18

IT HAD BEEN WEEKS since he had seen Mitchell or any of the gang. With Christmas break approaching, Karl was at last beginning to feel like he might be able to survive his freshman year. The time in the hospital had cost him dearly, but he had stubbornly refused to drop any classes. Since before Halloween, there had been little time for anything but classes and study, classes and study. He had been so single-mindedly immersed in the grind, that even the Kennedy assassination had barely registered on his mental radar.

He had managed to pick one of the coldest days of the month to interrupt his academic marathon and make the trek across to Boston. The weather had finally turned cold, giving Karl his first real taste of New England winter, no match for the frigid Upper Peninsula, but with a raw edge, nonetheless. He pulled his hood tighter and cursed the crosswind on the Harvard Bridge. He wished he had been able to talk with Mitch over the phone, but whenever he called there was no answer.

Outside the apartment building, there was no sign of Mitchell's decrepit van. Inside, Karl stomped the snow off his boots and started up the stairs. As he neared the third floor, he called out, "Hey, Mitch, long time no see. What's up?"

The stranger just closing the door to the apartment turned, a surprised and somewhat puzzled look on his face. "Hello?" he said.

"Sorry, I just thought you were someone else. Mitchell Rossing. You a friend?"

"Rossing? Oh, you must mean the guy who used to live here. Sorry. I just moved in. I never met him." He spoke with just a trace of a British accent.

"What? He's moved out? When? You know where he went, where I could get in touch with him?"

"I haven't the slightest idea. I think he went back to...to Minnesota."

"You mean Wisconsin?"

"Yeah, whatever. Back to what you call the boonies, at least that's what I heard. As I said before, I never met the guy. Sorry."

"No, I'm sorry. I was just taken by surprise. My name's Karl, Karl Lustig."

After an uncomfortably long pause, the man smiled. "I'm Paul. Pleasure." He nodded without offering his hand. "I was just on my way out. See you. Cheers." He strode past Karl and headed quickly down the stairs.

Odd, thought Karl, that Mitchell would just disappear. But then Mitchell always was a bit odd. I should try and track down Wasserman. He might know what happened. Haven't seen much of him either. Ah well, back to the grind. Two more quizzes, five labs, and four finals to go, then I'm free. Maybe during the break I'll look up that girl from BU. As long as I'm stuck here in the decadent Hub of the Universe, might as well.

He trudged down the two flights and out into the December winds.

We may become the makers of our fate when we have ceased to pose as its prophets. – Karl Popper

Part Two: Mitchell

19

1963 — MITCHELL HAD WATCHED the door close and listened to the uneven thump of fading footsteps on the stairs. When he turned to Jef and Deb he said, "It's nearly the end of October. The Israelis are getting antsy. With or without Karl I think we have to go ahead as planned. We don't want to be crossing the Atlantic in the dead of winter."

"We do it without Karl?" Jef asked.

"Yeah. He wouldn't have been able to keep up, anyway."

"And he would have been no help schlepping stuff," Deb added. "Besides, I don't think his heart was ever really in it. He just isn't the driven kind. He's the sort who just takes what happens to come along."

"You're right," Mitchell acknowledged. "But he does have a kind of loyal, dogged effectiveness that I admired from the moment I met him. I wish he were still on the team. He is absolutely the sort that you can count on when the shit hits the fan."

"It's okay," Deb said, putting a hand on his shoulder. "We can handle it. But we better get moving if we are going to stick to schedule. You have to clock in at the 'tute and we have to get all this stuff stowed. Everything has to be just right for The Party." 'The Party' at first was just the fictional excuse Jef had used when he called his uncle in Florida asking to borrow the Delft, but it had since become a code name for the entire operation.

Mitchell grinned. "We have plenty of time. In fact, I'll report to work a few minutes late, as usual. When I see Rocky, around about one, I'll tell him I need to leave a little early in the morning and get him to clock me out. Then I'm off for the week. And parts unknown. When I do get back, I'll just tell 'em I was really sick. They're used to that sort of thing. If they don't fire me, I'll just give them my two-weeks' notice." He laughed.

Jef looked at him and nodded gravely. "So, we're really going to do this, huh? A million dollars. Not bad for a couple of twenty-year-olds and a teenage sociopath. Tell me, Mitch, what will you do with the money? Go back to Wisconsin for some of that 'beer that made Milwaukee famous?'"

"No thanks, I'd rather have 'the champagne of bottled beers.'" He slumped down in the chair beside the door. "No, I'll probably come right back here, use my share of the money to start some kind of business, and get really rich. I hated being hungry and bored when I was growing up in the Midwest. I don't plan to be either again. What about you, Jef? What's in your future?"

"I want to finish my degree, like I planned, and design computer circuits. I'll probably just sock my share away in a bank account somewhere, save it for when the proverbial precipitation comes. I don't know whether it's such a good idea to come right back here, though."

"No, that's the whole idea. We come back and go on as if nothing happened. By the time MIT discovers something did happen, they will have no idea when, so the trail will be as cold as Juno in January. What's more, odds are they'll keep it really quiet. Can you imagine what having all that nuclear material unaccounted for would do for their reputation, to say nothing of future government research funding?

No, I'm willing to bet they will be as mum about it as the Is-raelis are about their end of things. It will never be in the news. By next week, this never happened."

Jef turned to Deb. "So, are you going to stay in Israel?"

"Nope. I've been looking into enrolling in the Technion in Haifa, but I would have to come back here and apply. Can't just swim ashore and say, 'Here I am.' It would draw attention to The Party and put us all in jeopardy. No, I'll come back, finish the semester. I'm thinking of going to Eng-land over the winter break. I have a cousin in Sheffield who just had a baby girl. It would be fun to see the country and help her with the baby, maybe pick up some extra cash."

"Do you Jews ever stop thinking about money?" Jef asked, teasingly.

Deb pulled a cushion from the couch and swung it at him. He ducked and Mitchell took it full in the face. "Oh, poor baby," she said kissing him repeatedly. "I'm sorry. And you, you little creep" she said, turning back to Jef. "After that crack, I am not going to sleep with you."

Jef scowled. "You mean you were thinking about it be-fore? You would, I mean you would have, but now you wouldn't?"

Deb narrowed her eyes at him but said nothing. From over her shoulder, Mitchell gloated, "I already got to first base."

She swung around again and caught Mitchell in the shoulder with the cushion, sending him staggering. "Do men ever stop thinking about sex?"

"Of course not," Mitchell said, "especially around you. But honest, you gotta believe me, you are so much more than a body to me. It's not just about sex. It's about your breasts, er, I mean your brains." He held up his arms in mock defense as he teased her. "Besides, we have work to do. Plus we'll be cooped up onboard for weeks with plenty of time to get to know each other better. Lots better, I hope." She hit him again.

"Look, I have a rehearsal at Hillel," she said. "They are starting a singing group. Israeli folk songs, that sort of thing. I'll be back in plenty of time after supper. Just stay cool and stay put, boys."

Mitchell left shortly after her to go get a pizza from Antonelli's. When he returned, Jef was sprawled on the couch, staring at the ceiling. "Is something up there or are you just mentally computing the expansion of pi to a hundred decimal places?"

"We don't do that sort of thing at Northeastern. We're engineers. We design and build stuff. Five place accuracy from the *CRC* tables is more than enough, and most of the time a slipstick will do. We leave the higher math and theory to you Tech types. Anyway, I was just thinking about The Party, maybe feeling a little uneasy."

"Don't sweat anything. We've planned every step. The whole operation is a walk in the park," Mitchell told him, his innocent grin never faltering. "Here, have some pizza. I'll get a couple of beers from the fridge."

The two ate without talking, standing up in the tiny kitchen. With Deb gone, they suddenly seemed to have nothing to say to each other. Perhaps, thought Mitchell, she was the wampeter. Or maybe the silence was more than just the absence of words. He knew they both had a thing for her.

In the living room, Jef flicked on the TV to catch the weather, and Mitchell joined him on the couch. The tropical storm that had been dancing around off the coast of the Carolinas had worried them, but the report said it was weakening and tracking out to sea.

"Okay, we are good to go. Our bearing takes us far enough north that we should have no problem across the Atlantic," Jef said.

Mitchell looked unconvinced. "You're the naval type," he said. "I'll have to take your word for it. All I've ever sailed are the MIT dinghies on the Charles."

He got up and changed channels randomly, twisted the rabbit ears, then returned to the sofa. They sat, staring in studied silence at the snow-speckled black-and-white picture, both unaware of time or even of what they were watching. They jumped when Deb opened the door at last and said, "Let's party, boys."

It took several trips to cart all the last-minute supplies down to Mitchell's van. When they were done, Mitchell led them down a flight of squeaky wooden stairs to the basement of the building. By the light of a single bare bulb in the ceiling, he undid the oversized padlock on a storage room. He pulled out two coveralls with "MIT" stitched over the left breast. "B&P combat uniforms: they'll make you less suspicious if someone happens to be wandering the halls. You can put them on in the van after you ferry all this stuff to the boat. Deb, you can wear my baseball cap to cover your hair. And here, throw this in the back, too." He shoved a heavy-duty moving dolly toward them. "I cumshawed this from my last job. There's another one at the 'tute that we can borrow."

"What's that?" Jef said, pointing to one side toward several large barrels that seemed to be filled with sawdust.

"Oh, that's one of Mitchell's many so-called business schemes. He sells Polaroid lenses to Italians who turn them into pricey sun glasses."

"I don't get it. Why don't they just buy them from Polaroid?"

"Because Mitch can get them cheaper, like for bupkis. He has a deal with the company that hauls away the Polaroid trash, which he sifts for discards. Right Mitch?"

"Yeah, yeah, but that deal's only worth a few hundred a month. I'll kill it after I get back."

"What else you got back here?" Jef asked as he started to poke around.

Mitch stopped him. "Some other time, hot shot. We got uranium to move tonight."

"Yeah, let's go," Deb said, as she bounded up the stairs carrying the coveralls, leaving the dolly for Jef and Mitchell to drag up the steep steps.

20

MITCHELL WAS WAITING at the tail board of the loading dock, arms crossed, when the van showed up at MIT. He looked at his watch. "You're almost 15 minutes late."

"Hey, no big deal. Deb wanted to call home. Didn't want to have worried parents calling the dorm while she was away. They got to talking. You know. Besides, there's still plenty of time. We don't sail until 5:30," Jef said with a sigh.

"Yeah, but sunrise is 6:12 and we don't want to be moving the stuff or loading in twilight. Plus, I don't like standing around looking like a conspicuous loafer. If a supervisor had happened by, we'd be screwed. Come on, give me a hand. Hold the flashlight for me." He pulled a wrench from his pocket and crawled under the van. "Hey, I need some light here."

"What are you doing?"

"Releasing the locking bolts."

Mitchell grunted with the wrench, then started banging at something. Suddenly, the left rear of the van sprang upward several inches. More grunts, a few bangs, and the other side bounced up.

"What was that?"

"I put in special load-leveling shocks last week. We can't have the bottom dragging with all that extra weight in back, but I didn't want to draw attention by riding around all week with the van raked like some hotrod. Deb, you grab the dolly and both of you follow me. Try to act casual, like we are just three coolies slogging through another night shift. If you act like you belong, you will."

He led them through a pipe-lined maze, stopping at each turn to stick a piece of masking tape on the corner at eye level. "So you don't get lost on your way back. Yes, I know you studied the floor plans, but we can't take any chances. And we can't forget to pull them off on our last trip." They reached a double door that opened into a main corridor. He blocked one door open with a wooden wedge. "Can't forget that, either."

He led them first to a supply closet where he grabbed a stack of corrugated cardboard marked "Suffolk Scientific" and another dolly, which he shoved toward Jef. Farther down the hall he stopped at an unmarked door, unlocked it, and heaved it open, motioning his companions in.

Mitchell propped his flashlight up against a cabinet to one side of the door, then pulled a paper from his pocket, unfolded it, and laid it on the floor, turning it to line up with the room. It mapped the position of each of the serial-numbered fuel rods, which ones would be removed, and how the remaining ones would be repositioned to disguise the removal. He nodded, and Jef and Deborah started shifting the nearest rods to one side to create a corridor to reach the ones in back.

They worked quickly and methodically. When they were ready to move the first fuel rods, Mitchell unfolded the corrugated cardboard and wrapped it around each shipping frame. Once on the dollies, they looked like cartons of equipment of some kind.

Mitchell waved the two of them off, then stood guard anxiously outside the door for the long minutes it took them to make the first run to the van and back. When Deb at last rounded the corner he looked at her inquiringly. She gave him a thumbs up.

The job went quickly, and they finished sooner than expected. On the last run, Mitchell went with them to pick up the tape and the wedge and to double back to return the borrowed dolly. Jef was rocking the last of the rods into place in the now packed van. "Good thing we didn't take more. We almost ran out of room as is. We should have dumped that big metal tool locker in there."

"Can't, it's welded to the floor," Mitchell said. As he turned to leave, two students, one in a fraternity jacket, the other in a sweatshirt, rounded the corner of the building carrying stacks of fan-folded printer paper under their arms. Mitchell signaled Jef with a shake of his head to ignore them, but they turned toward the van.

"You poor slobs have to load equipment all night?" one of them asked.

Mitchell hopped down from the loading dock and took several quick steps to get between the students and the van. "Keeping up with all you young Einsteins is a twenty-four hour job," he said, hoping that Jef would use the extra moment to shut the doors. Instead, Jef started pulling a tarp down over the cargo, but it caught on something and came down only part way.

The other student, who had slipped by Mitchell, was almost at the van. "What's this, guys?" he asked, pointing. Mitchell and Jef froze. Mitchell could see Deb just getting out of the passenger door. She had Mitchell's wrench in her hand. He looked right into her eyes and shook his head with a slow but definitive "no."

The student in the sweatshirt reached the van, then

turned back to his fraternity buddy. "Hey, Steve-o, beer!" he called. "These B&P coolies are hauling brews."

"Who you calling coolie, you little snot," Jef growled at him, hoping that three days' worth of stubble made him look old enough and sufficiently threatening.

"It's all right, Mac," Mitchell said, crossing to Jef's side and positioning himself to partially block the view inside the van.

Out of the side of his mouth Jef mumbled, "Sorry, I forgot to unload the case."

"I said it's all right. Look, boys, you don't tell our boss about the brews, and we'll give you some. Here," he reached behind Jef and pulled out four bottles, two in each hand, and handed them to the students.

"Hey, thanks. Maybe you B&P guys are not all bad."

"Right, but get out of here," Mitchell said closing one of the van doors. "Back to your computer stuff before we all get in trouble. Not a word about the beer, okay?"

"Right, okay," the student said, grabbing at his fraternity buddy. "Let's go."

Jef closed the other door and leaned against the van. "That was close. Good thinking, Mitch. Now, let's get out of here."

"No, I gotta return the dolly and make one last check. You pull out of the driveway and wait around the corner. I'll be out the side door in two minutes. If I am not there in ten, you figure there has been a problem. Get to the dock. If I'm not there by 4:30, go without me. You hear?" He scrambled up the ramp and pulled the sliding door closed behind him.

Twenty minutes of shivering later, Deborah insisted that Jef follow the plan and leave for the boat. He took the back way, turned, and headed down Mass Avenue, which was completely deserted, then continued across the bridge. On the other side he turned to get onto Storrow Drive.

"Where the hell are you going?" Deborah asked.

"I figured I'd take Storrow. What's the problem?"

"For one thing, it's not in the plan. For another, I think that's a cruiser behind us."

The confirmation came in the form of a brief burp from a siren as a patrol car pulled up beside them and the officer riding shotgun gestured toward the breakdown strip.

"Shit. Shit fuckin' shit. The MDC police. What now?" Jef pulled over quickly. The Metropolitan District Commission police had a reputation, whether deserved or not, for being particularly hardnosed with students.

As the officer approached, Jef struggled with the sticking hand crank to roll down the window. The policeman waited impatiently, then leaned in to look around. "Do you kids know that commercial vehicles are not allowed on Storrow Drive?" he asked.

"Yes sir, officer, but this is not a commercial vehicle. I mean, it's just for personal use," Jef said, trying to sound as polite as possible.

"I'm sorry, son, but this is a delivery van, not a passenger vehicle, and your plate makes it a light truck. It's not allowed on Storrow. What are doing out at this hour anyway? What's with the coveralls? What have you got in the back?"

"We were at a costume party, you know, Halloween," Jef answered. Deborah, sitting in the middle next to him, elbowed him in the ribs. "We're heading back from the party with the leftover stuff, you know," he finished.

"Could you open the back, please? I want to see this 'stuff.'"

The two of them looked at each other. "Okay, okay!"

said Jef, pulling the keys from the ignition. He walked to the back, unlocked and opened the right-hand door, then stood back. "What's under the tarp?" the officer asked. Jef didn't answer. "Let's have a look."

Jef lifted one corner to reveal the case of Budweiser. "Like I said, officer, a party. We borrowed the van to ferry the brews back to my place. I guess we just weren't thinking about this being a … well, a van."

"Let's see your ID, son. You don't look old enough to drink."

Jef reached into his back pocket and handed over his license.

"Well, Mr. Jacob Miller from Providence," he said, reading from the license. "You may be old enough to drink, but I'm going to have to cite you. You're not allowed to drive this thing on Storrow Drive. Please wait in your vehicle."

Jef climbed back in, his hands shaking. "What are we going to do?" he asked.

"Just wait," Deborah said. "And hope to hell that they don't radio in for a trace on the van. Mitch doctored the plates."

They heard the crackle of police radio coming from the patrol car behind them. Suddenly, the siren screamed and the cruiser swung out around them, speeding away in pursuit of someone or something else. They followed its flashing lights in the distance as it exited and sped across the Longfellow Bridge, heading toward MIT.

"What the hell was that? Should we wait or what?" Jef asked.

"What we should do is step on it and get off Storrow Drive at the next exit. We're going a different way, the right way. I'll navigate."

21

THE FLINTY WIND BLOWING across the pier was not enough to erase the smell of the harbor, a pungent potpourri of old wood, dead fish, creosote, and gasoline. Jef fussed with the hood of his sweatshirt as he paced back and forth on the dock. "Where is he? It'll start getting light soon. How the hell is he going to get here, anyway? The T doesn't run at this hour, and I don't think he'd risk a cab. What were we thinking anyway, leaving him there. We should have waited for him."

"Hey, Jef, cool it. Mitch knows what he is doing. He'll show. He'll show. Let's get this thing on board. You drive." She tossed the keys back to him.

The boxy war-surplus LCVP that served as the yacht's dinghy was moored at the end of the dock, looking like it might have just disgorged a jeep and a platoon of troops to invade Boston. Jef cautiously edged the van forward toward the ramp formed by the opened bow of the boat. Even with the tide high, the ramp angled sharply downward, and the van scraped bottom as the front wheels cleared the edge. Jef quickly shifted into reverse and squealed the tires as he pulled back for another run. This time he gunned the engine and shot the van over the lip and down the steep incline. He slammed on the brakes but still skidded into the bulkhead, smashing the left front headlight on a protruding fitting.

There was not enough room to open the driver's-side

door, so Jef slid to the other side and kicked open the sticking door. It banged against the side of the boat. "It was a piece of junk, anyway," he said, squeezing past the van and back onto the dock.

Over the wind, Jef could hear a distant, high-pitched buzzing that reminded him of one of his little brother's model airplanes. It grew slowly louder. A helmeted figure on a Vespa rounded the corner from the street and rumbled down the rough boards, racing toward them without slowing. At the last second, the rider throttled back just enough to step off and stumble into them, letting the scooter fly off the end of the dock in a long arc just to one side of the LCVP. The buzzing ended abruptly as the scooter splashed into the water and quickly sank.

Mitch took off his helmet and tossed it to Jef. "I always wanted to try something like that."

Jef looked down at the helmet, then up at Mitch. "You nuts? You could've ended up in the harbor with the scooter. And that looked like a perfectly good scooter, too."

"It was hot. They'll never find it now. It'll just be another Vespa gone missing from behind Grad House. Happens all the time. I'm just glad I had these with me to cut the chain." He pulled a pair of folding bolt cutters from his pocket. "Where's the van?"

Deb gestured toward the boat. "We already drove it onto the LST," she said. "We were just waiting for you."

"Not an LST," Jef corrected. "An LST is a huge sort of armored barge. This is just 36 feet of plywood, a glorified swamp boat. Anyway, let's shove off. What happened, Mitch?"

"Nothing. I had to take a leak and I ran into Rocky in the john. He just likes to talk and talk, and I always just listen and listen. Didn't want to put him off, 'specially since he'll be clocking me out at the end of the shift." He followed Jef onto the landing craft. The three of them squeezed past the van and climbed up to the cockpit. "Hey, this is pretty neat. And just the thing we'll need for the other end. Like Normandy, only without the enemy fire, right?"

"I told you we had everything covered. Like you said, a walk in the park, just a walk in the park."

Jef cranked the big diesel engine, which was reluctant to start. Finally it chugged into deep-throated life. Ever so slowly, he backed out from the pier. "You're going to love this." He deftly steered the craft until he was clear, then shifted into forward and accelerated out into open water. He shouted above the growl of the engine and the slap of the water. "As planned, I had a harbor pilot take the Delft out Saturday so we can load and leave without drawing attention. Told him it was for a party this weekend. I paid him in cash, of course. He wasn't a bit suspicious. Yakked on about his college days. I gave him a bottle of Johnny Walker and told him it was from my uncle. Said he wished he'd had a rich uncle, too. Oh, yeah, and the fuel is topped off—maxed out everybody's credit cards. Soon as we hoist this baby on deck, we are ready to go."

With the lights of the harbor and the city behind them, they headed through the light chop toward a distant dark spot barely discernible against the horizon. The yacht, as they approached it from the stern, was neither very beautiful nor impressive, but as they pulled alongside Mitch almost gasped. The gleaming white hull, longer than a football field, seemed to be lit from within in the predawn glow. "Holy shit, this is one big mother."

"Wait until you see the insides. It's another world." Jef

cut the engines to dead slow and edged alongside the yacht.
"When we get close enough, you two get those lines around
those cleats there and there." He cut the engine, climbed on
the gunwales, and deftly stepped from the boat to the rungs
of a ladder welded into the side of the yacht. He clambered
up toward the deck, shouting orders as he went.

Once the LCVP was hoisted by the davit and secured on
deck, Jef lowered the bow ramp and opened the back of the
van.

"We need to get the stuff stowed right away. Once in the
open ocean, I wouldn't worry, but here close to home there
is always some chance the Coast Guard will want to snoop."

With only one dolly, it took the better part of an hour to
unload all the rods, ferry them to the elevator that had once
lifted ammunition, and get them below deck. Then began
the laborious process of winching each one by hand down
into shafts conveniently left in the lead-laced concrete bal-
last that had been added when the ship had been converted
into a yacht. When they finished, Mitch told them to wait
and ran back up on deck. He returned with the scintillation
counter, which he checked as he walked slowly in circles.

"Look's good, hardly even a twitch," he said.

"Okay, crew, let's go up to the bridge," Jef said, waving
them toward a flight of stairs. "We're ready to sail."

22

2003 — MIGDAL TURNED FROM the sweaty men in the tiny room to look out the narrow window for a moment. The sun, just set, had left the sky above the Old City ablaze. He let the beauty of it wash over him, let the whispering voices of Jerusalem's winding streets and jumbled buildings remind him of his promises, remind him of why he was here, in this small room, with these people.

When he turned back, he was smiling, but Hashim knew him well enough to know this did not mean he was happy.

"Migdal, Migdal, is this really so big a thing we ask?" Hashim spread his arms in a dramatic gesture that turned his robe into a black sail in the slight breeze coming through the window. "It's just another business deal."

"I cannot, you know that, Hashim. It is simply impossible." He thought of tearing the paper in his hands into small pieces but instead simply placed it on the table and slid it across to Hashim. Hashim pushed it back.

"Since when was anything impossible for Migdal Rozeyn? You have done it before. The impossible. *This* impossible thing, in fact. Oh, yes, we know all about it. You can do it now for us, for us all. It is about balance, about restoring balance." A resonance had entered Hashim's voice, as if the bass boost on a boom box had just been turned on.

"It is not the same, Hashim, and you know it. Your client will use it. Israel did not, will not."

"And since when do you know the Minister of Defense? Or those ultra-orthodox jackals who surround him and howl in his ears? Since when do you know his mind or his heart?"

"I know him well, like a brother. Didn't you know he actually *is* my brother," Migdal said, trying to lighten the tone.

"Ah, so your family tree has branches I would not have imagined, my American cousin. And did you not once call me brother? Have we not traded as brothers, with trust, with fairness?"

"I am not your American cousin. I am an Israeli citizen. And this would not be a fair trade. It would be treason, betrayal, not just of me, but of the whole organization. It would be an abrogation of what *we* are all about. For me to agree would betray you as well, Hashim. Were such a thing ever to be discovered, even hinted at, Trade Now would be doomed. You would be out of business.

"No, we do not trade in death. I will not be a part of this, not in any way."

"You misread the request. It is for medical research. The lab is a legitimate scientific endeavor. The research they undertake will enhance the prestige of the Palestinians in the eyes of the world scientific community. It legitimates us as contributors to learning and progress."

"Hashim, you yourself do not believe that. How can you expect me to believe it? You know. All of you know." He turned to the two silent men seated just beyond the dimming light from the window. "This is one shipment that would be returned to Israel, in a different package, a package with death stamped on it. Do you take me for a traitor?

"The answer is no, Hashim. I do not know what web you may have become caught up in, my friend, but I will not be lured into it."

One of the two men in the shadows stood. "Some of your own already call you traitor," he said with contempt. Speaking in Arabic, he turned to Hashim, "This is a waste of time. Remind him that he has no choice. Remind him that he has a wife and a young son."

Migdal understood. "You threaten me? You threaten my family? And still you would pretend this is about trade? No, I think we are done for today. Perhaps we are done for more than today." He began stuffing papers into his briefcase, among them the document that was the focus of their dispute. Perhaps I am already a dead man, he thought. No, they think I am their only source. No, that is doubtful, but I am their choice of the moment.

Hashim turned to glare disapprovingly at his companions. "Tariq, please. Business that is born of threats is bad business."

To Migdal he said, "We will leave aside this business— for now. Let us speak instead of other trade. On what might we be more in agreement, friend, brother?"

Migdal, looked down at the papers in his hand, unsure of whether to continue or to make a point by walking out. The price of either option might be far higher than he could compute at the moment. At long last he said, "Okay, okay. Ga'ash Lighting has a pending contract for fixtures at a new park in The Netherlands, but they are already working to capacity. Perhaps there a small metal shop in Gaza that could subcontract for the poles. This is interesting work with some new materials. It could be lucrative and a learning opportunity. Is there anybody? Could Rashid and his crew handle something like this."

"I think a better fit would be Mediterranean Metals."

Tariq spat. "They collude, they cower. Give it instead to

Rashid, who at least has a spine."

Hashim stiffened. "This is about trade, about the well-being of our people. Our peoples," he corrected. "This is not about politics."

"And is standing up to the Zionist oppressors not about the welfare of our people." He emphasized the last word to make clear it was singular.

Migdal shook his head slowly as he began again to return papers to his briefcase. "Am I your oppressor now, Hashim? I don't know what is happening, but this may be a matter for the Committee. Perhaps you ... no, perhaps neither of us is any longer well-suited to this work. You know that Trade Now can never get involved in contraband or weapons. As it is, there are rumors, accusations. And it must be neutral, always. We must all negotiate for freer trade, for mutually beneficial business arrangements that build the Palestinian economy. Not good deeds, but good deals, as it says on our website." He snapped his briefcase shut.

"Still, I will work on the Ga'ash deal. I will pretend you never made the other request. I hope we can do better as brothers and as businessmen next time, Hashim. I look forward soon to sitting down, as we have so many times, just you and I, building a better world for our sons."

"*Inshallah,*" Hashim said with a slight nod of his head.

"Yes, God willing. *Salaam.* And to you also, Tariq, and to your silent friend there. Go in peace." Migdal pushed past the two seated men, half expecting to be stopped. Outside in the twilight, he headed downhill, striding quickly over the cobblestones until he was just beyond the view of the window above. He turned into a narrow alley before retrieving his cell phone. He scrolled down through the address book until he found an entry with only the initial "L" and dialed it.

"It's me," he said as soon as he heard a click. He continued without waiting for a response. "Look, I hate this. I thought I was done with it all, but I have a package for you. It will be at the old drop. Better retrieve it tonight. You'll understand. And get the Institute to keep an eye on Shira and Binyamin for a while. I can't leave for Haifa yet." He closed the phone without saying goodbye.

In the window that Migdal could no longer see stood Tariq Mustafa, looking out over the city in the fading light. "This is a waste of time, a complete waste of time. We know he can do it, and you know we can make him."

Hashim, well aware of how effective Tariq and his people could be, nevertheless said, "In this case, I think not. Migdal will not piss himself and promise the moon like those cowards from the instrument maker that you coerced last month. He has proved himself resourceful and unshakable since he was barely more than a boy. Remember how he got here. You know what he did."

"Yes, yes, we know how he got here. We also know what he has been doing ever since, which is why he is the one to fulfill the contract. He is a known quantity, as the Americans say."

"You may have measured the quantity incorrectly, Tariq. I think it will take more than threats to persuade him."

"Exactly," he said, turning toward the door and gesturing for his companion to follow. "Exactly."

Once on the street he spoke again. "Sabir, my aptly named compatriot, your patience will be rewarded. We will get what we are after, and our Mister Rozeyn will help us. I want you to see to that, do you understand?"

"Of course, I do. It is done."

23

HIS HOTEL ROOM WAS SMALL and stuffy, and Migdal slept fitfully until he was awakened by the steady ring of his cell
phone. He looked at his watch: 2:20. It was Shira, crying,
almost in hysterics. He tried to calm her enough to figure out
what she was saying, although he was already making some
dreaded guesses. "Are you all right? Is Bini all right? Just tell
me. Are you both okay?"

"But they came into his room, they came into our home,
they cut our son. They cut our little boy. Do you understand,
they carved an X into his hand." She continued to cry.

"Look, take care of his hand first."

"I already did. It's not too serious. I put a sticking plaster
on it."

"Okay, then both of you get over to Avi's. Now. I'll call
and tell him you're coming. You'll be safe there. I'll get a taxi
for you. Don't use the phone. I'll have the taxi wait around
the corner. Go down the fire escape when you see the taxi
waiting. It will be all right. The driver will be one of Lev's
people. Everything will be fine."

"Mig, what's happening? I thought it was over."

"I did, too," he said quietly. "I'll meet you at Avi's when I
can. I love you. Everything will be okay. Now hang up and
take care of Bini. Take care of him, he needs you." He knew
that giving her that charge would bring out the best in her.
When she was taking care of others, she could be anything,

she could be superwoman.

He made two quick phone calls to arrange for Shira and Binyamin, then dialed a third number. A sleepy voice answered. Migdal said nothing.

"Hello, who is this? Is it you, Tariq?"

"No. Migdal."

"What are you calling for? It's the middle of the night. You've awakened the baby."

Migdal was silent for several more seconds, then said, "Tell Tariq that he and his crew can pick up the goods in Europe. I'll provide details later. Remind him that I am the only person who can get him what he wants. The only one. And remind him that I may have left Mossad, but that does not mean that I am without friends. They do not look kindly upon acts of terrorism inside Israel, however small those acts or small the targets. Tariq and his goons have miscalculated badly."

"I do not follow what you are saying."

"Tariq's men attacked my wife and son." The sound of a sharp inhale came over the phone. Migdal continued, "They are okay, but it will be regarded as a direct affront to Mossad. I do not know what or by what means, but my old colleagues will, I know, exact revenge. And warn Tariq that if any of his men are ever spotted within a hundred meters of my wife or son, I will see to it that this becomes a matter of utmost priority. Tell him his entire family will be wiped out—his wife, his children, his brothers, his nieces and nephews, his cousins—everyone. If I cannot do it myself, I will arrange it. Did you get that, Hashim? And don't ever, ever expect to deal with me again. I will start over from scratch. I will build new contacts, starting from nothing again."

"Migdal, I had no choice but to deal with Tariq. Like you, I had no choice."

"We Jews have an expression, Hashim. You should learn it. No choice is also a choice."

"I don't think I understand. I…"

Migdal disconnected, cutting him off, then dialed the L entry from his address book. As before, there was nothing more than a click on the other end.

"It's Mig, again. I assume you got the document. We need to meet. I'll be in Haifa tomorrow, lunch at the café." He snapped the phone closed.

He lay back on the bed, staring through the ceiling, imagining the stars beyond, shining as they had, unchanged, through all of the troubled history of the city. I can no more escape my past than can you, he thought. We cannot change what is fated.

Bashert, he thought. My fated one, Shira. He slipped off his wedding band and rolled it between his fingers, imagining, though it was almost black in the room, that he could read the Hebrew inscription engraved inside: *Zeh dodi, v'zeh rei.*

My beloved, my friend, he thought. How can I take care of you and Binyamin now along this uncertain road, this road ahead? "This Uncertain Road." What an apt title. I wasn't so keen on it at first, but I am glad your brother suggested that poem to read at our wedding. Yes, I know it well.

> This road ahead I do not know.
> I know not into what valleys
>   Or past what shadows it may lead,
> But I will walk with you, Beloved,
>   Along its wide turns and through its straits.

Whatever course,
  Through storms and lulls,
  I will go.
Even to the ends of the Earth,
  Even to the end of life,
  I will go.
And I will keep watch, my Fated One.
I will straighten the road or change the course
  of rivers.
For you, I will rewrite the words of Fate.

He wiped his eyes in the dark, then sat up. How do you re-write the words of Fate, he wondered. "How?" he said aloud into the chill silence of the night.

24

1963 — JEF STARTED AT A TROT up the stairwell to the bridge. By the time they arrived three stories up, Mitch was winded. Jef held the door for him and bowed. "Age before beauty, old man."

Mitch, in turn, stepped aside with a gallant bow and sweep of his arm as he let Deb pass, saying, "Ladies first. Besides I'm the youngest one here although there are others who may be older but lack my maturity."

Mitch felt like he was entering the top-floor boardroom of one of Boston's old firms in the financial district. The walls were paneled in exotic dark woods with burls and tiger stripes, oversized black leather chairs faced forward, and everywhere were polished brass fittings. The bridge offered a panoramic view over the bow and to the sides, wrapping around enough so that by going all the way to one side or the other one could also get a view astern. A chart table, which appeared to be mechanized in some way, and a wooden wheel, straight out of an old movie, dominated the center of the room. But the real beauty was the view outside. Mitch could think of only one word. "Wow!" he said. Deb nodded and Jef smiled.

In the early light, the calm seas stretched to the horizon like an endless pewter platter, dimpled by a hammered finish. Deb and Mitch just stood and stared while Jef unlocked the controls. He pressed a large button, then waited for a light to signal the anchor was weighed before starting the turbines that powered the ship. The entire ship shuddered as he engaged the twin screws and the Delft began, ever so slowly, to make headway.

"This," he gestured around the room, "is the bridge. That's the radar scope, and over there," he pointed toward the central table, "is the plotter that shows where we are and where we are headed. Here are the engine controls, and this is the helm, or, for you landlubbers who don't know port from starboard, the steering wheel."

"I'll give you guys the full tour below later. Right now I want to put as much distance between us and MIT as I can. We'll man the bridge until we're clear of the last of the Harbor Islands, past the tip of Cape Cod, and well out to sea, then the wonders of modern technology take over. This thing just about sails itself. My grandfather hired Honeywell and GE and Sperry-Rand to custom design the control systems so one person could run the whole damn ship from up here. My grandfather was not a very sociable guy.

"Anyway, for now though, we keep one eye out and one eye on the radar and both hands on the helm."

As they watched, the rising sun slowly began to separate itself from the water, creating a golden highway ahead. Within minutes, they encountered the first commercial traffic: a cargo ship, it's deck stacked high with brown and green shipping containers, headed in toward Boston Harbor. As they passed it port-to-port, they could just make out some crewmen waving to them. They waved back, automatically, even though they couldn't be seen inside the bridge. Over the next several hours the sightings became less and less frequent until it seemed as though they were alone in an empty, gray world.

Mitch looked down at the compass and frowned. "Shouldn't we be heading sort of south? I mean we are headed for the Straits of Gibraltar aren't we. Last time I looked at a map that was, like, east and south of New England."

"We're not sailing on a map, genius, we're sailing on a globe. The bearing to sail is a geodesic, a great circle route, the shortest distance between two points on the globe. But we're not heading for Gibraltar at the moment, anyway. We are headed for the Azores. Santa Cruz de Graciosa is our first landfall."

"We're going to stop in the Azores? I thought we were going non-stop for Israel. Can't we make it in one run?"

"We are going non-stop, but it is some 3,000 nautical miles to Gibraltar and we don't want to miss it, so we pass Santa Cruz as a way point, a check, just to be sure we are on target. From here, our bearing to Santa Cruz is 82 degrees, which is somewhat north of east, past Nova Scotia. And as of now we have," he looked over toward a relay rack filled with electronics, where banks of nixie tubes flashed their glowing neon-orange figures, "only 1844 nautical miles to go. In this leg, that is. All told we cover some 5000 nautical miles before we turn tail and come back rich.

"Okay, everything is hunky-dory up here. Time to take you guys on a grand tour."

"Shouldn't somebody, you know, stay up here and stand watch or something?" Mitch asked.

"What for? Like I said, this thing sails itself. Besides, what would you do? Do you know any of this stuff?"

"No, do you?"

"Yeah, obviously. Or mostly. When I was sixteen my uncle took me and my folks on a cruise in the Caribbean. He showed me how to work everything. Even let me take the helm. You can do it manually if you have to, like we just did coming out of Boston. And we'll need to do it again as we go through the Straits of Gibraltar and the Mediterranean, which gets pretty busy. But, for now, it's just chug away at 28 knots over open water. The autopilot will keep the heading, the radar will warn us of obstacles, and we can take it easy. So, welcome aboard." He winked. "Allow me to show you to your cabins."

He held the door from the bridge to the outside open. Deb started down the steep metal steps, but Mitch hung back. "You go ahead, I'll stay up here and keep a look out. I'll have plenty of time later to see the rest of the ship. Besides, I like it up here. Great view!"

"Okay, suit yourself," Jef said and followed Deb down the steps. The metal door slammed behind them.

As soon as they were out of sight, Mitch started studying the equipment. He didn't like being either ignorant or out of control.

25

LULLED BY THE STEADY VIBRATION of the engines and absorbed in reading, Mitch was unaware of passing time. He was sitting cross-legged on the floor with a stack of manuals that he had found in a drawer under the chart table when the door to the bridge swung open, sending a blast of chill air across the room. He looked up from the manual he was reading and gasped. "Wasserman! What the …? How the hell did you get here? Oh, shit!"

"Your friend told me to go someplace, and I knew you were going someplace, so I got in the van. But then I thought that maybe Jef or you might be mad at me, so I decided to hide. I wanted to find out where you were going. I didn't want you to leave me alone. Did I surprise you? Are you mad?"

"My God, you did. You surprised me, all right. Yes, yes I'm mad. Shit, this is a problem. We're already, like, a hundred fifty miles out. We can't just drop you off at the next T stop. And I still don't get how you got here. Where did you hide? Where were you?"

"I was in the toolbox in the van. But it was getting too cold, and the wind was getting louder, so I came up here to tell you to turn around and take me back. I don't think I like boats."

"Wasserman, we are not going back. I just don't know what we are going to do with you." Mitch stood up and started pacing back and forth. When he looked out the windows he realized that the wind had picked up, blowing the sea into a latticework of frothy waves. Now, with the horizon as a reference, Mitch became aware that the ship had developed a small but definite roll.

As Mitch turned in his pacing, he noticed a blinking arrow beside one of the orange numbers. He frowned.

"I don't know what that means; I'll have to look it up."

"That's millibars," said Wasserman.

"I can read the label, I just don't know what it means."

"A bar is one atmosphere, one hundred kilopascals. Average normal sea level pressure is 101.325 kilopascals."

"Look, damn it, I know all that, or I mean I don't care how many pascals make a millibar or a Hersey bar or a sand bar. I just don't know what that," he pointed at the blinking arrow and the number next to it, "means for us and for the ship."

"It's obvious," said Wasserman, starting his nervous habit of rocking back and forth. "The pressure is falling. It's already well below normal at 997 millibars. We should turn around. There's a storm coming, you know. We need to get into port. We don't want to be in a ship in a storm. It could be a big storm, like a hurricane."

"Wait a minute. What did you say?"

"It's obvious, the pressure is falling. It's already well below normal at 997 millibars. We…"

Mitch cut him off. "No, about the storm."

"I said it could be a big storm, like a hurricane."

"That's it! My God, it must be Hurricane Ginny. It must have turned north. I've got to get a weather report." He looked around. "Okay, this must be the shortwave radio. No, wait, this is what I want. " He flicked a switch and suddenly the room filled with a thundering hiss, like the sound of Niagara Falls from the observation deck. He quickly turned down the volume, then started slowly twisting a knob, scanning across the dial. When he finally found what he was looking for, the news was not good. The storm that had been tracking almost due east out to sea only the day before was now racing north-northeast at more than 20 knots, picking up energy from the warm waters of the Atlantic.

"Look, Wasserman, I just want you to stay here and watch out until I get back. I have to go find Jef. He'll know what to do."

"But what do I do?"

"Just watch. Pay attention. Listen to the radio. But don't touch anything." Wasserman took his hand off the railing by the window that he had been holding. "No, just don't touch any of the equipment. When I get back with Jef, you tell us about whatever you saw and heard. Okay?"

"Okay."

Mitch's heart was pounding as he raced down the stairs. He suddenly realized he had no idea where to go. They could be anywhere, and the ship was huge. It had originally been built to carry a crew of two hundred. Jef had said that, after conversion, there were 12 large staterooms plus a master suite. Mitch took a guess and headed down the first hallway with the lights on. He opened a door with a nameplate that said "Agneta." It opened on a bedroom finished in bright yellows, a room so large it dwarfed the enormous four-poster bed to one side and the desk, bureau, and vanity along the other. It was empty.

The next door was marked "Bertina" and was finished in shades of pink and peach. It, too, was empty. By the third room, "Catrijn," he had figured out the pattern: Dutch names of girls. By the time he reached the quiet greens of the "Linde" stateroom, he was doing no more than swinging the door open, giving the room a perfunctory sweep, and closing the door again. That was it. Nothing. The corridor ended at another set of stairs. Up or down? he thought. Up, of course. he bounded up the flight and stepped into a short hall that ended in a small foyer. It was dark, but by the light spilling over from the stairwell he could see the wide double doors ahead, each with a bright brass knocker at its center. He reached for one of the knockers, then hesitated. He tried the knob. It turned, and the door swung open.

The scene before him resolved slowly, like a photographic print in a darkroom tray, the image gradually darkening and sharpening as the chemicals gently washed over it, pulling the hidden picture from within. Across an expanse of blood-red oriental carpeting was yet another four-poster bed. But the bed, ornate though it was, was not what drew Mitch's attention. He stared instead at the rolling waves in the muscles of Deb's back as she arched and twisted, arched and twisted. He had never in his short life seen anything so hypnotic, so painfully beautiful. A small, choked cry involuntarily escaped from his throat.

"Jesus, Mitch! Knock, will you," Jef barked at him.

Deb slowly turned and gave Mitch a lopsided smile. "It's all right. Mitch is cool, aren't you, Mitch. We'll be up top in a bit. Okay?"

Mitch stared at her breasts for a moment, watching a drop of sweat fall from her left nipple. "I …" He took a deep breath. "I think you better come up to the bridge. Now. I … oh shit, this … this … not another." He started to shake.

Deb pulled herself off of Jef, who protested and tried to hold her back, but she crossed the room and put her arms around Mitch. The sharp pungency of her sweat and the musky smell of sex washed over him as she held him. He tried to straighten up, to stop the shaking, but he was suddenly cold.

"It's okay, Mitch. It's okay. Everything is all right. The trip isn't over you know. You never know what might happen next. Right?"

Mitch bit his lip and pulled back. "Look, I may look like just a kid, but I'm a big boy. I don't need charity. Or sympathy. It's just that, well, a lot is going wrong. You better come up to the bridge and see for yourself."

"Can't it wait?" said Jef impatiently from across the room. He had a pleading, expectant look on his face, like a puppy eager to chase sticks.

"Fuck! You do what you want. You fuck until your dick falls off, for all I care, but I'm going back up to the bridge. Maybe Wasserman and I can figure out what to do about the hurricane." He stomped out and slammed the door behind him. Before he could start up the stairs, Jef rushed out, pulling his pants on, trying to get his penis stuffed in.

"What the hell was that about Wasserman? And what hurricane? That thing down off the Carolinas was heading out to sea and petering out."

"Well, it changed its mind, then, because now it's making right for us and kicking up 90 mile-an-hour winds. The barometer is already falling, and if you guys weren't so busy with your bedroom pushups you might have noticed the seas have picked up, too."

Jef reached out and put his hand on Mitch's shoulder. "Look, I'm sorry. It just happened, you know. Win some, lose some. Who can fathom the female mind, right?"

"I heard that, Jef Vries," Deb said, straightening her hair

as she emerged from the bedroom. "Nobody won or lost anything." She pushed past him and took Mitch's hand. "Come on, sport, let's go up to the bridge and see what we can do. Wait a minute. Did you say Wasserman? Wasserman is on board?"

By the time they reached the bridge, Wasserman looked like he was on the edge of panic. His rocking had increased to a dizzying pace. "I did what you said. I watched and listened and I didn't touch anything. I waited, like you said."

"Good. That's good, Wasserman," Mitch said, giving him a gentle pat. "So what's up?"

"Well, the barometer is still falling, down to 995 millibars. I heard the radio, too. There was a warning from the Coast Guard that Hurricane Ginny was a category two now. That means winds over 100 miles an hour."

"Did they say where it was? Do you remember?"

"Well, they had a picture of it on TV, they said. They used the new satellite to take a picture of it from space. It's the first time. It covers half the ocean."

Jef paced impatiently. "I don't care about a goddamn picture from space. We don't have a television, and it wouldn't help if we did. Just tell me where it is."

Mitch stood next to Wasserman and told him to go on about what he knew.

"Okay, at 18:00 GMT it was at 35.1 degrees north and 71.5 west and the pressure in the eye was only 968 millibars. 968!"

Jef shook his head in disbelief. "Does he remember everything to three decimal places?"

"That's all they gave," Wasserman answered. "They only gave three decimal places."

"That's not what I meant, you idiot. Mitch, you tell me

what's happening."

"Well, the storm turned north last night, then started really picking up speed early this morning. At this rate I'd guess the edge of it could be right on our tail by nightfall."

"Well, we can't guess." He walked over to the chart table where a pen plotter was making small dots on a vellum overlay, marking their path across the ocean. Jef slid a parallel ruler across the chart, lined it up, then grabbed a mechanical pencil from Mitch's pocket and made a mark. He repeated it at another point on the chart, then drew a line. "That's the eye of the storm now," he said. "That's where it was this morning, and that, over there, is my best estimate of where it will be by midnight." He punched a couple of buttons on a control panel, then entered a number on a keypad, and the plotter suddenly sent its pen skidding across the chart and back. "We should be there." He pointed to the new mark. "At our present pace, and assuming the storm doesn't accelerate, the eye should be more than a hundred miles behind us. We could still get some wind and high seas, but we should be okay."

"Should be, but the weather report says it's accelerating," Mitch said. "What's the worst case scenario?"

"Okay, if it picks up to say 26 knots and tracks like this." He traced a faint line on the vellum. "We would be in the soup."

"What are the options?" asked Deb.

"We could head for Halifax, ride out the storm there, but the way I see it, that's how the storm is tracking. Besides, we could lose a day or more, which we don't have. Look, I think we can outrun it. If we keep on the current bearing and go flat out, we should be able to squeak through with just a spanking from behind."

"And if we can't, or we've miscalculated?"

"Then we take a hell of a beating and hope and pray for a miracle, because that baby is already kicking up winds of a hundred miles an hour and the radio just reported thirty-foot seas. So," he crossed over to the engine controls, "so it's full speed ahead." He shoved the two handles all the way forward.

"That's 34 knots, right? Under the best conditions, in calm seas, right? And how long can we push the engines like that?"

Jef pursed his lips. "Don't know. Never asked my uncle."

~ ~ ~

By early evening, the cloud cover had thickened and the seas had picked up. At full speed, the ship slammed into the waves, sending spray exploding high over the foredeck. Wasserman stood at the window, holding the railing, rocking and mumbling.

"What's he mumbling about?" asked Jef. "Gives me the creeps."

"Leave him alone," Deb said. "He's scared. Me, too. Some."

Wasserman turned to Deb. "The important thing is not to be afraid," he said. "Rabbi Nachman of Bratislav. All the world is a narrow bridge." He looked around. "Hey, that's funny. Get it, a narrow bridge?" He went back to his rocking.

Jef shook his head again. "No, Mister Quotations and Quantities, I don't get it."

Deb scowled at Jef. "I said leave him alone. He's talking about a famous saying in Hebrew. All the world is a narrow bridge; the important thing is not to be afraid."

"Whatever. Look, Wasserman, if watching is bothering you, why don't you go below. Pick a room, any one of the rooms on the second deck, and close your eyes and get some nice sleep. Mitch will show you the way."

"I know the way," he said. "I studied the plans of the ship when you brought them over to the apartment to show Mitch. I know where to go." He made his way, hand over hand, along the railing and reached for the door to the exterior stairway.

"You sure you're all right pal?" Mitch asked. "I'll walk down with you if you'd like."

"No, that's okay. I remember where things are. I like the room named Jaclyn. That's like Jacqueline. Like Missus Kennedy. It's on the port side, at the end of the passageway. I'll find it." He opened the door, stepped through, and was gone.

26

THE SEAS PICKED UP even more over the next few hours. Jef and Deb eventually headed down for the comforts of the stateroom and each other's arms, but Mitch never left the bridge. There was nothing for him to do but sit in the padded leather captain's chair and watch the blinking lights and listen. Against the sound of wind and waves muted by the thick glass was the nearly constant whine of the servomotors that spun the wheel first left, then right, then back again, responding to silent instructions from the rack of computers tirelessly crunching numbers to maintain their heading against the shifting winds. The rocking of the ship and the pounding of the spray that sometimes clattered against the windows kept him from sleeping most of the night, but he finally drifted off as the winds began to subside and the seas calmed.

The sky was already lightening when he awoke with a start to find Deb leaning over him. She kissed him slowly, gently on the forehead. "Rise and shine, bos'n. You're not supposed to sleep on the watch."

"Hey, didn't Jef say this thing could run itself?" He stretched and looked around. "Where are we? How are we doing?" He stood to get a better view.

"We're in the middle of the North Atlantic, right there." She pointed to a spot on the chart where the plotter pen had just made a tiny cross at the end of a long string of them.

"Right. But where is that, and is that where we are supposed to be?"

"Jef says he thinks so, but we need to shoot the sun to be certain. Unfortunately, it's overcast this morning."

"Wait a minute. I thought this thing did everything itself. Do any of us know how to, what did you say, 'shoot the sun?' Don't you need an astro-something to do it with?"

"It's just a check. Jef says we'll probably be all right without it, but he doesn't want to miss Santa Cruz. Jef says there's this telescope thingy that is linked to the navigation computers, so you just spin those dials to aim it at the sun, and, since the computers know exactly what time it is, they can figure out where we are and correct any errors that might have crept in. Jef says..."

"Jef says," Mitch echoed. "Jef says a lot. What does Jef say about breakfast? I'm starved. I haven't had anything since that sandwich yesterday afternoon."

"Jef's out looking for Wasserman. He said to meet up in the lounge, and we could all have breakfast together. He ..."

The rest of her sentence was drowned out by a discordant blast of an alarm horn. Mitch and Deb pitched forward, as if the ship had hit something. They both looked around, trying to figure out what might have happened. Mitch reached over and punched a button on the main console and the alarm stopped. Deb, who had gone around the corner to look astern, called out, "The engines must have stopped. There's hardly any wake trailing us."

"I think I found the problem," Mitch answered. "Something to do with the turbines, something overheated." He pointed to one of the gauges.

Deb came over next to him. "Great, what do we do now?"

Just then Jef threw open the door. "Which one of you turkeys did that?" he said, crossing the room and elbowing them both aside. He looked down at the instruments. "Shit. Gobble, gobble. I'm the turkey. I should have cut back the engines once we were in the clear from the hurricane. Now, I'm not sure what to do. We need to be underway or we just drift."

Mitch cleared his throat. "There's an auxiliary system of some kind. If the main turbines fail, you can turn on this little extra engine, but you can only do something like five or six knots with it, just a crawl."

"Since when are you the nautical expert, Mitch?"

"Since reading all the manuals, which Captain Turkey should have done, too."

"Okay, genius, how do we turn on this spare engine?"

Mitch went over to one of the relay racks and slid out a keyboard just below a small monitor screen. He typed a few things, and letters appeared on the screen. He waited, then typed some more, waited and watched for a while, then pressed one key dramatically. They could hear a distant growl as the ship slowly started to make headway again. "See, just like that," he said, bowing with a flourish.

"Alright, already, I'm impressed, but what did you do? And how did you know what to type?"

"I didn't. Your grandfather wouldn't have either. But he had the engineers who built the control system create what they called a help tape. You type 'help' on the keyboard and then type what you want help about, and it reads the tape until it finds what you are looking for and tells you what to do. Cool, huh?"

"Cool. We're moving. But we ain't moving very fast. At this rate it will take weeks to get to Israel. We're going to have to fix those engines. And I for one don't know the first thing about engines."

"I do," said Mitch. "I'll go down to the engine room and see what I can figure out." He left through the inside stair-well.

Deb was leaning on the railing, staring out over the ocean. Jef went up behind her, reached around, and cupped her breasts.

"Is your middle name Randy?" she asked, squirming out of his grasp. "Why don't you do something useful and find Wasserman so we can all eat breakfast."

Jef walked over to the console and picked up a micro-phone attached by a coiled black cord. "Theo Wasserman, paging Theo Wasserman." His voice boomed out over the whole ship. "This is the Captain speaking. Report to the lounge immediately. Report to the lounge immediately. That's an order. Theo Wasserman, report to the lounge im-mediately." He slipped the microphone back into its cradle on the console. "There," he said to Deb. "Let's go wait in the lounge."

They had just reached the lounge, with its big picture windows on three sides, and were about to sit down at the ebony bar when the ship shuddered and creaked. The main engines had started again. A few minutes later, Mitch walked in, grinning.

Jef spun around on his barstool. "Okay, mechanical mas-termind, what did you do? And how did you do it so fast?"

"I just pushed a big orange button marked 'Restart.' It seemed like the logical thing to try."

Jef slid off the stool and started toward the door. "I better get up to the bridge and throttle back on the engines so we don't overheat them again."

"Don't bother," Mitch said, walking up to the bar and twisting a handle just under the lip. A section of the bar top sprung up an inch, and Mitch swung it all the way open to reveal a set of controls. "You can do most anything you want from here. And from duplicates in the night stand next to your bed and a couple other places on deck. Permission to speak frankly, Captain? You really should have studied those manuals, sir." He smirked.

Wasserman didn't show up for breakfast, so after they finished, Jef suggested they start a stem to stern search. Mitch agreed. "If I know Wasserman, he's in some hidey hole somewhere, pissing in his pants. He looked pretty green last night. We just need to check all the places he might be huddled. My guess is he didn't answer your page, Jef, because it sounded like you were ticked off. Wasserman is scared of you."

They started at the stern, checking every hatch and door and calling out as they made their way along. As they rounded onto the starboard side, Deb, who was in the lead, gasped.

"It's gone!"

"What?" shouted Mitch, who was just behind her. Then he saw. Some splintered pieces of plywood and a length of chain hanging over the side were about all that was left of The LCVP. "God, we're screwed."

Jef came up behind them and looked over their shoulders. "Shit. We must not have lashed it down properly. It must have worked loose and gone overboard in the storm. And we didn't even hear it."

The three of them walked listlessly toward where the LCVP should have been. It was clear from the wreckage strewn on deck that it had come loose and been battered repeatedly against the ship before finally being washed or blown overboard. Mitch kicked at the few pieces that by chance remained. "We are screwed," he said slowly and emphatically.

Deb and Jef stared in silence as Mitch bent to pick up something wedged in a fitting. He turned away and pressed his forehead against the side of the stairs to the upper deck. No one moved or said anything. Finally, Mitch raised his head, looked skyward, and then turned back to them. "We don't have to keep looking for Wasserman," he said, his voice so quiet that it was almost lost in the wind.

"Why," asked Deb. "You don't think …"

Mitch held something out toward her. She took it, turned it over in her hand. "Wasserman's?"

"Yeah. His slipstick case. Open it up, and you'll find a broken Keuffel and Esser log-log duplex decitrig slide rule, a birthday present from his parents who thought he needed something like that. He was never without it. Never. He carried it hanging from his belt. It must have gotten caught when … when …" He covered his mouth with his hand.

"Couldn't we go back for him?" Deb asked.

Jef shook his head. "Don't be silly. Back where? We don't know where or when this happened. Could be anywhere over hundreds of miles of open ocean. And this is the North Atlantic. It's the end of October. You fall in and you don't last a long time, even if you are alive and conscious when you hit the water. Most likely from the look of this mess, he was already dead."

They stood in silence for several minutes just looking out over the waves.

"Poor Wasserman," Deb said. "He was a little weird but he didn't deserve to drown at sea. Barely more than a kid.

How old was he? He thought he could win the Fields Medal someday. He thought he could prove the Four-Color Theorem. Conjecture. He corrected me on that." She started to cry. Through her tears, she continued, "We never should have come. We never should have done this. This whole thing is crazy. We're college students, for God's sake. What the hell are we doing stealing nuclear fuel? This is stupid. We could go to jail. We could," she choked, "we could die. We could all die, like Wasserman. What have we done?" She pushed past Jef. He tried to hold her, but she shrugged him off and ran down the deck.

Jef started after her, but Mitch reached out and stopped him. "Let her go. Let's clean up this mess and figure out what we do next."

~ ~ ~

They found Deb at the rail on the upper deck, holding an egg carton bound with string, staring down at the water rushing by below. Jef walked up beside her, and Mitch went around to the other side. "What are you doing?" he asked gently.

"It's his slide rule. I thought he should have it." She held the carton straight out over the side. "We should have a minyan. He should have had a son. But, here we are." She closed her eyes. "*Yitkaddal v'yitkaddash sh'meh rabba,*" she began. Jef started to ask what she was saying, but Mitch put his fingers to his lips, and they both just stood and listened until she finished. "*Oseh shalom bimromav hu ya oseh shalom alenu v'al kol Yisrael, v'imru amen.*"

"Amen," they said, as she threw the carton out as far as she could. It blew, tumbling, back in against the side of the ship, then into the water, where it shot backwards and disappeared in the churning wake behind.

"Kaddish," she said. "You were going to ask. That's the Mourner's Kaddish, a Jewish prayer for the dead. He was Jewish, too, you know. He should have made it to Israel."

Mitch didn't know what to say, so he put his hand on Deb's shoulder. She turned into him and started to cry again as he held her. Jef gave him a disapproving look, but Mitch ignored him and gently stroked her hair.

"Well," said Jef, "we have a ship to run and uranium to get to Israel. The sun's finally out, so we can check our position. Let's go, guys."

"I'm not a guy," Deb said with an edge to her voice. "And I don't think we're going to Israel. We lost our LVDP or whatever it's called. We have no way to deliver the fuel. We can't row it ashore one rod at a time. Let's just dump it here and go back and hope no one ever saw Wasserman anywhere near the boat. Anyone asks and we'll just say we don't know where he is. He'll be just another missing college student. Maybe they'll connect him with that missing Vespa you rode into the harbor. We go back now and people may still believe we just had this thing out for a joy ride, an extended party. Nothing we can do now. This will just have to be something we live with. For the rest of our lives."

"Deb, we don't have to go back. There's no problem. Everything is fine."

"Everything is not fine," she said, spitting out the words.

"Everything is fine," Jef repeated. "The ship carries two LCVPs, one on each side."

Mitch and Jef looked at each other, both thinking the same thing. They took off together at a run, heading for the port side to check if the second LCVP was safe. Deb slumped down by the rail and started to cry again.

27

2003 — SHORTLY AFTER TAKEOFF on the flight from Tel Aviv to Vienna, Migdal looked out the window at the crowded shipping lanes of the Mediterranean below and thought back to the voyage on the Delft that had started it all. He may have changed his name, but inside he knew he was still that kid, Mitchell Rossing, who bluffed his way through life.

After Wasserman had been washed overboard, it seemed like none of them had much to say to each other, at least when all three of them were together, which was not a lot, since Deb and Jef spent much of the time holed up in the master stateroom. Mitch finally had to switch bedrooms to one farther away from the sounds from above that kept reminding him of where and with whom he really wanted to be.

The crossing had been dramatic, at least at the start, but threading their way through the Mediterranean ultimately proved far more challenging. They slipped through the Straits of Gibraltar nearly half a day behind their original plan, which forced them to plow ahead almost recklessly. He remembered more than one near miss with a tanker or a cargo ship and one time off Cyprus when they almost ran right over a trawler after Jef decided to change course somewhat abruptly. As it turned out, it was a good decision, because they narrowly avoided running aground.

Then there was the night that Mitch was at the helm. By

this point they all were pretty good at steering the yacht, which may have lulled Mitch into paying less attention than he should have. He should have been trying to match everything on the radar scope to the lights he could see around him, but he was thinking instead of Deb, who had kissed him at the end of her watch the way she had that time back at Antonelli's Pizza—a teasing kiss that seemed to promise but never delivered. She had kissed him just before bounding down the stairs to Jef. Mitch never could figure her out. She was always so sweet to him, but it was Jef she was sleeping with.

What did I do wrong, he thought then, just before a shape the size of a mountain appeared in the dark ahead. A horn that could wake the dead blasted across the rapidly closing gap. The radar alarm went off, and the servomotors tried to turn the wheel out of his hands. Without thinking, Mitch kicked the switch to kill the servos, spun the wheel all the way to starboard, shoved the port engine all the way to full, and threw the starboard screw into reverse. The yacht lurched and heeled sharply, then shook as he put the starboard engine ahead full again and spun the rudder back to neutral.

No one can turn a three-hundred-foot yacht on a dime, but Mitch came close to it, with just enough of a turn and just enough extra forward speed to angle across the bow of the oncoming ship with mere meters to spare. A sailor on the bow could have spit and landed a gob on the stern of the Delft as it passed below. Mitch thoroughly expected Jef to come storming up to the bridge to chew him out, but Jef had a one-track mind when he was with Deb, and it would have taken more than a near collision at sea to derail him.

The rest of the watch and the rest of the rush to reach Israel had gone without any more close calls, at least of the nautical kind.

~ ~ ~

Migdal pulled his thoughts back to the present and the plane for Vienna. He looked around at the tourists and business travelers on their way to Austria and thought about his own dirty business there. He pressed his face to the window and strained to see below as the ships shrunk and the sea lightened.

He hated to leave without first seeing Shira and Bini, but he did not want to risk tipping off anyone as to their whereabouts. As long as they were at Avi's and he didn't try to contact them directly, they should be all right. He hoped that Shira would not decide on her own to go back to the apartment. During the three days he had spent alone there, he had several times spotted men watching. He only hoped that Tariq's people were not clever enough to be able to have monitored his Web surfing. He didn't even want Lev to know what he was up to, but he also knew that if Lev wanted to track him, Lev would succeed. They had both been trained by the same man, and Lev had always had far better access to their common mentor.

The plane banked and Migdal got a brief look back toward his adopted country, the coastline of Israel sparkling in the winter sun.

28

1963 — MITCHELL'S FIRST GLIMPSE of Israel had been little more than a red slash on the horizon: the sandstone cliffs of Ga'ash Beach painted scarlet in the last light of the setting sun. Behind him, he could no longer see the Delft. He throttled back and reached for his binoculars. Despite the calm seas, he found it hard to compensate for the gentle roll of the LCVP. Finally he got the knack of it and brought the beach into focus. Beautiful, he thought, too bad Deb isn't here to see this. She'll get her chance soon enough, though.

He closed the throttle and drifted as the sky darkened. The instructions had been very explicit. The Delft was to keep her distance, to stay far offshore and not draw attention. The material was to be brought ashore in the LCVP at a secluded beach near the twin kibbutzim of Ga'ash and Shefayim.

He continued to drift as he waited for the signal. Through the binoculars he watched the brightening moonlight slowly turn the sand at the base of the cliffs to a band of silver. On shore, a tiny light flashed twice, then twice again. Mitch swung the bow around and headed at half throttle toward the spot where he had seen the flash. His heart started to pound. They were waiting. Mossad. This was it, what they had crossed the world for, what, without knowing it, Wasserman had died for.

With almost no wind, it was easy guiding the boat in. As

he approached a gap in the rocks on the shore, he cut back to dead slow until he felt the bottom scrape. He gunned the engine briefly to slide smartly up onto the beach before shutting down. He pulled the release and the winch rattled and whirred noisily as the bow lowered and slammed onto the sand.

Mitchell climbed down and walked out onto the soil of Israel.

Looking up and down the shore, he saw no one. He was alone on a secluded beach, with nothing but the soft sound of the waves and the crunch of his own feet on the sand. Then suddenly he was surrounded. Four men, two on either side, seemed to come from nowhere. Then he spotted two more abseiling down the cliffs. All were dressed in the same black turtlenecks and black trousers.

"Welcome to Israel, Mr. Rossing," said one of the men on his left. Mitchell turned toward the voice, which continued. "I am Novikov, Avram Novikov. Tsvi tells me you have a package for us. Where are the others?"

"They're back in the yacht. We thought it prudent to leave someone on board."

Novikov sucked in a breath. "But we told you explicitly that all of you were to come ashore together. All of you." In the darkness it was difficult to read his face, but a note of distress had definitely entered his voice. The man behind him leaned forward and whispered a few words into his ear. Novikov shook his head. "*Lo,*" he said, "*Lo!*"

"That means no, doesn't it?" said Mitchell. "No to what?"

"It matters not. What's done is done. You should have all done what you were told."

Mitchell tried to control his voice, to seem at ease. "So, everything is fine, right? Well," he said, starting to pace back and forth in the sand, slowly edging toward the open bow of the LCVP. "Let's get this thing settled so I can get back to the yacht, and you can get on with your nuclear ambitions." He reached casually back into the shadows of the open hull. His fingers closed on the Verey pistol stashed there. Suddenly a hand grabbed his wrist and twisted his arm up behind his back. The flare gun clattered to the deck.

"Not a good idea," the man holding his arm said. "And no use anyway."

Novikov walked over to them and put his face mere inches from Mitchell's. "Forget about them. They should have come. Forget them." Over his shoulder he said a few words in Hebrew to the others, who started unloading the fuel rods from the LCVP.

"What about the money?" Mitchell asked.

"Ah, yes, the money. Give him the money, Ari." Two small duffle bags were casually dropped onto the wet sand in front of Mitchell. "It's there. It's yours. All yours. Israel's little note of appreciation for your contribution so far."

Mitchell didn't like the sound of that and said so.

"Well, perhaps someday you will even join us, Mitchell Rossing. You even remind me a bit of my own son. You're smart, resourceful, and capable, just the sort we would want in Mossad. It would not make sense to speak of recruiting you now, not under these circumstances. You're too young, for one thing. But time will fix that. You lack training. And judgment. But a few years in the IDF, the army, will take care of that. In the meantime, we'll take care of you. We'll find you a place to stay and something to do."

"You seem to assume that I am staying in Israel. What if I don't want to?"

"We do not assume, and we did not ask you what you

wanted. We are used to getting what *we* want."

"What about the others?"

As if in answer, a bright spark of light flashed far out on the water, quickly followed by two more. The Israeli's seemed as surprised as he was, and started talking rapidly among themselves.

"What the ..." Mitchell stared out over the sea, watching as the light flickered and dimmed. He waited, his heart pounding, as long seconds passed before a muffled drum roll swept over them. "What happened? What did you do?" he shouted, although he had already guessed what had happened.

Novikov looked down at the sand. When he raised his head again, he said nothing. One of the others, it was hard to tell who, spoke first. "We told you to come together. We told you. This was not exactly as we planned, but now there is nothing to be done."

"They're gone, aren't they?" Mitchell said, feeling stupid and angry. "You killed them, just like that. And you expect me to stay in this fucked up country?"

Novikov and his companion looked at each other but said nothing.

"What if I refuse?"

They laughed. "It is not like you have a lot of options. You have no passport, and you are here illegally. There is no yacht to go back to; your little rowboat will be gone as well in a few minutes, once we finish unloading; and there is no one else around on this beach to hear or see anything that happens. Where are you, Mr. Rossing? Where exactly? Does anyone know where you are, anyone except us, your new Israeli friends? Who else will ever know anything? No, you are gone. And, now you are here. As I said before, welcome to Israel, Mr. Rossing. With time, I think you will find much to love here."

Once more, one of his men whispered something to Novikov. He responded in Hebrew. "Yes, yes, Mr. Rossing. Now we are beginning to wonder whether you are very clever or very stupid. But, what's done is done." He gestured and a man picked up the two bags, hefted them, and set one back down. He walked away with the other before Mitchell could protest. Novikov reached for the remaining bag and shoved it at Mitchell before he and the others walked away.

Mitchell looked out over the Mediterranean and thought about Debbie, who would never make *aliyah,* and Jef, who would not design computer circuits, and Theo Wasserman, who would not win the Fields Medal. He stood in silence on the shore of his new homeland, tears streaming down his cheeks.

No choice, he remembered Deborah saying, is also a choice. It seemed to fit, although as yet he had no idea just what it meant.

29

2003 — MIGDAL HAD SLEPT THROUGH MOST of the flight from Israel to Vienna. At the airport, he had rented a car and driven back east towards Hungary, through the gently rolling wine country of Burgenland, and to a crumbling warehouse at the border that had served many purposes but now was just an address, an isolated place to which to invite people. Two hours passed, and there was still no sign of his contacts. It had taken days to convince them, and now the trip to Austria was beginning to look like a complete waste of time.

"Mitchell. Mitchell Rossing."

Migdal reached for his gun and turned toward the voice speaking English with an American accent, coming from somewhere in the shadows. "Who is it? Who's there? Not Mustafa?"

"What? You don't recognize my voice? Has it changed that much? I would know yours anywhere. Don't you recognize an old friend from college? Have you forgotten all the debates in your apartment, our arguments as we crossed the ocean together?"

Migdal turned left and right, trying to pinpoint the voice amidst the echoes. "Jef? It can't be. Is that really you? I thought … I thought you were dead."

"Well, you thought wrong." Jef stepped out of the shadows, a semiautomatic in one hand, a length of pipe in the other. In the harsh overhead light, his face looked pocked and gnarled, splotched with patches of red and purple as though a circus clown had been interrupted before finishing his makeup.

Migdal backed away.

"You? Afraid? It is so unlike you, Mitch. You of the quietly confident smile. But what are you afraid of? Of me? I'm alone. I told the others I could finish this, one way or another. Besides, I owe you my life. Don't you know that? Or maybe you don't know. Maybe you don't know what happened that night, that night off the coast of Israel, that night of unexpected betrayal. So, I will tell you.

"I was standing at the stern when the first of the three explosions went off amidships, just below the wheelhouse where Deb was standing watch. I was thrown overboard, my femur shattered as I was slammed against the railing. In the water, I was disoriented but felt no pain at first. The wind was knocked out of me by the explosion and the impact with the water, and I struggled slowly to the surface with my leg dragging uselessly behind me and my lungs screaming for air. I got my face above water just as the next charges exploded. The blast seared the skin from my face and knocked me back underwater. Above, the sea became an inferno of burning oil and debris. With my lungs bursting, my face in searing pain, and my leg sending electric shocks through me each time I tried to kick, I still somehow managed to swim underwater far enough to clear the edge of the fire.

"To this day, I do not know how I survived those first minutes. Even from a distance, the waves of heat from the fire burned my face, and the saltwater, though cool, only increased the pain. I was delirious but somehow managed to drag myself onto a section of paneling from one of the staterooms. There I drifted for hours.

"I would have soon died were it not for the Lebanese fishing boat that, drawn by the fire, arrived and took me aboard. Even then I wanted to die. The pain was not merely unbearable, it was beyond description. They had only aspirin, which was useless, and some greasy unguent that one of the old sailors concocted. But worse than the physical pain was knowing that Deborah was gone. I wanted to be dead, too. But you kept me alive, Mitch. It was not until I thought of you that I could think of any reason for living. I hated you for betraying us, and I turned the hate into a drive that would keep me alive, that would enable me to endure the pain of healing and the shock of seeing myself in the mirror. Hate would help me learn Arabic, would make it possible to avenge myself on Israel, that land that had betrayed its own, its daughter, that had burned alive the only woman I would ever love."

"I didn't know," Migdal said. "Really, I didn't. Mossad planned it all along, but I had no idea. They wanted to wipe out the tracks. You and Deb were supposed to be on the beach, with me. Their plan had been only to scuttle the ship, not blow it apart, but the vapor in those huge, near-empty fuel tanks exploded. And you can't imagine the guilt I felt all these years. I always blamed myself, but I didn't know."

"You expect me to believe that? Who was it who argued that somebody should stay behind with the ship? Who said he could handle the drop alone? Who? And I see that nothing changes. Here you are, with none of your friends. You still think you can do it all alone, and you still cannot be trusted."

"Jef, when we first reached the coast of Israel, we all agreed. It was the most prudent thing, safer. I really didn't know."

"No, I don't buy it, Mitchell Rossing, not for one minute, which is why I have followed you all these years. Zurich. Ulm. Sheffield. Wherever you went, I was there, which is why you are alive today and so many of your colleagues are not. I taught myself to think like you. You didn't see me or feel me, but we have been attached at the hip for decades. I have been Israel's public enemy number one and no one knew, least of all you. I had so many faces, though never my own. Not until now.

"All I had to do was think like a traitor, like the traitor you are, and I could be waiting around the corner when the papers were exchanged, standing in the alley when the as-sassin made his move. You were the lucky one who made it home because I let you. You were never anywhere near as smart as you thought you were, never half as smart as Deb-bie. You lived until now because I wanted you to. And now I want something else from you.

"You know, your wife reminds me somewhat of Deb-orah. Not quite as beautiful, not nearly as smart, but small and filled with creative energy. And your son, he is beautiful, too, though he is marred by those little scars on his hand. What a pity it would be if I had to send Sabir to give him more scars. Perhaps his face this time?"

"I don't think you will be sending Sabir. Mossad arranged a little accident for him, as they will for you soon enough." Migdal took a step forward. "Besides, your business is with me, not them. I'm here. They're not."

"Yes, I know. But where are they? I seem to have lost touch with your sweet family. But they'll turn up. Your Shira has too much curiosity and not enough caution. After all, she married you, didn't she? She allowed herself to be drawn in by that enigmatic smile of yours, just as we did, Deb and I, so many years earlier.

"As for accidents, I have more than enough practice eluding you and your inept friends at the so-called Institute."

Migdal took another step. Jef fired, clipping him in the shoulder. Migdal's gun clattered to the concrete and he fell to his knees. As he reached toward the gun, Jef swung the pipe in a low arc, striking Migdal just above the knee. He crumpled to the floor and almost blacked out.

"A taste, just a taste for you, Mitchell. Ah, but now you look so uncomfortable there, with your leg under you at such an odd angle. Here, let's fix that." He kicked violently, sending waves of fire through Migdal's leg. "There, a little something extra to keep the memory fresh for you, like it has been for me all these years. And next time don't jerk us around. We have no more patience for wild chases. So, go now, but remember, we want delivery, not an empty warehouse." He turned and walked away, his limp slight but noticeable.

Migdal realized he had badly misjudged his opposition. There would not be an easy way to end it now. He would have to fall back on his research, his guesses, on his long days holed up alone in the apartment looking for a way to rewrite the words of Fate.

He slowed his breathing and waited, but there was no sound other than the distant barking of dogs. The silence was broken by his cell phone ringing.

"Yes?"

"Hashim here. I…"

"We have nothing to say or do, Hashim. It is over."

"I know. Still, we are brothers, children of Abraham, and you have done me no ill. I feel terrible about what has happened. I wanted to warn you about Tariq. He would have me killed if he finds out, but I must tell you his plans. He knows about the rendezvous. He …"

"Too late. You're too late. But for calling me, for that I am grateful. May our sons know more peace than we have. *Salaam.*"

"*Salaam.*"

He closed the phone, pulled himself erect, and shuffled, slowly and painfully, out of the warehouse. The long, hard drive ahead would now be doubly difficult, but he knew what needed to be done, and he would have to arrive in Frankfurt with plenty of time.

There is no chance, no destiny, no fate, that can circumvent or hinder or control the firm resolve of a determined soul. – Ella Wheeler Wilcox

Part Three: Shira

30

1986 — HER NAME WAS SHARON. She was a distant cousin of Lev's visiting Israel before returning to finish graduate school in England. Her father, Saul Markham, describing her as a bit of a wild pony, had asked Avram Novikov to look after her. He, in turn, had asked his son Lev to take her on one last outing before her flight back to London. Not wanting to be stuck alone trying to make conversation with some college kid, Lev invited Migdal along.

Migdal and Lev had served in the army together but lost touch while Lev traveled abroad for a few years. When he returned to Israel and decided to follow in his father's footsteps in intelligence work, there was Migdal. Under Avram's tutelage they had risen together through the ranks of Mossad and become friends.

They picked Sharon up at her hotel, a slightly rundown place that appealed to young people who had grown too old or too well-heeled for the youth hostels but couldn't quite afford a really decent hotel. Sharon was petite, with curly, jet-black hair, and she fairly bounced out to meet them. She gave Lev a big hug, as if they had known each other since childhood.

"That's the American style Mum taught me," she said. "My father preferred us to be less demonstrative." She turned to Migdal, took his hand lightly, then kissed him on each cheek, continental style. She stepped back, looked him in the eye for a few seconds, and then hugged him, too. "I think Mum had the right idea, don't you?

"So, will this do for today?" she asked, stepping back and turning slowly. She was wearing jeans and a peasant blouse. "I wasn't sure what was in the offing, but I for one hope it's outside. I head back for jolly old you-know-where on Sunday, and this may be my last chance to see the sun in a fortnight."

"Well, then, little cousin," Lev said to her, "what do you want to do? Where do you want to go?"

"It's your country. What would you want to be doing on an afternoon like this?"

"Lying on the sand, swimming, doing nothing," he answered.

"Splendid! So, then, let's do it. I've heard of a beach north of here that's supposed to be beautiful. Ga'ash. I think that is what it's called."

Lev and Migdal looked at each other, choking back sniggers.

"What? Did I mispronounce it or something? Hebrew school was a long time ago, and I am still getting used to Israeli Hebrew, but certainly my accent can't be all that bad."

"No, well..." Lev, clearly uncomfortable, studied his feet.

Migdal jumped in to rescue him. "You see, it's a nude beach. It's way back from the road and shielded from view by these cliffs. It's popular with, you know, that sort of crowd. I don't think you want to go there."

"Oh, but I do. That's perfect. They do have naturist beaches in England, but I've never been to one. Who wants to skinny-dip in ice water and then stand around shivering on a rocky shore under an overcast sky? Ga'ash sounds like it would be great fun on such a beautiful day. And I do so like getting off the well-trodden tourist path."

Migdal shook his head. "I really don't think so. I don't want to go myself. If you two want to, go ahead. I should duck into the office anyway."

"Father told you explicitly not to show your face at headquarters today. Come on, what's the harm. You're not embarrassed, are you? I've never known you to be shy about much of anything."

"I just don't want to. I have my reasons. I don't like the place."

"Come on, I don't believe you've ever been there. How do you know you won't like it? We can stay the afternoon and watch the sun set over the sea."

"I've been there. Once. That was enough."

Sharon grabbed his arm and started pulling him toward the car. "You don't have to go in if you don't want to. Just tag along." She smiled at him with such guileless enthusiasm that it was impossible to resist.

They stopped on the way and bought sandwiches, which Lev put in a wicker basket that he produced from the trunk. "No, I didn't plan this," he said. "I just never clean out the car. It's left from a picnic last month."

Despite his claim that he knew where he was going, Lev managed to go past the turn off from Highway 2. What should have been a twenty-minute drive turned into over an hour of wrong turns and conversations that meandered from topic to topic. By the time Lev finally found the right turnoff near Ga'ash Lighting, the three of them were talking like old friends.

They drove a short way down a dirt track to where a cluster of cars were parked and from there followed a footpath to the beach. Although they were hardly alone, the narrow beach stretched so far that it seemed uncrowded.

Sharon stripped and ran into the waves before either of the men could get their pants down. They followed her in and swam for a few minutes, but then returned to the pile of clothes and sat down to bask in the sun.

"So, what is this thing you have about Ga'ash?" asked Lev. "How could you not like it here? What happened here?"

Migdal smiled and stared out to sea. "It's Mossad business."

"Then you can tell me. Remember, your office is just down the hall from mine. We work on the same cases."

"No," Migdal said, pursing his lips. "This would be on a need-to-know basis. Besides, it happened a long time ago."

"Now you do have my attention. You can tell me. What is it?"

"No. I can't. It's about Dimona. You understand. You know I can't say more."

"Speaking of Dimona, I want you to start working with me on the Vanunu operation." He spoke in a near whisper. "How's your Italian?"

"It isn't. German, English, several Arabic dialects. And, of course, Hebrew. That's it."

"Well, maybe we can use you in London, then. We'll talk tomorrow. But remember, we didn't have this conversation today. Okay?"

"Don't worry, little brother, I won't tell Abba." He winked. The elder Novikov was not only above them at Mossad but had become Abba, father, to Migdal ever since he and Lev had returned from military service.

Lev, changing the subject, nodded toward where Sharon was splashing in the waves. "What do you think of my cousin?" he asked.

"I don't know. She seems like a nice enough kid." His eyes followed her as she ran back and forth.

"You like her."

"Don't be silly. She's just a college girl. She was probably just born about the time I came to Israel."

"You do. You do like her, I can tell. You say no, but your anatomy says yes." He nodded toward Migdal's crotch.

"Reflex, that's all. She has a nice body. I may be of a certain age but I'm not so old that I can't appreciate a young woman with a firm body. From a distance, anyway."

"Uh huh," Lev said, looking down at Migdal again. "I see your scar has healed nicely. Why in hell did you do it?"

"To convert, why else. I wanted to be a Jewish citizen of a Jewish country, not an unclean heathen who had wrangled some kind of deal."

"I would never do that." He shuddered. "I would not convert. I would not slice off part of my johnson."

Migdal laughed. "Where did you get that old slang? And what are you talking about? You're circumcised. What do you mean you'd never do it?"

Lev was busy watching a young woman toweling off. "A gingy. Mmm. Very nice. There is something special about red hair. And you can tell hers didn't come from a package." He turned back to Migdal. "But, we were talking about ritual mutilation, weren't we. Look, I don't remember my *bris*. Thank God. But I had no choice. If I had a choice, I wouldn't do it. It's an atavism. I'm not observant and neither is my father. I don't know anyone in our family, outside of my aunt Sadie, who even believes in God. Yet we, we secular Jews, keep doing this to our sons. Covenant of the flesh." He shook his head. "Strange."

"You know damn well it's required for an Orthodox conversion, and that's the only kind that really counts. Look, it's just part of the initiation rites for entry into the club. That's all. In the final analysis, I don't believe any more than you do, and you know damn well I'm not a practicing Jew. But I am a Jew. I have the paper to prove it. And because I served in the IDF, I am no longer an American. What an irony. I have a real Israeli passport and a fake American one, courtesy of the Institute. One club boots me out and another takes me in."

"Well, then, welcome to our club." He looked down at Migdal once more and shook his head. "God, I bet the first erection hurts like hell." He turned left and right, looking for something. "Bugger all, I left the food in the car. You hungry? Me, too. Now I have to get dressed again and trudge all the way up and back." He reached for his pants, pulled them on, and headed back toward the path.

With a breeze picking up, Migdal moved himself up the beach to a more sheltered position. Suddenly Sharon came scampering up from the water and planted herself in front of him, legs apart and arms thrown to the sky. "This is awesome, simply the greatest. I do love feeling this way. Free. Turned on."

With the sun directly behind her, she was outlined in brilliant, sparkling beads of water. Her pubic hair, matted and dripping with saltwater, was right at eyelevel. It was hard for Migdal to look any place else. He tipped his head back and shaded his eyes with his hand to look up and see her grinning down at him. Her eyes were on his growing erection.

"Well, it would be a shame to waste that, wouldn't it now," she said. Before he could say anything, she straddled him and lowered herself into his lap, then wrapped her legs around behind him. She reached down and expertly guided him into her.

Suddenly self-conscious, Migdal looked around, but there was no one in sight. They were nearly at the cliffs, and a slight outcropping hid them from the view of the others farther down the beach. She must have sensed his tension, because she whispered, "It's all right, we're alone. And, no, I have never done anything like this before. But, don't worry, I'm on the pill."

They made love like that, that first time, sitting on the sand, in the open, with a slow gentle rhythm that matched the waves coming on shore. In the end, for the longest time, she just held onto him, saying nothing, not moving. Then suddenly she pulled herself off and stood, reaching down to take his hand. "Let's swim," she said, and tugged him toward the waves.

They swam and dived and floated and splashed until the sun was just kissing the water and Lev finally returned from the car. They ran back down the beach toward him.

"I see you two have been having fun," he said, setting the basket on the sand.

"We have," she said, pushing tight ringlets of wet hair back from her face and sending a big grin Migdal's way.

"So it seems. I did come back earlier, but you must have been off somewhere, so I went back and listened to the radio. I just hope the battery is not too drained to start the car." He scowled at Migdal. Migdal scowled back as he opened the basket and pulled out a wrapped sandwich.

They ate their sandwiches in silence, lost in reverie, transfixed by the purples and pinks and oranges strewn across the slowly darkening sky.

Sharon finished, wiped the crumbs from her stomach,

and stood again. She pulled Migdal up after her. "Let's go for a walk down the beach," she said. "Is that okay, cousin?" Lev, his mouth still full, grunted and nodded.

As they strolled down the long stretch of sand, she started telling Migdal about her life—about school and her studies in psychology, about her friends in Sheffield, and, lastly, about her secret passion, her art. She talked quickly, as if in a hurry to get it all in before dark, before they had to leave.

On the way back up the beach, just before they reached Lev and the picnic basket, Migdal stopped and turned to her. "Look, I know where you are going with this, but ..." He put his fist to his mouth. "Oh, boy, this is awkward. Look, it was ... it was beautiful, but face it, this is not going to go anywhere. I'm old enough to be your father."

"No you're not," she protested. "You don't know, but my father is much older than my mother. He was forty when I was born in 1963, already old. So, just how old are you, oh ancient one?"

"Forty," He said. She didn't respond. "See. Like I said, I'm too old. And you're too young. In a few days you'll be back in England. You'll tell all your friends about Ga'ash and how beautiful it was, but leaving out some of the details. That's it."

"That's it? Okay." She abruptly turned and started up the path to the car. On the way back to the outskirts of Tel Aviv she talked only with Lev. Migdal felt terrible, but he didn't know what to say and realized that whatever he said, it would probably only make things worse.

After they dropped her off at her hotel, Lev drove in silence for several minutes, then finally spoke up. "You broke her heart, you middle-aged cad."

"Look, she initiated it. I didn't take advantage of her."

"I didn't say you did. I said you broke her heart. This is not what it may look like to you. You think it was a summer fling, an afternoon of last-minute acting out by a girl about to return home. But that girl, that young woman, is in love with you."

31

THE LITTLE STONE HOUSE on the steeply winding street in Shef-field was too cold. It had always been too cold for Sharon, but now, after her summer in Israel, its thick walls seemed to suck the heat from her, as if pulling the very life force from deep within her. Her yellow woolen jumper was not enough against the chill, and she hugged her arms tightly around herself as she made her way down the narrow stairs from her room on the third floor. The lower she descended, the deep-er the chill, until finally she opened the door into the sitting room with its cheery but barely effective fireplace.

Her father looked up from his reading. "Aren't you sup-posed to start classes this week? Mustn't dawdle."

"No. Classes began last week, but I have withdrawn from university. Now I am awaiting word about going to America. Has the post arrived?"

"Surely you cannot be serious," her father said, looking over the top of his glasses. "You simply cannot withdraw now. You have but this one last year and then your clinical internship and then you start practicing, and ..."

"And then I crawl slowly, ever so slowly, into the coffin of my chosen profession—chosen, I must add, not by me but for me, not by me but by my teachers and parents and men-tors. There I will molder until someday they nail the lid down and give me a right and proper burial. No Father, I am going to America."

"Always the thespian, eh? And what, may I ask, is in America? Did you meet someone in Israel? Is that what this is all about?" He turned his head a precise few degrees to the left toward his wife sitting quietly in the identical wingback chair next to his. They could have been mistaken for brother and sister, they had grown to look so much alike, with the same slate-gray eyes, the same wavy white hair. "Or is this your influence, Rachel?" he continued. "You Americans are always so impulsive, always taking off in some new direction on little more than a whim or a change in the wind."

"We Americans," she said quietly without looking up, "are no such thing and do no such things. I will remind you ever so gently that it was my handsome Brit who proposed to me mere hours after we met and that this particular American has remained steadfastly at his side for nearly thirty years now."

"That is not the point at all, Rachel. Our daughter is talking about throwing away a career, discarding the investment of years to go … to go to America." He said the last word as if it were an epithet.

"Father," she said, just that word. He was always Father to her, never Dad or Daddy.

He looked at her with his head still turned slightly aside. "It is the art thing, isn't it," he announced, a softness mingling with the disappointment in his voice. "You want to be a sculptress. Still. How is that possible? With such a late start, it is hardly reasonable. I had thought you finally had your head about you. Well then, how do you propose to go about it? Knowing you, you have a plan. Although you do your planning without great foresight. Tell me now, Sharon, what precisely that plan would be."

"Shira. Please call me Shira, Father. It is my name, after

all. And yes, I have a plan. I have contacted a sculptor in America who has offered to apprentice me. I want to make beautiful things, Father. That's all I have ever wanted to do. I have played the good girl and gone to school and earned the marks to make you proud, but now I am a grown woman. I don't have to earn marks or pass exams for you anymore. It is time I made my own life, and this is the life I choose—to bring beauty into the world."

"And so, then, when in all your travels abroad and your apprenticeships and your changing careers willy-nilly do you think you shall find the time to bring the beauty of a grandchild into the world? Do you think I shall live forever? Do you think you shall be an attractive young woman forever. I want to live to kiss my first grandchild."

Aloud she said, "Father, please. *Bashert iz bashert.*" To herself, Shira thought that if he had been so keen to have grandchildren, perhaps he should not have had a gay son as his firstborn.

Of course, she loved her older brother dearly, and had always accepted his oddities, even when, as children, he would borrow dresses from her to wear during the meetings they held in their secret clubhouse behind the garden shed. She would always remember the look of horror and fury in her mother's face when they were discovered one afternoon. "I won't tell your father," her mother said, once she recovered her voice. "It would kill him. But don't let me ever catch you wearing a dress again in this house. Or in this garden. I will kill you, Barry Markham, if you do. I will." Barry, of course, knew she would do no such thing. His mother adored him, and showered him with unquenchable love. Still, Barry promised her and kept his end of the bargain, making certain that he was over the line into the thicket of the neighbor's garden whenever again he slipped on a purloined pair of panties or tied a ribbon in his hair. As an adult, he never cross-dressed, at least as far as Shira knew, but there was never any doubt when he was with any of his many boyfriends who took which part in the relationship. The whole family also wondered when he might tire of moving from one all-consuming affair to another to settle down with one partner.

So it was Shira who fell heir to her father's longing for progeny. "Before we think too much about babies, Father, perhaps I should have a husband. Before that, I want to establish myself in my profession. And before that, I must learn. So you see, Father, it all fits together, and I shall soon be off to America to study art."

Soon, however, was not until the sullen winter had settled in over the Midlands and her father had ceased to speak to her save to ask for the salt or to read aloud some newspaper item about psychologists. And when confirmation finally arrived, he refused to see her off to the train for London to catch her plane. Thus it was her mother who gave her the small package from him.

"'Don't open it until you're on the plane,' he said. Please understand. You know your father. Ah, yes, and here are some sandwiches for the train. Promise you will write often."

"I will. I love you both." She slipped the packet from her father into the pocket of her coat and climbed aboard.

It was not until the flight to New York was nearly over that she remembered and retrieved the packet from her coat in the overhead compartment. She sat down again and carefully opened the folded and creased butcher-paper wrapping. A tiny Star of David on a fine silver chain fell into her lap. She recognized it as one that had belonged to her grandmother. Father, you are such a sweet, stubborn man, she thought.

At JFK airport in New York she wearily scanned the crowd as she emerged from the arrivals hall. She spotted a woman holding a hand-lettered sign with "Markham" written on it, and her heart sank. Regina Bosworth was not what she had expected and looked like no sculptor Shira had ever imagined. Her wild, gray-streaked hair erupted from beneath a drab blue headband. There were dark circles under her eyes and dirt under the fingernails of her big hands. A lumberjack of a woman right down to her plaid flannel shirt and scruffy, boot-cut jeans, she towered over Shira but spoke with the small, soft voice of a young mother crooning to a newborn.

"You must be Shira Markham," she said. "And you must be exhausted, poor thing! Let me carry those bags for you. My car's in the parking garage, and we have a hike ahead of us. And a long drive."

On the drive up to Regina's farm in rural Connecticut, Shira learned just what kind of a sculptor she had apprenticed herself to, a sculptor who welded steel girders and pipes into monuments to human folly that would grace a corporate headquarters in Michigan or break the monotony of a campus in Iowa, a sculptor who had found her audience in the moneyed enterprises of America. The turn onto the dirt drive that led up to her farmhouse was marked by a slender tower of rods and thick cables that stood with what seemed a brutish grace amidst the poplars lining the driveway.

"I call it 'Reach,' and it's only there because the damned high-tech company out in Santa Clara that commissioned it went belly up before I could deliver it. I thought of recycling the materials but decided to keep it around as a lesson in humility. However good you may be, Shira, whatever success you may obtain, no matter how many big commissions you might score, just remember not to become too full of yourself. An artist, a real one, is not a master but a servant, a servant of her art and of those who will love and appreciate her art. That is the first lesson and the last lesson. Now, let's eat and then get to work."

Shira worked diligently that year and the next, to learn the lessons that Regina had to offer. Regina taught her to use an acetylene torch and a bending brake, to polish and to hammer, to work from sketches and to improvise. And, most of all, to love working with her hands, to love seeing physical form emerge from the void of invisible thought. But whenever she was not working with or for Regina, Shira would turn the same tools and techniques to art on a smaller scale, sculpting miniatures and replicas of Regina's monuments, tiny wonders that charmed rather than awed the viewer. Regina, who had no agenda but to teach and to inspire, nurtured Shira's more delicate talents with her generous appreciation, her honest and focused criticism, and with new tools that she acquired for no other purpose than to help Shira assemble a portfolio of intricate miniatures that would get her into the Rhode Island School of Design.

As a going away present she handed Shira a small package done up in ribbon. Shira nearly dropped it.

"What is in here? It feels like lead."

Regina smiled at her and said, "Silver. Not quite a small fortune, but let's just say that much of my last commission is in there."

"I couldn't, I ..."

"Yes, you could, and you will. This was what you were meant to do. Use it well, to make beautiful things. And write, damn it. More often than you write your folks back in England. I don't know where you're going, girl, but I expect more than a post card. Do you hear?"

Shira loved it as a special student at the school, and learned to call it Risdee, as everyone did. Still, she quit after only three semesters. To her, time had begun to rush by, like the pages of a calendar in a 1940s movie blowing away in the wind. She took to jewelry as if she had been creating it all her life and used her work to get connections in Europe, then parlayed one deal into another until she could afford to start the studio in Haifa. Suddenly, time dragged, and she waited five agonizingly long months before calling her cousin and suggesting that they meet in Tel Aviv. She waited until she was there in person to ask about Migdal.

For Shira it had been different because she had known, instantly, what it would take years for Migdal to learn. Within minutes of taking his hand and kissing him lightly on the cheek, she knew that Migdal Rozeyn was her *bashert*. She knew that she would have to run to catch up to him, but she would. Still, it was always in the back of her mind that she might catch up, only to find that it was too late.

It was not.

32

1990 — LEV LEANED AGAINST the door jamb, hands in the pockets of his blue jeans, and waited for Migdal to look up from the case file he was working on.

"What?" Migdal said as he kept typing, his eyes still fixed on the computer screen.

"Nothing. Shira's in town, down from Haifa for the weekend. She asked about you."

Migdal finally looked over toward him. "Who?"

"Shira. That Shira. I know it's been a few years, but surely you remember Ga'ash beach."

Migdal still looked puzzled. "I have vivid memories of Ga'ash, all right, but I don't remember any Shira."

"The English girl you boinked in broad daylight. Now do you remember?"

Migdal nodded and smiled. "Now *that* I remember. That was, what, 1986? Just before we pulled in Vanunu. My God, where do the years go? You know my friend, we are getting old, too old for this business."

"Don't let Abba hear you talk that way. He wants us to be here until we drop. Anyway, that one, that one on the beach, you must have known her as Sharon, my distant cousin Sharon Markham. Well, now she uses her Hebrew name, Shira, and she asked about you. She asked a lot about you. She must have asked me four times whether you were married or not. I warned you. Remember that, when you are sending out wedding invitations. Remember that I warned you."

Migdal did not have to remember for long. He and Shira slipped into each other's lives as if the conversation started on the beach five years earlier had been interrupted by a short phone call or a quick trip to the loo. Something odd had happened in the interim. In a strange way, it seemed to Migdal as if she had caught up with him, as if he, already grown up, had stayed in a chronological holding pattern, while Sharon—Shira—had matured. There was no longer a chasm of years between them. It was the same number but not the same size. In defiance of fact, they had become contemporaries, and when they were together, Migdal could not imagine that he had ever miscalculated so badly. How could he have ever thought that he was too old for her?

Of course, it had been different for Shira.

33

1999 — THE FIRST YEARS OF MARRIAGE to Migdal were the ful-
fillment of a dream, a plan Shira had formed and shaped on
the drive back from Ga'ash and on which she had been
working for years. For Migdal, a middle-aged bachelor who
had always lived alone and never expected otherwise, their
life together was a wind from an unexpected quarter, and
those early years mixed trial with pleasure.

Aside from casual sleeping-bag snuggles, which had
been an all but compulsory part of training back when he
was in the army, Migdal had not been with a woman until
that afternoon in Ga'ash with Shira, not since that one furtive
time with Deborah on the Delft.

He had not known what to make of it then, and he still
did not know. He had just been relieved from the helm by
Jef, who, much to their surprise, had volunteered to stand
watch on the very last leg of the voyage. Deb had stopped
Mitch on the way to his bedroom and dragged him into the
nearest room. It was over almost too fast for him to decide
whether it was good or not. As she left him lying there,
sprawled out atop the yellow bedspread, she had said, incongruously, "You know, Jef's not such a bad guy after all,
Mitch. Remember that." It was the day before they reached
Israel, so he never had a chance to question her about what
she meant.

With Shira, from the very beginning on the beach, there

had never been much ambiguity about sex, although every so often she would suddenly turn cold, and he would find himself sleeping alone for weeks or months before being invited back into their bed. Most times, she would eventually open up and tell him what it had been about, but there were times that he never learned what the issue had been. After Binyamin was born, she no longer kicked him out of the bedroom, but just turned her face to the door before turning out the light. Migdal, who would have preferred the sofa in the living room to the silence in the bedroom, was invariably patient or stoic, although even he didn't always know the difference. Eventually, Shira would some night turn back and draw him into her in that same artless way she had on the sand at Ga'ash.

As the years piled up, Migdal began to believe that he, too, had known from the beginning that they were meant for each other. Things that had never made sense before seemed to come together for him in a cohesive narrative that gave order and meaning to his life.

At first, after the wedding, they both kept their apartments, and Migdal commuted between Haifa and Tel Aviv. On the strength of her artistry, Shira's studio had been an almost instant success in Haifa, and they both concluded that it would be ill-advised to risk trying to relocate to Tel Aviv. But Mossad was based there, in its big, faceless building. When he had been a *katsa,* doing field work, Migdal hardly cared where his apartment was, but once he was doing analysis, it began to matter. At the same time, he was starting to lose faith in the mission of Mossad, beginning to doubt that his country was doing what was right. Ironically, it had started with Lev.

Lev had just returned from overseas and came into Migdal's office with a solemn face. He threw a stapled folder down on Migdal's desk and said, "Fuck!"

"What's this? Oh, the 'Italian Job.'" It was the code name for a preemptive strike against a family of bomb-making experts that served as indiscriminate consultants and suppliers to anyone willing to attack Israel. It had taken years of shoe-leather and analysis to put all the pieces together. A bit of casual name-dropping by an informant who was known to work both sides had finally allowed Mossad to begin tracking the bomb-maker's movements and to plan an attack.

"This is great," Migdal said as he flipped through the first pages. "It looks like a textbook operation that went off like clockwork. And the press and everyone else thinks it was sectarian rivals who set off the bomb in the Cooper Mini. Even the collateral damage was acceptable; the street was virtually deserted. I'd say you have cause to celebrate."

"Yeah, lets chant *Shehechiyanu*. Everything went precisely according to plan. Perfect. We just hit the wrong house. We were just too cocky, too full of certainty, too full of ourselves. Fourteen innocent people, including nine children, died in the explosion and fire. None of them had anything to do with bombs or radical Islam. They just were in the wrong house, so we blew them away.

"God, I hate this kind of thing. Whatever happened to *tikkun olam*? We Jews are supposed to heal the world, not blow it up."

Migdal fiddled with his pencil but could think of nothing to say at the time.

It was not, of course, the only such mistake. Ever since his landing at Ga'ash, Migdal was particularly keenly aware that small missteps could carry immense consequences, that the price of misjudgment was often paid by the innocent. But with the debacle of the "Italian Job," Migdal's doubts grew deeper. It began to seem to him that the time-honored responsibility of Jews to set a moral example for the world was becoming lost amidst the hysteria over terrorism. Then Binyamin was born, and his world changed utterly. Being away for four or five days at a time was out of the question, so he quit Mossad, and moved to Haifa.

Avram, who felt personally betrayed, was furious with him. "You don't just walk away from us, from me, not like this. You don't quit The Institute, you retire after a long and distinguished career. You leave quietly when you are no longer of use to Israel, when the secrets you know no longer matter because they are no longer secrets or because they are in the distant past and are no longer of consequence."

Migdal started to object, but Avram went on. "Yes, there have been others, of course. People leave. But you are not like those others who work for a while and quietly go on to new things. You have a history that makes you both special and suspect. That history may have been forgotten by some because of the work you have done, but it will be remembered the moment you go out the door. Surely you know that you would be watched for the rest of your life. Your every move would be scrutinized. People who have quit under the wrong circumstances or who have misbehaved after leaving have disappeared. No, I am not being melodramatic. You know too much. Dimona, for instance, and that is just one of many instances. Outside the Institute you become a potential threat to Israel just by walking around. Leave the country and you become a ticking bomb."

"I am threatening nothing," Migdal said. "I am simply quitting."

"We are not even having this conversation. You are like a

son to me, Migdal, you and Lev went through the IDF to-gether. I trained you both. You called me Abba. Abba. Do not put me in such a terrible position."

Migdal took a deep breath. "Lev already said all that to me last night. I know the risks. I simply can't be part of this anymore."

"Are you judging me? Are you judging us? Are you saying what we do or how we do it is wrong?"

"No. I don't know what is right and what is wrong, ex-cept for me. All I do know is that I want to heal rather than rend. I want to build something that when Binyamin is older I can point to with pride and say to him that I built that."

"What about all this?" Avram gestured around himself.

"I didn't build this. It's just a building, anyway, filled with computers and files and papers. I wrote some of those pa-pers. I created some of those files. But what are they? No-thing, ciphers, meaningless."

"You have done some brilliant work. You, you and Lev, were responsible for taking down that cell in Germany. You helped us get Vanunu. You…"

Migdal stopped him. "Yes, I killed people and put others in jail. I ferreted out lies and liars, then I spread my own lies to cover other lies. Maybe it was right. I just don't want to do it anymore." He stood. "You do what you have to, Abba. I'll do what I have to."

Of course, neither of the Novikovs were ready when, shortly after the move, he started Trade Now with some of the friendly Palestinian contacts he had made while still with Mossad. To him there was no such thing as justified terror-ism, and he harbored no illusions about Palestinian "free-dom fighters" as the good guys—the Israelis did not strap ex-plosives around the waists of their children and send them into a crowd to become martyrs—but he truly believed that helping to lift the ordinary Palestinian out of cycles of poverty and ignorance and violence, that building bridges of mutual interdependence, was the best way he could serve the interests of his son and his people.

Lev and Avram were both livid, and their superiors were beside themselves. Surveillance stepped up and Migdal began thinking that he might be the target for more than just surveillance. But gradually things settled into a kind of détente, just as Migdal had planned, just as Migdal knew they would.

He had two factors working in his favor. The first was the openness and visibility with which he conducted himself and carried out the mission of Trade Now. He was keenly aware of the irony. For the first time in his life, after years of living within layers of deception, he was doing business openly. He knew that the more public he was, the more the books of the association were wide open, the safer he would be. The second factor was the very brilliance and skill of his colleagues back at Mossad. He, of all people, knew well what they could do and what they could not. He knew precisely the bounds of their abilities, and he planned to stay, from then on, within those bounds. He knew they would find out about whatever he did, be watching every move, reviewing every deal. All he had to do was be completely above board and scrupulously honest about everything, and they would know it. The longer they trailed him, the more they would learn that he was no threat. He wanted them to be taping him when he met with a Palestinian businessman in the West Bank. He wanted them to be photographing his contacts in Germany and tracking his phone calls. He wanted them to be shuffling and sorting and correlating the data.

What he did not want was for their imaginations to take over.

The last time he saw Lev was at a small café in Haifa, *Yafeh Nof.* They sat at a table outside and looked out over the harbor in the distance without talking. It was warm but windy, and Lev placed his hand atop the paper napkin under his cutlery to keep it from blowing away. Migdal tucked his under the edge of his plate.

Lev had made clear before they met that it would be the last time, that it would not be good for either of them to be seen together again. They sat for several minutes without ordering, without speaking.

"Why?" One word, just one word. That's all Lev said.

Migdal didn't know what to say. What was cause, what was effect? Had he quit because of the move? Did he start Trade Now because he had quit? Migdal only knew that it all fit together. It made sense. It seemed right. Like being with Shira, which seemed the most right of all and which made everything else more right.

"Bashert," he said, a one word answer for a one word question.

Lev stood, turned slowly, and left. On the napkin where his hand had rested there was a faint image of a string of digits. Migdal casually picked up both napkins, crumpled them, and threw them into a waste container. As he walked away he entered the digits into the directory of his cell phone under the letter *L.*

34

2003 — SHIRA TUCKED BINI into bed and kissed his hand. "It will be all right," she said. "Those bad men won't come here. No one will hurt you."

"But what if they had Uzis and they grabbed Uncle Avi and put him in a box and then they used big machetes to chop down the door and come in here?"

The mind of a five-year-old, she thought. "It's okay, my imaginative boy. Uncle Avi and I will both protect you. No one will hurt you. Now, close your eyes. It's almost light and you need to sleep." She kissed him again, then left and gently closed the door behind her.

Avi, who was no relation to Shira but was Uncle to everyone, opened his arms. "Come, my Shira, my singer of silver songs, you look wretched." He hugged her lightly. "I'll make some chamomile tea for you. With honey. It will help."

"I'm sorry to drag you into this. Migdal told us to come here. He's into something, I don't know what. I thought he was through with all that stuff, but something with Trade Now must have blown up in his face."

"Don't tell me about it. That way if the bad men come with Uzis and put me in a box they won't be able to get anything out of me."

Shira laughed. "Okay. I'll take that tea now."

They sat in the tiny kitchen and sipped their tea and talked until daybreak, speaking of everything except Migdal and Trade Now.

"You go get some sleep now," he told her. "I'll take care of Bini today. He can stay home from school one day. I'll introduce him to some of my old IDF buddies who will show him some of their souvenirs and give him history lessons."

"Oh, just what he needs. More war stories to fuel his imagination." She went around the table and kissed Avi's neck. "Someday you'll have to tell me one of your war stories. I still don't really know how you and Migdal met, what got you together."

"I never met Migdal. I did meet a Mitchell Rossing once. Served under my command. Nice young man—spoke wretched Hebrew—but he was a good soldier."

"You are such a tease, Uncle Avi. But he's not a young man anymore. He'll be 60 in a few years—hard to believe. I keep finding myself thinking that he and I are the same age, that we're just an ordinary young couple with a boy in school. Then I'll look at him and notice how white his hair is and realize it's the illusion I cast to keep from thinking about him getting old and me losing him. And then something like this happens, and I realize age has nothing to do with it, that I could lose him tomorrow." She started to cry. Avi stretched to reach a tissue from the box on the counter. She wiped her eyes, then took a slow, deep breath. "British training," she said. "My father never let us cry. He was army, too. The War, that was the only way he ever referred to it. The War, in capital letters and italicized. He never talked about it, just referred to it, except for how he met my mother. They both liked to tell that story, although actually the war was over by then.

"I do go on, that's for sure. Well, I'm off to bed for a few minutes. You may think you will take Bini today, but believe me, he'll be by my bed fifteen seconds after he awakens, asking, as loudly and happily as only a five-year-old can, whether I am awake."

35

TO KARL, THE STAINLESS STEEL and stone of the arrivals hall at Ben Gurion airport in Tel Aviv looked much like any other modern airport. Aside from the Hebrew letters on the multilingual signs, it could have been almost anywhere in the world. But it was not. It was the gateway to the Land of Israel and differences quickly became evident. Aside from the uniformed guards and officials, there were those in plain clothes who simply stood around and watched. Every so often one would approach a passenger singled out for no obvious reason and start up a conversation. And there were the soldiers, in pairs and armed with Uzis, who were everywhere. They stood to one side as an official flipped rapidly through Karl's passport like a Las Vegas hustler dealing cards. They followed with their eyes when Karl was told to take the line to his left. One look at the line and Karl knew he had been profiled. Ahead of him were two men in the white robes of traditional Saudi dress, ahead of them, a young man in coveralls and hair down below his shoulders leaned on his guitar case, and waiting at the yellow line a dark-skinned young woman in blue jeans and a loose sweater nervously picked at the edges of the *hijab* that covered her hair. They had all been singled out for special treatment.

When Karl finally reached the immigration official, the questions began, polite but insistent. Why are you in Israel? What do you do? What kind of a consultant are you? Is this your only passport? How long were you in Switzerland? Did you like it in South Africa? Where are you staying in Israel? How long will you be in the country? What was the weather like yesterday in *Bayern*? This last was asked in perfect German, which threw Karl for a moment.

"*Schön, aber zu kalt,*" he stammered.

The agent handed him back his passport, then looked over his landing card. "You did not declare your laptop. It is required, you know."

"I don't have a computer with me."

"What kind of a consultant did you say you are?"

"I told you already, information systems."

The man looked up at him, his face pleasant yet nearly expressionless, but the tilt of his head conveyed disapproval.

"Information systems," Karl repeated. "I'm traveling light. I figured there must be Internet cafés somewhere in Israel. I can file blog entries and do email from …"

"Please, just answer. And where are you staying?"

"As I said, Tel Aviv. I'm staying in Tel Aviv."

"Where are you staying, Mister Lustig?" He pronounced the name as if it were German.

Karl reached into his jacket and withdrew his PalmPilot.

"That's not allowed in here."

"Yes, of course, I forgot. But the name and address of the hotel is in here. I travel so much I never remember those things."

"And you are visiting whom in your consulting?"

Karl, unprepared, thought quickly. "Siemens," he said, certain that they must have offices in Israel.

"Which office of Siemens?"

"Headquarters." More quick thinking.

"But you're staying in Tel Aviv. Siemens Israel is located

in Rosh Ha'ayin."

"It's not that far. I'm renting a car." He bluffed, figuring that nothing was all that far in tiny Israel.

The agent stared at him for several seconds, then handed over the declaration card. "Please take your bag over there, we want to check it."

After his bag was x-rayed again, they opened it on a table and began methodically removing its contents and laying them out neatly beside the bag.

"And what is this?"

Karl froze. What had Ulrich done to him? "It's a laser pointer. You know, for pointing at things when you make a presentation."

"It is prohibited on board. It could be used as a weapon." Karl started to protest a rule that he had never heard of, but then stopped himself. "Please open it," the agent said, handing it across the table.

Karl unscrewed the cap and dumped the batteries on top of one of his shirts on the table. The agent looked over the batteries, then took the pointer back and inspected it carefully. He called out to one of the other agents, who came over.

Be calm, Karl told himself. As Ellen used to say, the important thing is not to be afraid. Breathe slowly, act indifferent. He waited while the two inspectors talked in Hebrew.

"I checked with my colleague. The power on this laser exceeds the limit allowed for import into Israel. In fact, it exceeds standards of the European Union, so you should not have brought it with you from America. We will have to confiscate it."

"Sure, okay."

The inspector lifted up the empty bag, studied it, and ran

his hand around the inside. "Is this your bag?"

"Yes, it's mine."

"And these letters written on the inside—U. B.—what do they mean?"

Karl shrugged. "I have no idea. They were there when I bought it in a second hand shop." He was beginning to enjoy himself.

"And where was this shop?"

"In Cambridge—Cambridge, Massachusetts."

"Are you sure you did not get this in Germany? It is a German brand."

"Yes, that's why I bought it. Good design. A lot of the stuff on sale at the shop must have been from foreign students."

"What is the name of this shop?"

"I don't remember. But I could take you there. It's right near Harvard Square." Karl smiled at the man.

"Okay, you may put your things back." He handed Karl his passport. "Have a nice stay in Israel."

After Karl picked up his rental car, he got on Highway 1 toward Tel Aviv, then drove directly to his hotel on the beach front. It was expensive but offered the anonymity of a high-rise that appealed to affluent American tourists and well-placed European business travelers. In his room he locked and chained the door before zipping open his bag and dumping the contents on the bed. He studied the rolling duffle Ulrich had given him, looking for clues, for anything that might distinguish it.

He squeezed the release on the telescoping handle and pulled it out until it locked in place with a metallic click, then squeezed again and pushed it back. He opened it once more to inspect the broad rectangular tubing. It was held open by the usual arrangement of spring-loaded ball bearings in the inner tube that engaged small holes in the outer one. Karl squeezed them and tugged at the handle. It gave, and the whole assembly slid out. He took out his keychain with the little blue LED flashlight on it and shown it down into the tube protruding from the bag but couldn't see anything. He upended the bag and shook it, but nothing came out. Then he turned to the other section. Unlike the sheet metal outer tube, the inner tube was a thick-walled extrusion. Odd, Karl thought. He tried to pull the handle from the tube, but then saw it was held firmly in place by blind rivets. He studied the other end. The spring-loaded ball bearings were in a kind of carrier assembly fitted inside the tube. He squeezed hard on the ball bearings, pressing them in as far as possible. The carrier wiggled. He reached for his keychain with his free hand and used the blade of one key to pry at the assembly. It sprang out and landed on the bed along with the magazine from Ulrich's Glock. Karl shook the other parts out onto the bed.

"What have you done to me, Ulrich Bremer? What have you done?"

He put the pistol together and did some pretend target practice until the moves and the feel of shooting returned from the deep recesses of memory, until the long travel and extra force required by the Glock's signature trigger-embedded safety became familiar. Then he took the time to run through assembling and disassembling the custom Glock several times before carefully returning the parts to the telescoping tube. It might as well stay with him, he figured. It might yet be needed. If it could get past multiple x-rays and Israeli security, it could go anywhere. But if he was right and it were to be more than just a symbolic comfort, he would have to get ammunition. Back home he knew he could just walk into a Wal-Mart for a box of ammo, but here he had no idea where to start. Well, it can wait, he thought as he clicked home the handle of the luggage.

Although Shira Rozeyn had said nothing about contacting her first, Karl wanted to let her know that he was in the country before he drove up to Haifa. There had been two telephone numbers on her Web site, and he figured one of them must be a home phone. He dialed each on his cell phone and let it ring a dozen times before giving up. Well, he thought, I've come this far, I might as well go the distance.

He waited until morning to drive up to Haifa. Under normal circumstances he would have taken great pleasure from the drive—new sights on a new road in a new country—but he was so anxious and so preoccupied with his current predicament that everything passed in a blur. In a sense, he still was not in Israel. Usually, Karl preferred smaller and more distinctive hotels, but in his room after checking into the hotel in Haifa, another high-rise, he thought about the advantages of the hotel hegemony, the few giant multinational chains that could be found everywhere. Once inside any such hotel, you could be anywhere —across town or across the world—and the surroundings were familiar.

He grabbed the remote control off the night stand, turned on the television, and stepped through cable channels looking for CNN, hoping there might be an update on the sniper in München or the FBI agent killed in Boston. He watched with the sound muted and ordered room service as the abbreviated headlines crawled across the bottom of the screen.

The war in Iraq, America's Bushwar, as Karl referred to it, dominated the news and pushed out the smaller stories.

Karl turned the television off and sat on the bed. He was thinking about what to do next when his cell phone beeped: an incoming text message. It was only three characters long, from Ulrich: "???" Karl sent back an equally terse response: "!!!"

He lay back on the bed and stared at the ceiling until the faint pattern in the plaster melted into smooth pudding as he dozed off. Suddenly, his eyes opened. Who said that? Must be imagining things, he thought. He looked at his watch and did some quick math. You're slipping Karl, you forgot to re-set your watch to local time. It's time, time to go meet Shira.

36

THE CAFÉ WAS CROWDED inside but only three people braved the late afternoon chill to sit at the outside tables. One, a dark-haired woman, sat alone, her head turned toward the restaurant as if she were reading something on the bare wall. As Karl approached, she turned and looked up at him with reddened eyes and a grim, tight-lipped smile.

"*Slicha,* he said. "Shira?" She answered him in Hebrew. "I'm sorry, I don't speak Hebrew." He pulled a Berlitz phrase book from his pocket and held it up. "Just a few words I picked up on the plane, that's all."

"Of course, I'm sorry," she said. "Yes, I'm Shira. And you must be Karl. Please, sit. We can talk here."

Karl sat opposite her and started absent-mindedly straightening things in the middle of the table before taking a menu card. "Oops, more Hebrew," he said.

"Turn it over for the other language of Israel."

"What's that, Arabic?" he said, flipping the card. "No, English, of course. I don't really want anything but a coffee anyway." He turned and stared at the wall, as she had been doing a moment before, then faced her again. "Okay, so, I'm not sure just how to say this, but your husband …"

"I already know," she said, lowering her eyes. "A friend … a friend of ours called me a few hours ago and told me what happened. The … the friend is arranging for his body to be shipped back." She choked back tears.

"I am so sorry. I don't know what to say. I still don't even know why I'm here or what any of this has to do with me. If you'd rather I just go, I'll understand."

"No. I'll be all right, at least for a little while. My training in British stoicism just needs to kick in. There will be time to fall apart later, but for now I have my son to worry about and too much stuff to sort out." She paused, studying her folded hands for long seconds before beginning again. "My husband always led a somewhat dangerous life, Mr. Lustig. I suppose none of us should be surprised by something like this. You just always tell yourself that it is not going to happen to you. At least I did, and I suspect Migdal did, as well. I suppose by now you know that he was with Mossad, which was dangerous enough, although he never really talked about it. Then he started Trade Now, which I think was even more dangerous. I don't know why he was killed, but I am pretty sure it had to do with that. Maybe one of his Palestinian clients was angry over a deal gone bad, or maybe the Israeli far right took him out, as you might say, because they wanted to end his work with the Palestinians. Sometimes Migdal even thought that Mossad was after him for quitting."

"Forgive me for interrupting, but that is interesting," Karl said. "Maybe they, the Mossad, are after me, too, although I can't imagine why." He told about being followed, about his apartment being ransacked.

"I am sorry that you've been dragged into this, but your apartment does not sound like the work of Mossad. Unless they wanted merely to frighten you, I suppose. It would be more like them to have gone through everything without you ever knowing they had been there. They are usually rather sophisticated in their methods."

"Yes, I think you're right about that. They managed to tap

into a colleague's computer, and I think they were monitoring mine. But I don't really know. This Novikov character told me that he was with Interpol and told my friend that he was with Mossad, but I suppose pretending to be what you are not is part of the job."

Her face lit up. "Did you say Novikov? Was it Lev Novikov?" Karl nodded. "He is our friend. He is the one who is making the arrangements for Migdal. Migdal worked with him at Mossad. His mother was a Moroccan Jew who married a Russian émigré. His father became like Migdal's Israeli father after Migdal learned that his own parents had died in a car accident soon after he arrived here. I think that is why he stayed in Israel, at least in the beginning. He had nothing to go back to. I don't know what brought him here, though. There was always something a bit mysterious about it, as if he were already working for Mossad, which makes no sense, since he was just a teenager."

Karl frowned slightly in concentration. "I knew him, briefly, back when I first started college, but I lost track of him. He was what we called a hacker—not the modern sense of a computer hacker. He pulled off stunts, practical jokes, like turning this big central dome at MIT into a giant pumpkin. Well, he didn't do that one, but stuff like that."

She shook her head slowly side to side. "Now, that was not my Migdal. He was always very serious, very—what might one say—applied? He had a smile that never left his face, but the smile was one of warmth not amusement. People trusted him. They knew they could count on him. The very moment I met him, I knew this man would be a good father to our children." Her voice caught. "Child. We only have the one. His name is Binyamin. He is five, and has this indefatigable imagination, which his father always fed with made up stories about spies and intrigue and adventure. Of course, maybe they were not all so made up. One never knew with Migdal. He led more than one life, one might say.

"Which is funny. I trusted him completely, absolutely, from the beginning, yet I knew he was not always telling the truth, or not what you would say, the whole truth. Sometimes I would catch him in some small slip, an inconsistency, never anything important, but some detail about where he had once been or how he knew this person, that sort of thing. I would just start to open my mouth and he would seem to know what I was about to say. He would simply stop talking, even in mid-sentence, and his smile would broaden, and he would say, 'Oh, well, you know.' And that would be it. It was as if I had stumbled on a secret vice or something, and we both knew not to say any more. The Mossad smile. That's how I always thought of it. The I-can't-say-more-about-this-darling smile.

"I knew Migdal better than any person on earth, I knew his soul, and yet I also knew so little about him. I knew the person and not the facts. Does that make sense to you?"

"Yes. I had a friend once say something very much like that about me. Only she said she knew all the facts but so little of the person."

"It is funny, this trust, isn't it? What makes us trust another person, sometimes all out of proportion to what we really know of them? Why am I talking with you about things that I have not spoken of with my friend Gila, who lives in the next building and has known me for years? Are you married, Mister Lustig?"

"No. Not for many years. But my ex-wife is a good friend. Would you believe it? I was the one who introduced her to her husband. She is the friend who said that thing about not knowing the person. Except, I think by now she does know the person, or maybe I am becoming less about the facts, nothing but the facts."

"Did you have children?"

"Thank goodness, no. I don't think I'm cut out for children. They always seemed to me like bewildering beasts, another species. I suppose that is a terrible thing to say, but I just never responded to them much, except to feel awkward around them."

"Now there, Mister Lustig, that is not a fact."

"Oh, it is, I assure you."

"No, what I meant is that it is not about facts, it is about the person, the person you are. Perhaps you are right, that you are changing."

A silence passed between them, like a soft breeze. She held his eyes for only a moment, but it was a moment longer than he expected.

"I think I could use that coffee, now," he said, with a sigh. "How do you get a waiter out here?"

"Oh, don't. The coffee here is terrible. The food is good, but I make better coffee. Come with me, I'll make you some. We can talk more on the way about this confusing calamity that has brought you to Israel. I hope you do not find me … find all this … too abrupt, but I have always been that way. I simply decide things and do things that seem right to me at the time. It is how I ended up here, in Haifa, in Israel.

"But for a cup of coffee you will also have to put up with one of those bewildering beasts, because my son will be coming home from his uncle's very soon. You watch out. He may make you uncomfortable. Or worse." She gave him a broad smile as she held out her hand and gestured for Karl to follow. "Oh, and please don't say anything about Migdal. I need to find the right way and the right time to tell my son. You understand. Right now he needs for things to be normal. As normal as they can be, anyway."

37

THE APARTMENT WAS SMALL and, by Karl's standards, unkempt. Dirty dishes were stacked by the sink, a blue stuffed bear lay under the kitchen table, and toy cars were strewn across the living-room floor. Perhaps that is part of it, Karl thought. Children are messy. They are Trojan horses bearing gifts of chaos. Let them into your life and order is lost, all illusion of control vanishes.

Karl was sipping his coffee when the apartment door burst open. A small boy with kinky blonde hair dashed toward the kitchen and skidded to a halt when he saw Karl. He turned and shouted something unintelligible to the elderly man just coming through the door. Both of them fell unexpectedly to the ground and started making chudda-chudda-chudda sounds as they sprayed Karl with imaginary machine-gun fire.

Karl stood to face them, then, suddenly inspired, grabbed at his chest and jerked his body repeatedly as he slowly shrunk to the floor. He lay still and waited. The boy stood up and came over to look down at him. He was just drawing his foot back to kick at the body on the kitchen floor when Shira returned from the bathroom.

"Binyamin! Avi! You know I don't allow gunfire in the apartment. Now clean up the blood and get rid of the body." They both laughed as she offered Karl a hand. He tried to keep from laughing as he continued to lie still.

"Now you have done it, you two," she said. "You have killed an American. President Bush will be angry. He will send troops to invade us. First Afghanistan, then Iraq, then Israel. Soon his troops will be everywhere."

Binyamin looked unsure of himself for a moment, then fell to laughing again. Avi crossed over to the kitchen and knelt beside Karl. "I am Uncle Avi. You must be the mysterious American. The dead mysterious American. Welcome to Israel. Please excuse the gunfire in the apartment."

Karl stood and offered his hand to Avi, then turned to Shira and said, "I hope that was okay. I don't usually act like that."

"No? Well then I was right, wasn't I, about changing."

Karl raised his eyebrows. "Are you always right, Mrs. Rozeyn?"

"Oh, absolutely," Avi said. "Just ask Migdal." Shira looked at him and bit her lower lip. "Well, I must be going. Bini and I had a grand day today. I'm sure he will tell you all about it—more than once, I would hazard. But I was there and know the story, so I'll be going."

Binyamin could not wait for dinner to begin to tell his tales. As Shira set the Shabbat table, he told about meeting the old soldier who had only three fingers on one hand but who could make a coin disappear and then pull it out of Binyamin's ear, about going to the harbor and seeing "real" ships, about catching a beetle the size of a bagel in the garden behind Uncle Avi's building.

As Shira readied to light the candles, Karl began to feel awkward. "Look, I'm intruding. I probably should get back to my hotel."

"Nonsense, you're staying. You even brought the wine, thank you. Besides, it's a *mitzvah* to have you join us. Sit down. You're our guest."

This is a woman who knows what she wants and gets it, Karl thought. He sat down at the small table opposite Binyamin, who again recounted his adventures. With each of the several retellings over the course of dinner, the number of coins, the size of the ships, and the length of the beetle grew.

After dinner, Shira told Bini that if he hurried into his jammies, he could pick out a story before bed. He emerged from his room a few minutes later in camouflage PJs carrying a book. He went over to his mother and gestured for her to bend down so he could whisper in her ear.

"He wants you to read about Kippi ben Kippod to him. It's a little young for him, but ever since … his hand, you know, he's been regressing a bit. Especially at night." She turned and spoke to her son. "I told him you don't read Hebrew," she said to Karl.

"Oh, but I do, I do. I just read it in English. And you can translate back into Hebrew. Here, give me that book."

He sat down on the sofa with Bini and Shira on either side and opened the book. He leaned over toward Shira and asked in a stage whisper, "What is that thing?"

"A hedgehog. A giant pink hedgehog who lives on *Rechov Sumsum*. Sesame Street, you call it. Are you sure you want to do this? I can read to him."

"No, I'm on a roll. Don't stop me.

"Once upon a time," he began, "there was a giant pink hedgehog named Kippi who lived with his pet orangutan in an apartment on, er, some side street in Haifa. Nobody knew he lived there because he only went out at night to steal bananas." Shira was trying to suppress a laugh. "Now, translate. Word for word," he said.

"I'll try," she said, "But I can't guarantee results." She translated. Bini looked at both of them skeptically, then said something to his mother. "He says that's not the way the story goes. Kippi has a pet goat, not an orangutan."

"Tell him that this is how it goes in American Hebrew."

Over the next twenty minutes Kippi took a boat to Rangoon, got captured by giant frogs, escaped in a kite pulled by porpoises, and returned with a week's supply of bananas for Igor, his pet orangutan. Bini clapped his hands and pounded on Karl's leg.

"He wants you to read it again. I told him you would tomorrow night."

"Oh, no. Now I am in trouble. I'll never get it right a second time."

She carried Bini into his room, where they talked for several minutes before she turned off the light. She eased the door closed and came back to the sofa.

"Bini likes you. He doesn't like everybody, so take it as a good sign. I think he knows, in a way young children often know, who is a *mensch* and who is not. I think he is right. You are a *mensch*."

"It's Yiddish, isn't it?"

"Yes, it means …"

"I know what it means. I speak German. Some. It's the same word."

"Yes, but then you probably know it does not mean the same thing. There is a difference between simply a man and a *mensch*, a *real* man, a genuine person. It is a high compliment."

"Well, thanks, then, although I probably don't deserve it. He just likes my goofy storytelling. But I do think your son is a great kid. His father must have been a *mensch*. I just wish I knew what this was all about, why and how I got dragged into it."

"If only you had not lost the mezuzah. From what you described, I think Migdal may have created that scroll as a message of some sort. Too bad it's gone. I wish I could have seen it. Perhaps I could have helped figure out what it was about."

"Here, be my guest. Take a look." He reached into his pocket and held out his keychain with the thumb drive on it.

She looked puzzled.

"I took a picture of it when I sent off my first email to you. It's on the flash drive. All we need is a computer."

"We can use Migdal's. It's in the bedroom. After Bini was born, Migdal had to give up his Haifa office, as we called the spare room. Now it's Bini's room. I'm afraid the bedroom is a mess. I've never been much of a housekeeper, and Migdal was like a crow, always collecting shiny odd bits and stashing them here or there." She led the way into the cramped bedroom. The door just cleared the double bed when it was open. She started grabbing things strewn on the bed and stuffing them into a locker at the foot of it.

"That's Migdal's side," she said, gesturing toward the far side of the bed. A laptop was sitting open on a small table squeezed in between the wall and an old-fashioned chifforobe. She turned away from him and put her hand up to touch her face, then quickly turned back. "We bought the chifforobe for him to use after he moved up here because my stuff already filled the closet to overflowing."

Karl walked around the bed, grabbed a stool from the corner, and plunked it down in front of the table. He reached to close the door of the chifforobe, which was in the way, but something caught his eye. He glanced over at Shira who was biting her lip.

"Those were Migdal's things. You might as well know. He used them sometimes when he was working for Mossad. Disguises. It gave him freedom of movement, he said, made him harder to spot. That's what he told me. But even after he quit, he would sometimes, you know, dress up. He was really good, actually. I came home early one day when a buyer canceled a meeting, and I thought some strange woman was letting herself into our apartment. He probably could have fooled anybody. In fact, he once spent the better part of a year passing as a female student on a deep cover operation at a German university. That was before I knew him.

"It helped that his voice wasn't all that deep, and his face never really lost its baby fat. Actually, he was, well, kinda cute when he was all made up—in a boyish sort of way. I really didn't mind. I grew up with a brother who liked to wear my clothes, so I wasn't too shocked. But Barry, my brother, turned out to be a flaming homosexual, and Migdal was straight, at least as far as I could tell. He just had a few odd ways about him. Maybe having a brother who cross-dressed set the stage for being with Migdal. I don't know. I do think the English are more matter of fact than Americans are when it comes to little eccentricities like that."

"Thank you," he said. "Thank you for telling me all that, because I think it explains a lot."

"What do you mean?"

He told her about meeting Maryam Cashman in Germany.

"That does sound like Migdal. He must have lifted your driver's license and slipped the mezuzah into your pocket then. I think he trained for such things in his work. It all makes sense. Well, except for why he might do that in the first place."

Karl sat down and booted up the computer. "Do you mind if I check email first? I am a little concerned about a friend in Germany."

"No, I don't mind."

He opened a browser and started to type the URL for his Web-mail account. After the first letters, the dropdown opened with previous addresses and Karl stopped. "Your husband was stalking me. He was looking at my blog. And here," he pointed, "he was checking out the MIT alum records." He went to Google and clicked twice in the search box. The dropdown was peppered with entries that Karl recognized. "He knew my clients, he knew my friends, he undoubtedly knew where I was going and when. But why? And why, if he was so thorough, why would an ex-spook leave all these breadcrumbs? Unless he wanted them to be found and knew they would be.

"I'm beginning to get that creepy feeling again that none of this has been an accident. Let's take a look at that mezuzah scroll." Karl slipped the thumb drive into a USB slot, waited for it to install itself, then typed in a long pass phrase to open the encrypted folder. He found the JPEG he was looking for and put it up on the screen."

"So clear," she said, scanning it slowly. "My pictures are never this good."

"Technology. It's all just technology. With a macro close-up and six megapixels, your shot would look just as good."

She squinted at the screen and read, mumbling to herself. "Yes, I see. There are two extra words, as you said: *zachor* and *bashert*. Does that mean anything special to you?"

"You know, I can't say as I ever heard the word *zachor* before my friend David read it to me from the scroll, but I do remember where and when I first heard the other word, which is interesting, because it was in Mitchell's—I mean Migdal's—apartment, in 1963, my freshman year at MIT. That's where I met this girl, Deborah Geffner, who I had a crush on. She had this spiel about us all being part of a network or something. I forget what she called it, but she said it was *bashert*, fated that we all came together."

"I think I know who you are talking about."

"You do?"

"Yes, Migdal told me once about this girl he knew when he was young. I think he may also have been in love with her. She was killed on one of his first missions for Mossad, I think, something to do with our nuclear program."

"Nuclear program? God, now it all comes back to me. I must have completely blocked it out. I was in a kind of fog for part of that year. It was a tough time for me. I was in the hospital for a while and overwhelmed and away from home for the first time. But now I remember. There was this screwball plan that Mitch, er, Migdal and his friends were fantasizing about, to steal nuclear fuel from MIT. This girl, Deborah, was part of the group. But it was a game, a kind of oddball intellectual exercise. You know, sort of, 'Mitch-found-this-stash-of-nuclear-fuel-at-MIT-and-now-let's-figure-out-what-we-could-do-with-it.' Deborah suggested selling it to Israel. They had this boat of some kind they thought could deliver the stuff. It was a game."

Shira shook her head. "No, not a game. They did it, I think. They brought that stuff here, although Migdal never talked about details. He never talked about a lot of things. We were married for more than a year before I knew that he was with Mossad. I just knew he was away a lot. Germany, England, America. I thought he made children's toys. Would you believe that? Children's toys? And here he was fighting terrorists, spying on extremists, who knows what, because he could never talk about it except in sentence fragments and opaque references.

"I didn't know what to do after I first found out. I thought of getting a divorce. I wouldn't let him touch me for months. But I couldn't stop loving him. He was my soulmate." Her voice cracked. "Then … then the baby came along, and he was so good with Binyamin. Such a loving, understanding father he was. I fell in love with him all over again, and I didn't care what he did or who he had killed. I knew he was a good man. And eventually he left it, Mossad. Or so I thought. Now I don't know."

"Why did he leave it? Was it because of you?"

"No, not really. He seemed to lose faith in Israel for a while, in what we were doing and how we were doing it. He helped found Trade Now. You know what that is? Yes, well, he thought we brought the Palestinian crisis down on ourselves. When the first *intifada* started, he said, 'Now we reap what we have sown.' What should Israel expect, he would argue, after decades of treating the Palestinians as dogs and our own Israeli Arabs as second-class citizens—or worse. He never condoned the violence, but he passionately wanted to find another way."

"But he was American. And he wasn't even Jewish."

"Oh, no. He was Israeli. They made him a citizen. That was part of the deal with Mossad. And he converted. He was a Jew all right."

"Because of you?"

"No, I didn't care. I loved Migdal. He could have been an Anglican priest for all I cared, and I still would have wanted him. No, I think he just wanted to go the distance.

He did things, everything, with a certain quiet intensity, nothing halfway. It scared me at first—maybe it always did—but it also drew me to him. It was like we were part of this network thing, what that girl talked about."

"A karass. I remember now. A word that this American author made up. Kurt Vonnegut."

"Yes, I've heard of him." She looked down at her hands for long seconds. "I believe in God, I think. Or at least I did when I said the blessings at the start of Shabbat tonight. And I will again at the next Shabbat. In between I believe in Fate. I believe in something that steers us and guides us and whispers to us. It whispers about what we are meant to do and whom we are meant to do it with. Maybe that's what this Vonnegut meant?"

Karl shrugged. "Maybe. Maybe it's just us whispering to ourselves and each other."

"So, then, let's see what my Migdal tried to whisper to us." She turned back to the screen. "He must have been in a hurry. Some of the letters are blotched, like he pressed too hard on a quill pen."

"Wait, which letters. Maybe he meant them to be noticed."

"Well there's a couple of alefs and resh and…"

"Write them down."

She grabbed a scrap of paper and started writing. "So here are the letters that stand out."

תראהירק

"Tav, resh, alef, heh, yod, resh, alef, kuf," she recited. "It's not any Hebrew I know. None of these letters have a *sofit* form, so we don't even know where a word might end."

"Maybe it's not Hebrew. Maybe it's in another language, just written with the Hebrew alphabet, like Yiddish, right?

Help me," he said. "What are the letter equivalents in English?"

"Well, the most straightforward transliteration into the Latin alphabet would be t-r-a-h-y-r-a-k. Trahyrak." She laughed. "Mean anything to you?"

Karl laughed, too. "We have to assume it's something simple, because Migdal would know we would not have the key to the code. At the same time it would have to be something that would makes sense only to us, that anyone else would not be able to figure out. Like the extra words. Unless you knew the *shema*, you wouldn't know that this scroll was not legit. If it fell into Arab hands, for instance, they would probably be clueless.

"Hang on, you read off those letters and wrote them down right to left, didn't you, as if they were Hebrew. But what if they're not? What if it's English, which is written left to right? So let's turn it around. We get k-a-r-y-h-a-r-t. Now maybe we're getting someplace."

"But what's a karyhart?" She pronounced it with a British accent, with both vowels broadened as if it were caw-ree-hawrt. "Sounds like it could be a name. Do you know anyone with a name something like that?"

"Hmm. Cory Hart? Maybe. Seems vaguely familiar, but I can't place it. Let's Google it." He typed and waited. "Hah, misspelled it. The first two entries are for Corey Hart, a Canadian singer. He had a couple of hits back in the '80s."

"What did he do? I don't think I ever heard of him."

"Oh, you know him all right, even if you don't recognize the name. His first biggy was 'Sunglasses at Night.' Remember that? Pop paranoia, much misunderstood. It must have made it to England."

"Yes, of course. But I don't see what that might have to

do with Migdal. I don't remember him mentioning the song or the singer. And he was never much of a singer himself."

"Something to do with sunglasses, then. Sunglasses at night, sunglasses in the dark." Karl shrugged his shoulders then exhaled sharply. "You know, now I do remember another of Mitchell's many schemes. He was selling contraband lenses to some European manufacturer. They made sunglasses."

"I don't understand."

"This was a long time ago. Polaroid had all the patents and a monopoly on plastic polarizing lenses. They squeezed the market for as much as they could get, which kept the cost of polarized sunglasses high. Mitchell found some way to get factory rejects and sell them abroad at a big markup. He used to pack them up in sawdust in these mongo shipping canisters. Made a real mess of his apartment. He kept tracking sawdust all over the building. The building super went bonkers, so he moved the whole operation down to the basement of the apartment house."

"Is it still there?"

"Is what still there?"

"The building. The building where his apartment was. Maybe we should go there."

"Look, this could be just a wild goose chase. The apartment building was in Boston. A lot has changed in the Back Bay. And we don't really know what the clue means. It could be about the overseas company. Maybe we completely misread the message."

"No. I think my Migdal would construct the message so we could read it. Did you know that company in Europe?"

"No, but ..."

"You did know about the sunglasses, sunglasses in the

dark. That's got to be it. This is a message to you, remember. Migdal sent it to you, knowing what you did and did not know."

"But I don't know Hebrew. I needed your help."

"And you think it was an accident that you are here, with me? How did you get Migdal's mezuzah with my mark on it in the first place? Who gave it to you?"

Karl looked at her, holding her gaze in his. "You're saying your husband arranged all this?"

"Or God. I don't know, but I know something brought us together for a reason."

"Yeah, I guess you're right. I better go back to Boston, then, and see what I can find."

"Look, I'll go with you. I knew Migdal. I don't know how, but I have a feeling I'll be able to help you sort this out."

"No, this is my responsibility. You need to stay here and take care of your son."

"That's what I'm doing, taking care of my son. Listen, they killed my husband. They carved an *X* in my son's flesh. Whoever they are, they're monsters." She locked eyes with him. "This business is not going to just go away. We have to get to the bottom of it or none of us will ever be safe.

"I'll go pack. I can take Bini back to Avi's before it's light. It's a good thing that I haven't told him yet about his father or I would never be able to leave now. He'll be okay with Avi. For a while."

"You don't waste time, do you." It was said as a statement of fact, not a question.

"I told you, that is how I do my life. I don't think we have a lot of time. For Bini's sake we need to do something now."

"But we can't just go, I mean just like that? You'll have to get a visa. It takes time."

"No, I don't need a visa." She reached into the drawer of the nightstand and pulled out an American passport. "See, I'm the American, not Migdal. I grew up in England but my mother was born and raised in Atlanta. And I never bothered to become a citizen here. At first I felt guilty, as if I were holding back some part of myself while Migdal had given himself completely over to Israel. He burned his bridges. Or had them burned for him. But there I was, hedging my bets. Then Bini was born, and I realized that it was a gift to him to be an American, too. Migdal might be comfortable investing all his eggs in this one basket, but Bini and I might someday need an exit strategy.

"So, let's go to Boston."

38

SHIRA WAS SHIVERING beside him as they walked up Boylston Street from the Prudential Center parking garage. "I warned you that Boston was pretty cold this time of year," Karl said. "I should have gotten you a warmer coat when I went out this morning." He thought of telling her what he had bought at the Wal-Mart but then decided it would not be reassuring. "Let's go shopping now and pick up something for you."

"I'll be all right. I don't want to waste time shopping. We've already lost another day."

They had decided to fly into New York, rent a car in Shira's name, then drive up to Boston. Karl had planned to return to his apartment, but when they arrived, they found it sealed off with police tape as a crime scene. He next suggested staying with David and Ellen, but Shira persuaded him not to risk dragging them back into things, so Karl drove up to Woburn to look for a hotel.

"Why Woburn?" she had asked.

"It's no place in particular, that's why," he had told her. "Hell, half the people in Massachusetts don't even know how to pronounce it." Ironically, they ended up at an all-suite chain located in the same industrial park as David's office. Karl insisted Shira take the king-size bed, then tried to get comfortable on the lumpy sofa. After a largely sleepless night, Karl had reluctantly awakened Shira, and they headed back into town without stopping for breakfast.

The morning sun struggled to squeeze through the clouds as they crossed Massachusetts Avenue and continued walking. Karl kept looking around, squinting, and scrunching up his mouth. "I wish I could remember better. This is not the Back Bay I knew in college. A lot of this looks familiar in a foggy sort of way, but nothing jumps out at me. And a lot is completely new and unrecognizable. I wish I could remember the actual street address of Mitchell's apartment, but I don't think I ever knew it. I just headed across the bridge and walked right to it."

"Then why don't we do that? We could start at MIT and just walk. You turn when it feels right. I think our bodies remember things that our minds forget."

It turned out to be a great idea except for crossing the Harvard Bridge, which was gusty as always. As they huddled to blunt the wind, Karl explained the markings on the bridge and told the story of Oliver Smoot, the hapless fraternity pledge who had been used as a yardstick. Once on the Boston side, every so often Karl would pause, frown, and say something like, "It doesn't feel right. Let's cross the street." Or, "It feels like I should turn here." After passing a row of new buildings on one street, Karl stopped suddenly at the corner. "It should be here, right here, but it isn't. That's the wrong building. I must have made a wrong turn. No, I didn't. That's gotta be it, but it isn't." He continued around the corner, staring up at the building and shading his eyes with his hand. "Hot damn. It is the right building. They put a new façade on it at some point, but this is the building, I know it. It's still here, Shira. It's still here." He took her hand and pulled her back around to the front again.

The front entrance was far classier than the one Karl remembered. To one side was an engraved brass plate so brightly polished that it looked as if it had just been pulled from its box.

Property under management of
Adam Benjamin and Mark Hamm, LLC

Shira stood staring at the sign, then leaned over and whispered, "Do you see? This is Migdal's doing, another message. That's my son, that's Bini. See? His name is Adam Binyamin Markham. We're in the right place."

Karl pointed at an "Apartment For Rent" sign in one of the first floor windows. "We're in luck," he said, as he pulled out his cell phone and dialed the number on the sign. The real estate agent said she was in the area and would be right over to show them the apartment.

"You don't have any pets, do you?" she asked. "The management doesn't allow pets." Karl reassured her that they were petless. He snapped the phone closed, then held it between his teeth as he took off his jacket. He put it around Shira, then slipped the phone into his pants pocket.

"You'll freeze, Karl. I can't take your coat."

"Don't be silly. I've still got a sweater on. Besides, I grew up in the Upper Peninsula. Michigan. Practically in the Arctic. This is downright balmy by those standards. It's above freezing, a veritable heat wave." He tugged at his collar and fanned his face. Shira laughed but kept the jacket.

When the real estate agent arrived, she looked disapprovingly at both of them over the top of her half-frame glasses. "You must be freezing in just a sweater," she said to Karl.

"No, I'm hot blooded. Can we just take a look at the apartment?"

The woman made a point of looking at Karl's graying hair, then turned to give Shira the once over. She shook her head disapprovingly before leading the way to the door.

Karl and Shira feigned interest as they were shown the third-floor apartment, which might have been fine for a childless couple who wanted to pay way too much for less space than Shira had in Haifa. Karl asked if there might not be something else in the building a little bigger, but the woman assured him that nothing else was coming vacant and they had better snap up this little gem before someone else did.

On their way back down the hall, Karl nodded toward the apartment just at the head of the stairs and mouthed the word "Mitchell." As they reached the ground floor again, he said, "So, is there a back entrance to the building?" He headed down the hall with Shira in tow, bobbing his head and studying the walls and doors as if they were fascinating.

"No, not that way, you have to—"

"And what's this?" he asked, pointing to a low door under the staircase. "An apartment for short people?"

The woman grunted disapprovingly. "That goes to the basement storage area. It's not for use by tenants. It belongs to the owner. Perhaps I should say owners. The building changed hands recently. The woman who owned it for many years sold it to the current management, Benjamin and Hamm. They own most of the properties on this block. I suspect they'll do what they did with the other buildings and replace this with something a bit more upscale. She was always nice, that Mrs. Cashman, the few times I would see her."

Karl was studying the door as she talked. "I don't suppose you could show us the storage area, even though it's not for the tenants. You know, just out of curiosity. I'm an architect, and I like to see what kind of foundation a place as old as this has. You understand. Just a quick look."

"Oh, I couldn't, even if I wanted to, which I do not. No, it's off limits, takes a special key. Mrs. Cashman always kept it herself. I assume she turned it over to the new owners. You'd have to take it up with them. Now, are you interested in the apartment or should I show it to the next prospect who called this morning?"

Karl told her they'd have to talk it over and would call her right away if they wanted it. She warned them again that it might be rented by then, but Shira jumped in and played her part. "We really need to talk first, dear," she said, looking most seriously at Karl. "We can call this nice woman after-wards on your cell phone, if need be, but we should talk."

Back outside, Shira seemed eager to tell Karl something, but hesitated when she noticed a man shivering on the cor-ner, pacing and rocking from foot to foot as he held the hood of his MIT sweatshirt pulled tightly around his face.

"See," she said. "I'm not the only one not dressed for this weather." They were clear to the next corner before she spoke again. "By the way, I think I know the kind of special key that the door to the basement takes. Migdal called it a Mul-T-Lock. He told me they are for restricted access, which was why he had a jeweler friend of ours make one into a pendant for me, as the key to his heart. He had it gold plat-ed, with a photo of us cheek-to-cheek laser engraved in min-iature on the back. As a jeweler myself, I thought it was a pretty weird piece, but started wearing it because I thought it was so sweet of him to go to all that trouble. See?"

She reached to her neck and pulled out the key on its gold chain. She disentangled it from the tiny silver Star of

David that also hung on a chain around her neck.

Karl leaned close to study it. Unlike an ordinary key, the edges were smooth, but a series shallow pits were drilled into the flat face of it. Because of the plating, they caught the light and glittered almost like jewels as he turned it over.

"See, that's us," she said, pointing. "It was taken in one of those photo booths when we were still dating. But the laser engraving makes it look pretty good."

Karl let her have it back to slip down in her blouse again. "I have seen ones like that before. Not gold plated, of course. In Europe. They're not very common over here, though. You don't suppose?"

"It's worth a try. We'll have to come back when Mrs. Real-Estate isn't around. And did you hear who she said was the woman who owns the building? Cashman. Wasn't that the name Migdal used when you met him in Germany."

"Mmm hmm. Did own. Maybe we should spend some time in the library surfing the Internet this afternoon, seeing what we can come up with on Benjamin and Hamm. Must be something in real estate or tax records."

They crossed back over Mass Avenue and headed down Boylston toward the Boston Public Library. At the library, Shira surrendered Karl's jacket.

"So, now you give it back," he teased, "now that we are about to go into someplace warm."

They spent the next several hours searching the Internet but found nothing definitive. Every trail they followed just led to another trail. Or a dead end. They finally gave up and went in search of an early dinner instead. Karl suggested his favorite Indian spot on Mass Ave, but Shira told him that the only decent curry outside of Mumbai was in London. They settled on Thai at an overcrowded walk-down place on

Boylston, but both of them kept looking out the window and neither of them ate much.

39

THE SKY HAD CLOUDED over and was turning from dull silver to deep charcoal when they finally reached the apartment building again.

"How do we get in?" Shira asked.

"Simple," he said looking up at the lights in the windows. "There's somebody home on the third floor." He went over to the bank of names and buttons. "Let's try M. Hogue on the top floor." He pushed a button. Nothing. "Okay, maybe it's B. Sandelman." He pushed another. This time the release on the front door buzzed in response.

"Thanks! Forgot my key," Karl called up the stairwell when he heard a door open above. He waited until he heard the door close again before walking down the hall toward the storage area. "So, let's see this special key of yours again."

She slipped the necklace and key over her head and handed it to him. The key was the right shape and slid past the warding into the horizontal slot. Karl half expected it to bind when he tried to turn it, but the cylinder rotated easily and the door swung open. "So far, so good." Karl fumbled for and found a light switch. The steep stairs led down to what looked like a long narrow room. At the bottom of the stairs, Karl found a pull-chain fixture and turned on the overhead light. The room turned out to be a narrow corridor running beside a row of wire mesh storage cages. They could see a few objects in some—a chair in need of re-caning, a rusted wheelbarrow, a broken lamp—but most were empty, and, judging by the thick layer of dust, long neglected.

Thirty feet away, the corridor ended in a blank wall.

"Nothing here. A wild goose chase," he said as they strolled down the length of the room.

"Hang on a minute, that doesn't fit." She pointed. "There, through the cages, you can see the foundation. It's blocks of stone. The wall at the end is smooth concrete, obviously more recent. Let's check it out."

Up close, they could see that the wall only looked like concrete but actually seemed to be painted plywood that might have once been white. A door was set in it, secured by a hasp with a large combination lock. Karl jiggled hopefully, then shrugged.

"Now all we need is one of," he looked at the dial, "uh, 64,000 combinations. Then again, this door doesn't look too tough. I could probably kick it in."

She looked skeptical, but stepped aside to give Karl room.

Deciding to use his shoulder rather than kicking, Karl drew back and threw himself against the door. "Oh, shit, I may have broken my shoulder," he said. "It may look like flimsy plywood, but there's something underneath. It's reinforced with steel or something."

"Let me take a look at that lock," she said. "I think I've seen one like it before." She turned it over in her hand. "I think I may even know the combination."

"You what? How?"

She pointed to the back of the lock. It was inscribed in Hebrew. "Hafner Locks, Haifa," she read. "There's one exactly like it on the hasp for our storage area at our apartment building. Migdal bought it. I don't think it's any coincidence. What's this particular kind of Israeli-made lock doing in Boston? I'll tell you." She spun the dial a couple of turns, then carefully picked out three numbers in sequence. The lock slid open with a heavy click. "A woman never forgets her wedding anniversary. A smart woman has ways to make sure her husband never forgets." She lifted the lock from the hasp and set it on the floor.

Karl looked at the lock on the floor, then smiled at Shira. "You certainly were right about coming along. I did need you after all. Are you ready to find out the rest of Migdal's message?"

Shira nodded, then tugged at the handle. "It's heavy." She pulled again, this time with both hands. The door moved a little but didn't open.

"Here, let me try." He got both hands on the handle as firmly as he could manage, put one foot as high as he could on the frame beside the door, then pulled with all his strength. His face turned red, but ever so slowly the door creaked open.

Karl pulled out his keychain with the LED flashlight on it and shone the ghostly blue light around the room. There were stacks of magazines and, toward the back, three huge cardboard canisters. Karl picked up a magazine off the top of one of the stacks and blew the dust from it. "Hey, look at this," he said. "*Popular Electronics,* June 1959. And here," he wiped dust from another stack, "a 1953 *CQ Magazine.* That's ham radio. Your husband really was a geek. He must have been a serious collector. These are all sealed in plastic. Let's check out the barrels." He used his knife to work loose the lid on the nearest one, gradually increasing the gap until he could slip his fingers under it and pry it off. The barrel was filled with sawdust from which a few scattered pieces of dark plastic poked up.

Karl laughed. "Now that is really funny."

"What is it?" She leaned over and peered into the barrel. "What's so funny?"

"Mitch. Migdal. Your late husband. These are the contra-band Polaroid filters I told you about, the sunglasses in the dark. He just never made the last shipment. They've been here all this time."

"Thanks for doing my work for me." The voice came from the far end of the basement. Through the doorway they could see a man ducking down to peer at them as he came down the stairs.

"Lev, it's me, Shira. What are you doing here?"

"Hello, cousin. I'm just keeping tabs on you. And don't you two make a clever pair." He strode toward them, gun in one hand and a flashlight in the other.

"The joke's on you, Novikov," Karl said. "Migdal out-smarted you all. There's nothing here but old magazines and bits of plastic." He grimaced and looked at Shira. "Man, I think I hurt my back, too, when I tried to open the door." He arched his back and stretched as he reached around with his hand and pressed into the small of his back underneath his sweater. He seemed to tug at something as he said, loudly, "Ah, much better." Shira gave him an odd look, but he didn't react.

Lev ducked down to get through the low doorway and swept his light around the room. "Really? Just magazines and plastic?"

Karl reached into the open barrel and scooped up a handful of oily sawdust and brittle plastic. He sprinkled it back in. "See? Sawdust and plastic, plastic and sawdust." He dipped his hand in again, but this time struck something hard and much bigger.

"Migdal outsmarted us, all right," Lev said, nodding toward the barrels. "We tracked him all his life, we used every intelligence connection we could and followed every lead, and in the end he fooled us with nothing more than the old purloined letter trick. He never moved the stuff. He didn't put it in a vault or ship it off shore or work a deal with anybody. That's why we could never find a trace of it. He didn't do anything with it, just secretly bought the building and left it here practically in plain sight."

"Are you talking about plastic? No, I guess not."

"No, I'm talking about MUF, Material Unaccounted For. You see, Migdal shorted us. That night at Ga'ash, when he delivered the uranium to my father, he was three short of the promised delivery. He said that what he had was all he could get. But years later, when the theft was finally discovered by MIT, we found a little accounting discrepancy. MIT, of course, never acknowledge the missing fuel. Exactly as Migdal and his felonious friends had figured, MIT covered it up. It would have been a public relations nightmare and financial disaster for them to admit they had lost nearly a ton of fissionable material. A little creative accounting here, a fabricated experiment there, a change of dates on old refueling schedules and, voila, no MUF. But, as I am sure you can guess, we have our sources. We found out that they were, in truth, missing more of the original fuel rods than we received. Migdal had held back the others as a sort of insurance policy. As long as they were unaccounted for, we needed him alive and on our side. Of course, we couldn't prove anything or openly accuse anyone without tipping our hand and bringing a house of cards tumbling down around us. And, like MIT, Migdal never acknowledged the missing material. It was a threat, believe me. It would be damnably hard to make an atomic bomb with this stuff, but with half a teaspoon of intelligence you could make some really dirty explosives that could leave a small city uninhabitable for a very long time."

"What are you going to do to us?" Karl said. "Are you going to kill us now that you got what you were after?"

"We don't work that way," he said, returning his gun to the holster under his arm. "You know a lot, you two—more than you should—but I think we can trust you, at least as long as we can keep an eye on you. Which is why I would suggest, Mr. Lustig, that you consider moving to Israel. Despite appearances and the current political climate, it would really be ever so much safer." He paused. "For you, anyway, if you get my meaning. We do have a certain amount of leverage to ensure you'll both go quietly about your lives." He looked at Shira.

Karl took a slow breath. "But you killed Migdal, or had him killed, because he was dealing with the Palestinians, with the Arabs."

"Look, I won't pretend to condone everything that Migdal was trying to do with Trade Now, but he was one of ours. He was more than that, he was a brother to me. We wouldn't kill him because he quit, and we wouldn't kill him because we didn't like his politics. We just wanted to neutralize him, not take him out. We wanted to be certain this stuff wouldn't end up in the hands of terrorists. After he was killed, we worried that we would never recover it, but then you entered the story. Yes, we dogged him and kept the pressure on, but we didn't kill him."

"Then who did?"

"I did." The voice came from the stairwell at the end of the room.

"Tariq. I should have known you would be here."

"Yes, you should have, Lev. You should have figured it all out quicker and saved everyone a lot of pain and trouble. You know, just for a moment, there, in Germany, Mitchell thought I was you. It was his last moment, because I had given up on him. He was never going to deliver. So, Mitchell died thinking it might be Mossad who was after him." He laughed, a short, explosive laugh. "And you will die thinking that it is Tariq Mustafa who wants to kill you. But you both will have been wrong."

"Then who are you?"

"You could call me a dealer in antiquities. I trade in nuclear relics. I am also a promoter of free trade. And my wealth. Unfortunately, you have something there that I already bought and paid for, paid dearly." He stepped into the light where they could see his face. He was wearing an MIT sweatshirt, and Karl realized that it was probably he rather than some student that they had seen hanging around the apartment earlier in the day.

"You see, there was a survivor from the Delft. Your father must have told you about the Delft, Lev. One of his finest moments, blowing up a couple of college kids. But he missed one. Ah, and now you understand. Yes, here I am, Mitchell's shipmate, Jef Vries, and I've struggled all these years to get revenge and to get what I deserved. I finally got my revenge in Germany, and now I am about to get what I deserve. I already have a buyer for the last of the fuel. Mitchell refused to deal and kept playing games with us, so I lost patience and got him out of the way. It's been a hell of a chase ever since. Now you are in the way, Novikov." He raised his gun.

Karl twisted slightly to one side, his back toward Shira, and took a half step back farther into the darkness of the storage room. He was hoping that she would notice, hoping she would be able to see enough in the gloom to guess what he was about to do and to stay back. Lev was now almost directly in front of him, half in the light, half out, while Jef, at the other end, was right under the light fixture. It was now or never.

The important thing is not to be afraid, he thought. In one swift but unhurried seamless motion, he dropped to one knee, drew the Glock from where it was tucked in the back of his pants, brought his hands together in front of him, took aim, and fired. At the other end of the room, Jef's arms flew out and he fell backwards. His gun discharged twice, wildly, before he slumped against the wall and slid down to the floor.

Lev pulled out his gun and held it outstretched in front of him as he ran down to the other end. He kicked the body, which fell to one side, then reached down and felt for a pulse. "He's dead," he said. "That was some performance Karl Lustig," he continued, as he holstered his gun and started back toward them. "Do you always carry a handgun? And how did you learn to shoot like that?"

"Yes, I always carry a handgun," he said with a quick laugh. "At least in recent days. And, believe it or not, like much of everything else that I've found useful in my life, I learned to shoot at MIT, on the pistol team."

"You know, you can get up now," Lev said, reaching down to give Karl a hand.

"I've never …" Karl shivered. "I never did …"

"You did what you had to. And it seems he did get what he deserved, just as he insisted. But you, Mister Lustig, you were really taking a chance. I don't understand why you didn't just empty the clip into him just to be sure. It's a Glock, a semiautomatic, you know. How could you be sure that your first shot would be good."

"Just old habit, I guess. When I was doing target shooting we used single-shot Thompson Contenders. I wasn't thinking about a second shot. I just wanted to place the one in the chamber right in the center of that MIT seal sitting like a bull's-eye in the middle of his chest."

"Well, it looks like you did." He spread his hands. "Come on, you two, let's get out of here. Our people will be along soon to clean up this mess. We are not supposed to be here, and you don't want to be talking to the police, not with an unregistered handgun, not in the Commonwealth of Massachusetts you don't. You'll have to tell me sometime how you got it and how you got it here. Maybe over *shishlik* and a bottle of wine at a café I know in Haifa." He winked.

"Maybe we will take you up on that. But you're buying." Shira flashed him a brief smile. "But what are you going to do with the uranium?"

"Give it back. We don't need it, not anymore. MIT thinks they can find a way to put it to some use, although they long ago replaced the reactor with a better system. And they're smart. They can be just as clever with addition as they were with subtraction. By next week, the books will balance and none of this ever happened."

"Is it still any good," Shira asked. "I mean, after all these years wouldn't it be somewhat worn out?"

"Are you kidding?" He looked at Karl. "You, MIT graduate, tell the lady the half-life of U-235."

"What, me? I was a computer geek. I don't remember. Something like 700 million years. But lend me a laptop and I'll Google it for you."

40

2007 — Bini planted himself between Karl and the television and said something too fast for Karl to follow.

"English, Bini, use English. You need the practice."

"No, you speak Hebrew. You need the practice."

"Oh, now you're in trouble, young man." Binyamin ran from the room and Karl chased after him with mock anger. He tackled him onto the couch in the living room and started tickling and kissing him. Bini squealed. "Stop, stop. I'll do it. I'll speak English."

Karl looked up to see Shira standing in the doorway, smiling. "What?" he asked.

"I'm just enjoying having both my guys here. I know you have to go to Boston, but I wish you didn't have to go so often."

"Hey, don't blame me. You know whose fault it is. So many secret trusts and holding companies and foundations. We found two more charities that ultimately traced back to him: the Wasserman Scholarship for Young Mathematicians and the Geffner Foundation that sponsors college students going to Israel. Anyway, I think most of the Benjamin and Hamm business is finally straightened out, so you and Bini are set. It mostly ran itself anyway. And you'll never guess; we finally sold all the old magazines to a collector. Oh, yes, David and Ellen say hello. Turns out Ellen has a brother who now lives here, and they are thinking of coming over for

Passover. It was David who put me onto the buyer for the magazines, some guy who made his fortune in publishing. Would you believe, he paid five figures for the lot?"

"No way," she laughed. "I really had no idea what an entrepreneur Migdal was. All those years of wheeling and dealing. Another secret side to a complex man."

"Oh, that reminds me. I have something to show you. I'll get it from the kitchen." She returned, after a few minutes, holding an envelope. Now there were tears in her eyes.

"What is it? What's wrong?"

"This came in the post yesterday. From Tel Aviv. They recovered it when they tracked down the rest of the Mustafa group." She handed him the envelope. He opened it and fished out a chain. A silver mezuzah was threaded on it.

"It's Migdal's, isn't it? Yes, I see it is. Wow. That must be a shock for this suddenly to appear after nearly four years."

"Well, I think it is right that it took this long, because if it had come earlier, I might have put it in a drawer or even melted it down to make something new. But now I know what to do with it."

She took it from him and slipped it over his head, tucking it into his tee shirt. "There. Migdal would have liked that. After all, he went to a great deal of trouble to bring us together. We'll have to get a proper scroll, though, to replace Migdal's doctored version."

"No, I think I prefer this one. I like the message. *Zachor. Bashert.* And last but most decidedly not least, I wear my sunglasses at night."

Shira laughed and wiped at her tears.

"You know," he said, putting his arms around her waist, "I've been thinking. I think he always had more in mind than just leading us to the fuel. It's almost as if somehow he knew that it would work between us, yet he barely knew me—just for a few months and that was more than forty years ago. We were just kids."

She put her head against his chest, as if listening to his heart. "You're a lot taller than Migdal, you know." She pulled back a little to look up into his face, "Didn't you once say that you had a crush on that girl who died on the boat? Well, so did Migdal. We were all part of the same karass, doing the same piece of God's work. We already had some connection. And we are both artists. So, how could it not work?"

"Well, what I think is that when he read the writing on the wall, he set out to make sure you and Bini would be all right, taken care of. So he just thought about the most obsessively over-responsible person he had ever known. And here I am, just as he figured." He reached down and fingered the mezuzah through his shirt. "You know I can't wear this." He started to slip it off over his head.

"Why not? Because it was Migdal's?"

"No, because I'm not Jewish."

"That's what you think. That's what Migdal once thought. But just wait."

"No, you just wait. If you think I'm going to," he glanced toward Bini, "well, have a *mohel* do plastic surgery below my waist, you better think again." He looked back toward Bini, who was rolling his eyes.

"Don't mind him," she said. "It's a ten-year-old boy thing. He does that to me, too."

"It's not true, Abba Karl. I would never disrespect my mother. Only you." He ran from the living room glancing over his shoulder to make sure Karl was behind him.

~ ~ ~

They saw Bini off to school, then Shira went down to her studio and Karl set up his laptop on the kitchen table. He was just getting organized—still trying to make up his mind whether to be responsible and write his next blog posting or do what he really wanted to do and resume working on his novel—when she returned to the kitchen.

"It's too hot to work, today," she said. "Let's go to the beach. We can go to Ga'ash. It's a drive but we have time. Bini won't be back from school until 15:30."

"I've never been there. I hear it's beautiful."

"Yes, it is, and full of surprises. You'll like it."

"Great. Let me grab a towel and try to find my bathing suit."

Shira laughed.

"What?"

She came over to his chair and sat, facing him, in his lap. "Like I said, it's full of surprises."

~ ~ ~

~ ~ ~

Read all seven of the Homeland Connection novels:

Bashert
The Dome
Web Games
Chipset
Gasline
Flight Track
Exit Plans

Author's Note

ALTHOUGH THIS IS A WORK of fiction, I did not make it all up. This much is true. In 1963, a clever and inquisitive student—who had doctored his own high-school records to enter the Massachusetts Institute of Technology a year early—was working in a part-time custodial job when he stumbled on an unmarked and unguarded room in which was stored a cache of nuclear fuel for MIT's research reactor. Much later, in 1969, MIT actually discovered that a quantity of highly enriched uranium, along with depleted uranium, had indeed gone missing at some point in time. A graduate student had apparently used a master key to obtain the unsecured material, which was, according to some reports, recovered later.

Construction on Israel's first nuclear reactor, at Dimona in the Negev desert, was already completed by 1964, and it is now believed that as early as 1968 the CIA had concluded that Israel was producing nuclear weapons on a regular basis. Indeed, some experts suggest that Israel already possessed at least two fully functional atomic bombs by 1967, which were, it has been claimed, ordered to be armed during the Six-Day War. Many observers have speculated that Israel's nuclear weapons program was fueled, at least in part, by significant quantities of MUF—nuclear "Material Unaccounted For"—from the United States.

The speed at which Israel had entered the nuclear club, without an invitation and without ever applying for an official membership card, impressed many politicians and scientists alike. However, even after dissident Mordechai Vanunu in 1986 revealed photographs and other details about the Dimona operation, Israel still did not acknowledge its nuclear program or admit to possessing nuclear weapons. Vanunu was abducted in Rome by Mossad in September of that year and returned to Israel to stand trial. He remained in prison until 2004.

Although sundry bits and pieces have been assembled over the years, the full story of Israel's nuclear program is still substantially unknown. As for the what-if story in this book, it began as a solo exercise in speculation inspired by an isolated memory and quickly became a collaborative work that bears the marks of many minds. Lucy, my *bashert*, helped from the beginning when it was no more than a scenario in my head and guided me through the false starts and the numerous drafts that "needed work," as she would so bluntly but gently put it, all the way to the end and back to the beginning—more than once.

And we were not alone on this extended journey. Others—my "subject matter experts"—joined along the way to help me with fact checking and educating me in the many areas of my inadequate knowledge about firearms, about sailing, and about Israeli intelligence, and to assist with my clumsy German and Hebrew. I cannot thank them enough. Dale Constantine, Jim Hawkins, Alexandra Levich, Barak Turovsky, and Helmut Windl all did their best to keep me from egregious technical errors and, along the way, made suggestions that also helped me to improve the story and the storytelling. As well, Ed Powers answered my questions about police practices in Massachusetts, and Bill Eldridge set me straight about the Boston harbor. In all, it is a much better book for all their generous input, and what missteps remain or may have crept into the manuscript despite their generous advice are my responsibility alone.

I am grateful also to Tom Newton, with MIT's Nuclear Research Lab, for responding to my many emails with vital historical information, and to Amy Stout and Chris Sherratt with the MIT libraries, for going beyond their duties as librarians to deliver important tidbits to an alum burdened by imperfect memory.

And to my old college friend, Dave Tutelman, who surfaced suddenly and unexpectedly from my own dim MIT past, whose sharp observations and pointed suggestions helped add the final precision and polish and who managed to find typos that had eluded us all, I add one more *toda raba*. Thank you. Thank you one and all.

Heidelberg, Germany, November 2007
Funchal, Portugal, March 2010

Appendix:
An Inspiring Hacker

HACKERS. IN CONTEMPORARY USE, a hacker is someone who gains unauthorized access to computer systems or resources, and the term "hacking" has been generalized to refer to nearly any clever scheme or workaround that manipulates a system or situation—or even a person. But the word has morphed in meaning over the past half century. When I entered the Massachusetts Institute of Technology in the early Sixties, a hack was a prank or stunt. An elegant hack was one that was inventive, intelligent, caused no harm, and, ideally, received wide attention. There is a long history of hacking by students at MIT (see references below), everything from disassembling a car and reassembling it atop the Green Earth Sciences Building to transforming "The Great Dome" into an R2D2 replica. Although the people and events in this novel are fictitious, behind the fiction are facts as well as inspiration from the short but eventful life of my friend Dave Hahn, a master of the elegant hack and in whose memory the book is dedicated.

Dave and a few co-conspirators actually pulled off the hack recounted in the story involving the first Boston-bound morning train into Kendall Square, the subway station adjacent to MIT in Cambridge. Owing to a measured application of lithium grease over a precisely calculated stretch of the tracks, the train slid through the station without stopping until reaching the midpoint of the Longfellow bridge over the

Charles River. Although the transit authorities and police ranted about how dangerous the stunt was, the students had done their physics homework, taking into account all the parameters—mass of the train, its speed, brake efficiency, coefficient of friction, and the like—to predict the exact point where the subway train would safely come to a stop.

That was possibly the last of Dave's hacks in the older sense of the word, but that was not the end of his inventive and idiosyncratic approach to life. Dave was a do-it-all-yourself entrepreneur whose business interests were usually well outside the mainstream and whose practices often played loose with commercial convention.

He once worked a deal to buy scrapped polarized plastic lenses from the company hauling the trash from Cambridge-based Polaroid. These he sold to an Italian sunglasses company by operating an import-export business for a time out of the basement of my Boston apartment. But he was a restless operator who moved quickly from one opportunity to the next. He helped found The Boston Tea Party, a legendary venue in the local rock scene and early influence on the evolution of the so-called Boston sound. Using his engineering and hacking skills, he patched together one of the first computer-controlled light shows, then soon sold his share to move on to other projects.

He developed an interest in government surplus and worked out a scheme for gaming the auction system to buy serviceable equipment for low-ball bids. Some of his winning bids had surprising outcomes.

In the predawn dark of one spring morning, a light but insistent rap on my apartment door tugged me awake. It was, Dave. "I've just driven through the night from Philadelphia. I'm exhausted. Can I crash here for a few hours?" I let him in, tossed an extra pillow and blanket on the couch for him, and went back to bed.

Bright sun was streaming in by the time of the second round of knocks, a thunderous pounding accompanied by a commanding voice. "Open up, police. Open up." I scrambled for my bathrobe and opened the door to be greeted by two of Boston's Finest. "Is that your boat downstairs?" one officer said.

"What? A boat?" I mumbled.

Dave was now sitting up. "That's mine."

"Well, you got two minutes to get it out of there. You're blocking the street. Move it, now, or I'm going to bury it in so many tickets you won't even be able to see it, and it'll be towed at your expense. And that ain't going to be cheap."

I accompanied Dave downstairs to find that our narrow, one-way Peterborough Street was completely blocked by a double-parked beatup flatbed truck with a gray Navy surplus whale boat listing to port on the back, held in place by jury-rigged ropes the size of my wrist.

That boat lived for a time in a disused parking lot on MIT's West Campus while Dave built a cabin and added a mast and sail to the open-hulled motor launch. His plan, to use the small craft to film a circumnavigation of the globe for National Geographic, was eventually scrapped in favor of trying his hand at fishing for king crab off the coast of Alaska. After hauling the boat cross-country on the same rickety rig that had showed up outside my apartment, that plan, too, was abandoned.

This is not to say that his business plans went nowhere. Using patched-up government surplus buses that he bought on the cheap, he started the first regular rural bus service in Belize in what was then called British Honduras. He later rehabilitated a navy surplus coastal mine sweeper, converting it into a cargo vessel to establish an import-export shipping business in Central America. While working on repairs to the boat, he suffered a heart attack and died. He was thirty-one.

Of all Dave's early money-making schemes, the one that inspired this novel ranks among the wildest. After discovering that MIT was holding highly-enriched nuclear fuel in an unguarded storeroom—to which he had a key—Dave became the focus of a group of friends who fantasized about how the situation could, in theory, be exploited. Dave eventually concluded that the risks were not worth the rewards for him, since he was certain he would make many more millions from countless other business deals over his lifetime.

Oh, yes, the fantasy plan was to deliver the nuclear goods to Israel, and yes, the group really did have access to an ocean-going yacht converted from a surplus destroyer escort.

Rowley, Massachusetts, March 2020

Leibowitz, B. M. *The Journal of the Institute for Hacks, Tomfoolery & Pranks at MIT*. MIT Museum, 1990.

Peterson, T. F. *Nightwork: A History of Hacks and Pranks at MIT*. MIT Press, 2011.

About the Author

LIOR SAMSON is the pen name of a former university professor who has won awards for both fiction and non-fiction writing as well as for his innovative work in industrial design. He has more than two dozen published books, including thirteen novels and two collections of short fiction. As a consultant and teacher, he has traveled the world, lived in Australia and Portugal, and served on the faculties of two international universities.

He resides in Massachusetts with his family, where he cooks creative fusion cuisine and composes serious choral music. He is a freelance journalist and photographer and one-man technical support team for the three students in his life.

The readers who write with questions, kudos, and criticism are vital parts of the dialogue he seeks to spark through his writing. He enjoys hearing from readers and appreciates those who take the time to post reviews on Amazon and elsewhere. He can be reached by email at: lior@liorsamson.com